Courting the Vicar's Daughter

by Sally Britton

OTHER TITLES BY SALLY BRITTON

The Branches of Love Series:

Prequel Novella, *Martha's Patience*

Book 1, *The Social Tutor*

Book 2, *The Gentleman Physician*

Book 3, *His Bluestocking Bride*

Book 4, *The Earl and His Lady*

Book 5, *Miss Devon's Choice*

Forever After

The Captain and Miss Winter

Timeless Regency Collection: *An Evening at Almack's*
The Heart's Choice

Courting the

Vicar's Daughter

Sally Britton
http://www.authorsallybritton.com

First Printing: March 2019

Dedicated to my husband, my very best friend.
And to my aunts and uncles, for telling me how proud they are. You
have all inspired the very best of my characters in every book.

Chapter One

December 31st, 1820

T he snowfall in the darkening skies, and the surrounding blanket of white, made the ride from the Earl of Annesbury's house to Whitewood Manor eerily silent. The only sound beyond Harry and his brother-in-law's breath was the jingle of the carriage harnesses. Neither man spoke, though Harry knew he ought to say something. Normally he broke tension with a witty remark, but that was hardly appropriate in these circumstances.

"What if he won't let you help him?" Harry said suddenly, disturbing the silence.

"I have to try, Harry. I am a doctor; it is my duty to see to any who need medical attention." Nathaniel Hastings, Harry's brother-in-law, shifted in his seat. "Tell me again exactly what the footman said."

It was New Year's Eve, and both men had been attending a celebration at the Gilbert home, where their family and friends had gathered to feast, play games, and sing until the old year ended. No further parties would be had in the country for many months, as all the nobility and many members of the gentry would make their way to London for the Season.

Home from university for a short holiday, twenty-year-old Harry Devon had been looking forward to this night. But his desire to sing and tease his sisters had been forgotten with one urgent message sent from his father's home, Whitewood.

"Father had a riding accident this morning," Harry said, holding a hand up to rub the bridge of his nose. "A broken leg. No one knew of it until hours passed and he was found by a tenant.

He was brought home, the apothecary has been attending him, and they only sent for me when he requested it."

Harry's fear that his father might refuse any help that Nathaniel selflessly volunteered was well-founded; Mr. Devon had never spoken the name of Nathaniel Hastings, or even that of his eldest daughter Julia, since they had wed.

Never mind that Nathaniel is a respected physician. Harry knew his brother-in-law was well-published in medical journals. Really, most would consider it an honor to be attended by him.

"Perhaps it is not too serious," Nathaniel said, tone cautious. "You would've been called home sooner."

Harry chuckled, without much of his usual humor. "My father would sooner give up his fortune than admit to any weakness, in body or mind. The fact that he sent for me, instead of waiting until I came home in the morning, worries me." Harry tensed when the carriage turned into the lane leading up to his house.

Every window glowed with light, and the old butler threw the front door open as the carriage rolled to a stop. Harry climbed out first, Nathaniel barely a step behind.

Carmichael, the butler, met them on the landing and began to explain the situation in hushed tones. "Mr. Devon went on his morning ride as usual, sir. No one even thought to look for him until the farmer brought him to the door."

"It was an accident, nothing more." Harry swallowed and nodded. "And his injury, Carmichael?"

"When he fell from the horse, it apparently stepped backward. The lower part of his right leg is broken and protruding. Mr. Neeson has been here all day, tending to Mr. Devon."

Harry looked over his shoulder at Nathaniel, whose expression had turned very grim. "Show us to my father."

Carmichael bowed and then lead them to the hall of family rooms, where Mr. Devon's bedchamber lay. Harry stepped into the room, immediately overwhelmed by the heat within. The fire was blazing and scores of candles had been placed on every surface. His father's large four-poster bed was against the far wall, swathed in green velvet curtains, and Harry could see his father's pale face in the center of the bedding. His cold blue eyes leapt out, hostile even in the midst of misfortune.

Harry's eyes were a matching shade, but he hoped they never caused a person the trepidation his father's did.

Mr. Neeson, the village apothecary, came forward with a straight back and narrowed eyes. "I am afraid your father isn't doing well, Mr. Devon."

"Mr. Neeson, this is my brother-in-law, Doctor Hastings. Please, tell him everything about the injury and what has been done for my father." Harry gestured for Nathaniel to come forward, which he did, only to be met with an almost scornful huff from the old apothecary.

"Doctor Hastings," Mr. Neeson said, his tone one of disinterest. "Mr. Devon has suffered a riding accident. After falling from his horse, he was trampled upon. He has sustained a break just below his hip and a compound fracture in his shin. The bone was protruding by three inches. He was exposed to the elements for above two hours. I have treated his wound and stretched the bone back into place. There is nothing more for you to do here."

Shocked at the tone of the man, Harry opened his mouth to say something sharp, but Nathaniel began speaking, calm and collected.

"I understand your protectiveness of your patient, Mr. Neeson. Please answer just a few questions for me, as a professional courtesy. Did Mr. Devon have many bone fragments in the wound?"

Drawing himself up, Mr. Neeson spoke as though to a simpleton. "As a doctor, sir, you should know the danger of going into a man's leg and poking around. You must've read the work of Samuel Cooper in regard to the danger of gangrene should the wound be too disturbed."

Nathaniel closed his eyes and spoke with patience. "I am familiar with the esteemed Doctor Cooper, but I would rather not discuss medical theories. Did you clean any debris from the wound?"

"I packed the whole with the appropriate medicines and poultice," Mr. Neeson stated firmly. "As is recommended in cases such as these."

Although Harry didn't even pretend to understand the world of medicine, he trusted Nathaniel's reputation as an expert in medical care.

"Mr. Neeson," Harry said, breaking in before the argument continued. "I ask that you defer to Doctor Hastings in the care of my father. He's family, and I trust him." Harry exchanged a meaningful glance with Nathaniel before going to his father's side.

Mr. Devon, his dark hair flecked with gray, lay as pale as a ghost in his bed. He moaned as Harry approached, then appeared to come more to his senses. "Horace," he said, using Harry's given name.

Kneeling by his father's bed, Harry tried to offer a reassuring smile. He had never been particularly close to the man. For the most part, he regarded his father with distrust and regret, but in this moment, he needed to be supportive and compassionate.

"I'm here, Father. I brought Doctor Hastings with me. Julia's husband. I want him to look at your wound."

Nathaniel approached but came no closer than the foot of the bed, clutching his medical bag tightly.

"Hastings?" his father said and turned his fever-bright eyes to the foot of the bed. When he spoke again, he hissed his words. "Get this man out of my house at once. Remove him from this property."

Harry stiffened and his stomach clenched tightly. "Father—"

"Remove him," his father shouted, then coughed and sunk into his pillows.

"I can help, Mr. Devon—" Nathaniel said, his voice soft, but he was cut off.

"Be gone," Devon said, turning to face Harry. "Neeson will see to my needs."

Neeson came forward and took Nathaniel's arm, as though to remove him from the room himself. "You are over-exciting my patient, Doctor Hastings, and that will only make his fever worse."

Nathaniel carefully pulled his arm from the apothecary's grasp, then looked at Harry with a somber expression. "I cannot help him if he will not allow it, Harry," he said.

Harry looked from his father to Neeson, who preened like a pompous old goat. "Thank you for trying," Harry said, forcing a smile. "Please tell my sisters of the situation here."

Shaking his head, Nathaniel shared one last look of sympathetic irritation with Harry before he left the room, bag still in hand.

"How dare you bring him here," Mr. Devon whispered, his eyes closed tight. "If I live or die, it will not be because that man touched me."

"Yes, Father," Harry said, as he'd been trained to do his whole life. He settled into a chair near his father's bed. "What do you want me to do?"

"Wait." The injured man pressed his bloodless lips together. "If infection sets in, there will be a fever. The loss of my leg is a possible outcome."

Though Harry wasn't particularly close to his father, who possessed a cold and unfeeling nature, the idea of the man dying before his eyes unsettled him. "If it would save you to amputate—"

"Neeson has his orders," Devon said with a snarl, then he began to pant.

The apothecary shuffled forward quickly. "You shouldn't upset him, young sir."

Harry dropped his face into his hands and barely repressed a groan. Then he sat up and removed his coat. If he had to sit in the oven-hot room, with two old men he felt nothing but frustration for, he was at least going to be comfortable.

"It is a shame you were injured today, Father." Harry forced some lightness into his voice. The atmosphere oppressed him, but with nothing to do but sit, he needed some way to alleviate the building stress. "It is a fine night. My sisters and their families are all well, should you wonder, and anticipate the New Year with great hope."

His father snorted. "Foolish of them. All poor nobodies, except Rebecca." He started coughing. "I had hopes for this family. You see how that turned out. Everyone a disappointment to me."

Harry knew this line of lecturing well enough to give it to himself, though he never agreed with it. Their father's hopes had been to manipulate each of his daughters into advantageous marriages, enriching his coffers and social connections, with little care for their personal wishes.

In time, Harry would be forced to choose between bowing to his father's wishes or being cut off. Though used to the ways of a wealthy gentleman, Harry had never really considered taking on his father's responsibilities.

"Best not to antagonize him, sir," the apothecary whispered loudly across the room.

"I am sick, not deaf, Mr. Neeson," Harry's father muttered darkly, before he turned to cough into his pillow again. "And the boy needs to be aware of his legacy. If I die—"

Harry jerked a little straighter. "You will not, Father. You have a strong constitution." Imagining his father succumbing to anything, even illness, against his own wishes was a foreign concept.

"Be quiet, Horace." His father's frame trembled and he moaned. "You will find everything in order, ready for you to take up your duties when the time is right."

Swallowing, Harry leaned closer to his father's side and tried to sound certain as he spoke. "I am still studying, Father. And when I am through at university, I will come home. You will teach me how you wish things to be done." Of that Harry had no doubt. He would be thoroughly educated in his father's less-than-savory business practices.

"Foolish boy." His father squeezed his eyes shut and sighed, though it was a rasping sound that made Harry wince. "Let us hope you are less like your useless sisters than I suspect, or the legacy I leave you will mean nothing."

The legacy of a callous heart, a man who loved money and position more than his own children, was not one that Harry wanted. In truth, he distanced himself as much as he could from his father in all matters. His friends at school were the men on scholarship, not the sons of lords. His favorite pursuits were those that gave him joy, not income or prestige. His sisters, whom his father ignored, were dearer to Harry than his own life.

The thought of the party left behind came to him, and he wished there had been no cause to leave the circle of his family. What did it say about him, that he would rather be there again than at his father's bedside? He'd left behind a house full of joy and laughter for the bitterness of his only living parent.

His father would not make for a pleasant patient, even if the fever subsided in the night. Harry knew his sisters, for all the good they possessed, should not be exposed to their father on normal terms. With Mr. Devon ill, it would be best to keep everyone as far from the house as possible. Which left it all to Harry to care for Mr. Devon. The last several years of his life, Harry had acted as a buffer in the family, which meant he was quite used to the position.

Whatever the outcome of the illness, it was up to Harry to see his father through it.

Chapter Two

Four Years Later, September 23rd, 1824

Carrying a basket of gingerbread biscuits to a neighbor, surrounded by the scent of damp earth and the golden leaves of fall, was quite possibly the most perfect way to begin a morning. Augusta Ames, who privately preferred the childhood nickname of Daisy, was called Miss Ames since both of her sisters married. If she couldn't be called Daisy, she much preferred Miss Ames to Miss Augusta.

She swung her basket as she walked and took in the sky with a smile, not wishing to be anywhere else in the world. The bright shade of blue above promised a clear, beautiful morning. Those were the very best sort of mornings.

A cart turned onto the road from a lane and she waved to its driver, Mr. Rollins. He was a tenant farmer on the Whitewood property. He tipped his cap and pulled up his horse when they drew even. "Mornin', Miss Ames. Where are you off to with that cheery smile?"

"To the Thatchers'. Little Annie Thatcher has just turned six, and gingerbread is her favorite." Daisy reached into the basket, finding a biscuit beneath the napkin she'd used to cover her baked goods. "Would you like to sample the birthday treat?"

Though she was twenty-one, she appreciated the gingerbread as much as the six-year-old would. And what sort of person would ever pass up the opportunity for gingerbread?

"Oh, that's kind of you—"

She forestalled his polite declination by holding the biscuit up to him. "Please, Mr. Rollins? It will make your ride to the village more agreeable." She knew his destination quite well, as it was his habit to go for supplies and sundries every second Tuesday. The Rollins family were a people of routine, as were many locals, and no one knew their schedules quite so well as Daisy. It often fell to her, as the last of the vicar's children at home, to perform charitable acts in her family's name. Knowing the people in her community with some intimacy aided in that duty.

"What a treat, Miss Ames. You're an angel." He accepted the biscuit and immediately took a bite. The gingerbread, shaped like stars, boasted a little icing on each point. Her father would not approve of the extravagance of icing biscuits; he believed they were treat enough without depleting the kitchen's sugar supply. A vicar's family ought to be the very model of economy, after all.

"I'm not at all certain about that, Mr. Rollins, but I do hope you enjoy the biscuit." She curtsied and went on her way, hearing his cart continue down the road a moment later.

A breeze danced through the trees and across the lane, making the leaves above her shiver and twirl on their stems. Autumn had arrived, and all the world put off summer gowns in exchange for the golden splendor.

Daisy couldn't resist grinning to herself. Chancing a look behind her, she lifted her skirts a little higher than proper in order to skip. There was nothing so freeing as a good skip down a road. The basket bounced against her hip, the handle tucked tightly in the crook of her arm, but she didn't mind it.

Her bonnet fell back, but the ribbons kept it secure around her neck, and she tossed her blonde curls out of her eyes with a laugh.

On days such as this, her dreams took flight on the breeze. All of her plans to open a school for the local girls were beginning to take a more realistic shape. For years she'd saved every spare coin she could to make a start. She had enough to purchase the most essential books, and she was nearly ready to reveal her plans to the community.

She didn't want to open a boarding school for the children of the middle-class, for nobility. She wanted to give the little girls she saw every day a way to better themselves, to better their families present and future. Her father thought it a worthy endeavor, if not a very practical one.

That brought a frown to her face and her skips slowed back to a walk.

"Farmers will not see any point in educating daughters who could be home assisting in family work," her father had told her, almost gently. "And once you marry, no husband will appreciate your time spent with the children of others. You will have your own home to care for."

Daisy had spent a week trying to form an argument against such farmers. Without telling her father, she had also reaffirmed her decision to put marriage off for a time.

A man stepped out from between two hedgerows, not ten feet in front of her, and she drew up sharply.

It was her father's curate, Mr. Percy Haskett. He wasn't overly tall, or all that imposing a figure, really, but she nevertheless hesitated before greeting him. Several of the young misses in the neighborhood found him a good catch, despite a somewhat large nose and darker coloring. Yet when she spoke to him no sense of real connection formed. As good a man as he may be, Daisy never found herself wishing for more of his attention.

"Miss Ames," he said, tipping his black hat in her direction. "Good morning. I didn't expect to see you out of doors this early. What a surprise." His green eyes, a shade which reminded her of spring grass, testified that he counted it a *pleasant* surprise when they crinkled at the corners.

"Mr. Haskett," she said, curtsying. The curate was the very sort of man who would praise her idea of the boarding school as both morally righteous and terribly impractical. "I am on an important errand. It's Miss Annie's birthday."

His brows drew together and he shook his head. "Miss Annie?"

The curate had taken many of her father's duties well in hand the last six months, leaving Mr. Ames to slip into a semi-retirement from his responsibilities as a clergyman, but there were still some things Mr. Haskett hadn't managed. Remembering the names of his youngest parishioners was one such item he'd yet to accomplish.

"She is the middle Thatcher daughter. She's turned six today." Daisy tried to keep her tone helpful, even kind, but it grew increasingly difficult to maintain such attitudes when near Mr. Haskett. Honestly, he reminded her a bit too much of her father, though not yet as ponderous in his way of speaking.

"Dear me. An auspicious day for her, indeed." His smile, she supposed, could be counted attractive, but he turned it too often in her direction of late. Though Daisy insisted to herself his attentions were nothing but those of a clergyman coming to know his parish, the time might come for her to put a greater distance between them.

"Might I accompany you?" Mr. Haskett asked.

"Oh. Certainly. If you have nothing more pressing to be about," she said, inwardly wishing he'd had some prior engagement. "I know your time is valuable, Mr. Haskett."

His grin faded to a gentle smile and he came to stand at her side. "I can think of no better way to spend it than accompanying you on this errand." He offered his arm.

Thinking quickly, Daisy held the basket out to him. "Oh, thank you. It isn't heavy, but walking a mile or more with even a light basket can begin to tax one's strength."

His expression changed to one of perplexity, but he took the basket, and she tucked her hands behind her the moment he had hold of it. "Come, Mr. Haskett. Why don't you tell me about your sermon while we walk? I enjoyed the text you shared last week."

Walking beside her, Mr. Haskett's brow remained furrowed. "You did?"

Her mind stumbled and she tried to recall exactly what he had spoken about. She'd sat in her family's pew, quite alone, as her father had been ill. In truth, she'd been worrying over her father's health more than she paid attention to the sermon.

"Yes. Of course. Who wouldn't enjoy your sermons? You are such an eloquent speaker." That much she could safely say. Mr.

Haskett never used a word of a single syllable when one of similar meaning existed with three or four times as many.

His face relaxed. "The figurative language of Isaiah is often difficult to address in a way that allows all to comprehend it, but I felt it was adequate."

Nodding with what she hoped was a somber and thoughtful expression, Daisy turned her eyes to the road. "What will you present next Sunday?"

Without hesitation, Mr. Haskett discussed his coming sermon with enthusiasm, using his free hand to gesture before him as if he addressed a crowded room rather than a single person at his side. Although Daisy was tempted to tune him out completely, that would make it difficult to make an intelligent response where one was required, so she listened with half an ear while drinking in the morning sights.

A quarter of an hour later, though they'd arrived at her destination, Mr. Haskett had seemingly only scratched the surface of his topic. Daisy waited, politely, for him to pause in his explanation of metaphors in the Old Testament.

"Now, Mr. Haskett, you must tell me no more," she said when he at last paused for breath. "I have heard enough to make me look forward to your sermon. It will be most enlightening for all of us, I am certain. May I have my basket?"

Mr. Haskett's cheeks pinked. "Of course, Miss Ames." He handed it to her and then glanced around. "I didn't realize we were here. When I am in your company the time is too much of a pleasure for me to mark its passing." Had he more of the rogue in him, it would have been a clever thing to say, but as he spoke every word with the same tone he used to sermonize, Daisy hoped she was safe from his affections.

"Thank you, Mr. Haskett. I hope you have a pleasant morning." She dropped a curtsy and hurried through the gate, which he tried to open for her, but she was already on the other side when his fingers touched the wood. She walked rapidly down the path to the front door of the tenant cottage, not looking back.

Children burst out of the little cottage as she approached, and Daisy pushed the worrisome thoughts of Mr. Haskett away. At her age, she had plenty of time ahead of her for suitors, should she choose. But really, as no man in the neighborhood had caught her attention in that sort of way, her mind rarely turned to the possibility.

After sharing the gingerbread with the children, Daisy stayed to play with them, laughing as sweet Annie Thatcher lisped through a rhyming game due to a missing front tooth.

Rhyming gave way to a game of chase, and Daisy took Annie's hand as they ran about the clearing near the little girl's house. Daisy was never so happy as she was when she spent time with children. *If I could open my school, I could do so much to help them.*

There remained further plans to make on that score, so Daisy put that thought away. *For now.*

Chapter Three

Sitting in his middle-sister's parlor, Harry watched two of his nephews attempt to play spilikins. Charles, at eight, was constantly reminding five-year-old Hugh of the rules with rather humorous results.

"Harry," Christine Gilbert said, bringing his attention back to her. "What on earth does this mean? You wish to let the house?" She was the second oldest of his sisters and the only one who still lived in the neighborhood where they had grown up.

Harry sat back more comfortably in his chair, noting his sister's confusion. "It is a big house, Christine. Too big for a man on his own. I would much rather take smaller apartments, for the time being. I do not need all that room, and it is a waste for Whitewood to sit empty."

"What about the tenants already on the land, Harry?" Christine asked, not looking away from him. "And where will you live? In London?" The skepticism in her voice was quite clear. She knew how he felt about London. He hated being in the city, with its filthy air and polluted streets. Though he had the means to lease rooms and set up bachelor quarters there, he didn't wish to step foot in the city unless there was a need.

Their father had spent more time in London than anywhere else, which also detracted from any charm the great city might have.

"I thought I would stay nearby, or perhaps take a house near Rebecca and Christian, or Julia and Nathaniel." He named his other sisters, thinking of how far away they lived. Rebecca's husband had several estates, but they spent most of their time in the house nearest London. Julia and her husband lived in Bath, where he practiced medicine. "If I didn't stay nearby, the steward would do well enough looking after the tenants, as he has for *years.*"

Christine frowned. Of his three sisters, she was the most outspoken, and she would not mince words with him. "It doesn't sound as though you have any sort of plan at all, other than leasing the house to a complete stranger. I understand it is done, and there is nothing shameful in it, but is it truly necessary?"

Harry tensed. "Not financially necessary, if that is what you mean." Indeed. Harry could likely afford to buy up several estates with his inheritance. When his father died four years past, succumbing to infection and fever from a riding injury, Harry had been shocked to learn of the wealth the hardened gentleman had accumulated. For someone not of the nobility, the amount was obscene. Which left Harry in a confusing predicament.

He had no need to work for a living, or even to be careful in a life of leisure. But what, then, ought he to do? He'd never admired his father's business methods, or his morals. Now that Harry had finished his studies at Oxford, and spent a little time on the Continent, he wasn't entirely sure what to do with himself.

"If you're going to let the house, then why stay? Why not visit faraway lands and exotic destinations?" Christine asked, half-smiling at him.

Travel. He'd considered it briefly. "I would miss my sisters too much," he admitted.

"And us," Hugh said from his place on the floor, then grinned unrepentant when Harry raised his eyebrows at him.

"Children are always listening," Christine informed him with a grin that was nearly the same as her son's. "Yes, Hugh. I imagine your uncle would miss you, too."

Charles and Hugh both looked up at Harry, their eyes widening in a way that reminded him of puppies begging for attention. He didn't bother hiding his affection for them. "It is true. I would miss you both too much. I cannot possibly go far, for that very reason."

The boys shared a smile and went back to their game.

15

"Don't do it, Harry. If you are staying in England," Christine said, holding the paper out to him, "then you should keep the house. Look after the tenants. Be a good landowner."

Harry sighed and took the lease he had drafted with the help of a lawyer. Tucking it back in his leather satchel on the floor, his mind searched for another argument to make. "I haven't the first idea how to be a good landowner. That's why I have a steward."

"You are talking about Mr. Simmons," Christine said, adjusting baby Jason in her arms. "He's a good man, in terms of business sense. That's why he worked for father. But he's nearly sixty years old and ought to retire. And do you think he has the tenant's best interests at heart or your bank account? You need to be more responsible for the people under your care."

Little Jason started to whimper, and the sound swiftly grew to a wail of discontent.

Christine stood, holding the baby against her chest. "If you will excuse me, Harry. I must tend to the baby. We can discuss this later, with Thomas if you like." She swept through the room, calling for the other two to come with her to the nursery.

The boys jumped to their feet and followed, their game forgotten on the floor.

Harry sighed, alone in the room, then crouched down on the floor to scoop up the jackstraws and put them back in their little pouch. He gathered his satchel and put it in the Gilbert office. Christine and Thomas used to share the house with Thomas's father and mother, but the senior Gilbert couple had recently moved in with their daughter five miles away.

No one had seemed to mind *them* leaving one house behind in favor of another.

After stashing his belongings, and finding his hat and gloves, Harry made his way outside.

What Harry needed was to organize his thoughts. As the day promised to be fine, with blue skies above and no mud in evidence, a walk would be the very thing he needed. His eldest sister, Julia, was fond of comparing a muddled mind to one filled with cobwebs. A brisk walk and the September breeze ought to do a fair job of clearing those away.

Harry went to the lane and, by habit alone, chose to walk in the direction of Whitewood Place, his family's estate, which abutted the Gilbert property.

With no destination in mind, Harry had little need to focus on more than putting one foot in front of the other.

Christine's idea is only one opinion. It really isn't a terrible idea, to lease Whitewood.

Though as he'd spoken to her, he realized his plans for Whitewood were rather short-sighted. And not entirely thought out. Even though he'd had four years to consider what he wished to do with the property, he'd spent most of that time trying not to think about it. He really couldn't put off a decision any longer. Deciding what to do with the estate, and the rest of his life, must take precedence until both issues were resolved.

The future hung before him like a question mark at the end of a page. He needed to move forward with his life, but how did one do that when one couldn't decide in which direction to go?

"Stop right there, you horrid beast!"

Harry scuffled to a stop and lifted his head, looking around in shock. Had someone been addressing *him*?

"You know you're too old and fat to climb any higher, and I am too old and refined to come climbing up after you," the voice continued, feminine frustration coloring every word. "Come down this instant."

The voice came from the other side of a hedge, where a birch grew with branches stretching over the bushes to reach toward the trees lining the road. He went that direction, without much thought, and peered through a narrow break in the leafy shrubbery.

At the base of the tree, half out of sight, he saw a woman in a blue-gray gown. Her head was tilted as she stared up into the tree, and her hands were on her waist.

"I mean it, Jezebel. You come down this instant, or I will leave and you will absolutely *starve.*"

Glancing up, Harry saw a fat feline perched on a thin branch, perhaps fifteen feet above the ground. The cat was staring balefully down at the woman, tale twitching, as though calling the woman's bluff.

The woman circled around the tree, out of sight, muttering to herself. He could barely make out the words. "Feline...stubborn...useless...."

The cat remained unimpressed.

The woman came back into view, her back to Harry, her bonnet now dangling down her back from ribbons. He could make out a head full of golden braids and twisting curls escaping above her ears and at the nape of her neck.

Appreciating her lovely hair and shapely figure from behind a bush wasn't the act of a gentleman, however, especially when the woman he ogled obviously needed assistance. Harry stepped forward, pushing through the bush. The rustling sound brought the woman's attention to his presence and she whirled around as he approached.

Her blue eyes were wide in surprise, and pretty, too. As was her finely sculpted face. With round cheeks and a narrower chin, her features were almost elfin. Her eyes swept over him as he struggled to emerge from the clinging branches of the hedge.

"Good afternoon, miss," he said, giving one last lunge in order to stumble out of the bushes. "I couldn't help but overhear—are you in need of any help?" He looked up into the trees where the fat feline still sat, its attention fixed on him. The furry beast licked its lips and narrowed its eyes.

The woman sighed, a touch dramatically. "Perhaps. But you've already fetched this wretched creature down from the trees for me once. It doesn't seem fair to ask such a thing of you again." Her eyes sparkled playfully, and then she smiled.

The whole world lit up with that smile. Harry's heart sped up and warmth crept up the back of his neck.

"I have?" he asked, not daring to look away from her. His mind had turned into a sluggish machine, trying and failing to catch up with his need to understand what the woman meant.

Surely, he'd remember meeting her, let alone rescuing her cat. Where had he seen her before? Studying her more carefully, noting the impish upturn at the end of her nose as well as the blonde lashes framing her eyes, his memory finally heeded his desperate need to know her identity.

"An Ames daughter," he said at last, rocking back slightly on his heels as he continued to stare at her. The vicar's children, as young girls, hadn't exactly been in the same social circles as he, even when he came home on holiday.

Her smile widened. "But which one? My father has three, you must remember." She turned her eyes up to the cat, finally breaking the spell he'd fallen under the moment their gazes connected. He released a breath, his lungs protesting that he'd held onto it for too long.

"The eldest is in India," Harry said, thinking aloud. Christine had written him about that exciting happening. "She married a missionary."

"Mm-hm," the young woman agreed, stepping away from him to get another view of the cat.

His mind immediately protested the distance between them and he followed her, taking in the speculative tilt to her head and her lowered brows.

"Miss Gabriella—"

"Is now Mrs. Robin."

He blinked. Was he addressing a married woman, then? If she was married that made him a cad, admiring another man's wife in such a manner. Harry quickly looked down. Seeing the state of his coat, covered in leaves and twigs. He started brushing off his sleeves to avoid looking like a walking shrubbery.

The young woman glanced sideways at him, narrowing her eyes. "She married a naval captain, actually."

"She did?" Harry asked, jerking his head up hopefully. "And you are not married to a naval captain?"

"I am not married to anyone," she stated, appearing unbothered by that fact. "I am too busy taking care of that fat beast in the tree to entertain suitors." She pointed upward and he saw the cat had decided to move up the branch to an even more precarious seat.

"Fat *and* unintelligent," she muttered to herself. "Not at all the sweet kitten she was last time you rescued her."

"Kitten?" Harry said, and then the memory came back to him. Years ago, he could not even remember how far back in the past, he'd come upon Miss Gabriella and the younger sister. What was her name? The vicar's younger daughters had been beside themselves, as they tried to convince their tiny new kitten to come down from a tree very similar to this one.

What had they called the youngest?

As if she knew his thoughts, the woman took pity on him at last. "I am Miss Augusta Ames."

"Miss Augusta. Of course. I apologize for not knowing you at once. It's been several years since we've crossed paths."

She met his eyes for a moment and offered a most friendly smile, then made a dismissive gesture with one hand. "Think nothing of it. Except, with two older sisters married, I am Miss *Ames* now. It is good to see you again, Mr. Devon."

Harry winced at that title of address. "Indeed." He looked back up into the tree. "That thing was the kitten I climbed into the tree to retrieve?"

"Yes. Time has not improved her temperament, I'm afraid. Bell is an absolute hoyden of a cat, which is saying something given that all cats misbehave."

"Bell?" He couldn't help raising an eyebrow. "I thought you called her something different a moment ago." When he looked down at her, he had the pleasure of watching her cheeks turn pink.

"Oh, it is only a joke I shared with my sisters. We called her something indecent, I'm afraid, considering we're the daughters of a vicar." She cleared her throat and folded her arms. "What do you think? Ought we to leave her up there?"

He tried not to smile at the obvious attempt to avoid any further questions on the cat's name. "Can she not come down on her own?"

"I'm afraid she will refuse to do so. She rarely climbs trees, at her age, but the last time she did she stayed up for two days until I bribed one of the earl's under gardeners to go up after her."

Though tempted to laugh, Harry took off his coat and went to the tree, draping the article over a branch before beginning his climb.

"Oh, Mr. Devon, you really shouldn't—"

"It's perfectly safe, Miss Ames." He went further into the tree, though his clothing was ill-suited for his adventure. Still, closer to the cat than the ground, he continued on. The animal noticed him drawing near and set to making an awful sound, part-growl and part-yowl. Nothing about the noise was friendly.

Harry reached up with one hand, the other holding tightly to a thick branch above his head. "Come, Bell," he coaxed, hand nearing the animal's wide-eyes and snarl. "I'll help you down."

She hissed and puffed out her fur, then raised one paw in an obvious threat, claws extended.

He froze, realizing this exact thing had happened years before, only he'd been better suited for climbing trees and the cat had been much smaller.

Of course, he'd grown a little wiser, too.

Crouching down on his branch, he held his hand out. "Throw me the coat, Miss Ames."

Much to her credit, and despite her frown of puzzlement, she tossed his coat upward with a great deal of force. He caught it by a sleeve and then went about finding his balance again, teetering as he had to snatch the cloth out of the air.

Harry stood again, gripping the branch above him, and studied his precarious perch as well as the cat's stubborn position.

"Maybe we ought to leave her," the lovely Miss Ames said from below, obvious worry in her tone. "It would teach her a lesson."

Judging by the malevolent gleam in the cat's eye, Harry very much doubted the truth of that statement.

"Miss Ames, I am a gentleman. I will not leave man or beast in distress." He angled himself to look down at her and shared his most charming smile, the one which made many a young woman blush and flutter their fans. But Miss Ames only stared at him, wearing an expression that appeared to question his sanity.

21

Harry faced the cat again, then carefully swung his coat in the animal's direction. Distracted, the cat turned its hissing and growling toward the cloth, batting at it with a paw. But, as Harry suspected, the animal didn't move from her chosen spot.

"Right." He swung the jacket in a wider arc, then another, and finally tossed it onto the cat. The horrid little beast froze, though its strange noises continued, now muffled by the fabric, and Harry reached out with his free hand to scoop the jacket, wrapped around the animal, up into his arms.

Immediately, Bell started writhing within his grasp, howling with rage. One clawed foot emerged. Harry tightened his hold on the cat, pulling it against his body in an attempt to keep it from moving. At least a dozen claws dug through the jacket and into his chest.

"Careful," the young woman from below said.

Harry gritted his teeth against the pain, realizing he hadn't grown as wise as he'd hoped, and tried to make his way down with one free arm. It was slow going, and his rescued prize didn't tire of thrashing and digging claws into his jacket. He heard an astonishingly loud rip.

"Oh dear." Miss Ames must have heard it as well.

He was on the branch closest to the ground when the cat came through the coat's collar, claws in his shoulder, and sprung to the ground at the same moment he meant to swing down. The animal's unexpected maneuver threw him off balance and Harry tried, through flailing his arms, to find purchase.

His boots slid off the bark and he tumbled backwards, five feet to the ground, and landed on his back and shoulders.

His breath left him with an "oof." He laid there, his body stiff as a board, staring up into the branches of the tree. Miss Ames moved into view, brow pinched with concern and eyes full of worry. She knelt beside him and reached out, her slim fingers brushing against his cheek.

"Mr. Devon? Mr. Devon, can you hear me?"

At last Harry's lungs loosened, and he sucked in a deep breath of air. "Jezebel."

Miss Ames drew back her hand, her concern replaced with affront. "Pardon me, Mr. Devon, but I had nothing to do with your fall. Calling me names—"

Harry couldn't help the laugh that escaped, even though it made the muscles in his body contract in a way that told him of bruises sure to come. "Not you, Miss Ames. The cat." He folded his hands over his chest, in no hurry to get up. "Jezebel. It suits her."

"Oh." She covered her lips with one hand, but not before he saw the flash of her pretty smile. "She is a terribly ungrateful creature. She's already streaked away like a bolt of lightning. I am so sorry you were hurt in her retrieval."

"I've fallen out of trees before." Harry at last started to push himself up, into a sitting position. He managed not to grunt, though the ache in his back promised to stay for some time.

"I would hope you haven't had much practice at that feat recently." Miss Ames stood and held her hand out to him. He considered it for a moment, wondering if he ought to allow a woman to help him up. He had little pride left to lose, so he wrapped his hand around hers.

She leaned her slim form away from him, providing just enough leverage for him to come easily to his feet and stand taller than she, looking down into her eyes. He admired the pert tilt of her nose and the slight pink in her cheeks, and the fingers resting against his gloved palm.

"Mr. Devon," she said, blonde eyebrows drawing together. "Are you sure you are all right?"

Realizing he ought to have released her hand some moments before, Harry reluctantly did so now and reached up to adjust his hat—only to find it missing. "My hat."

Miss Ames tucked her freed hand behind her back and her eyes swept the ground around them. Harry watched her search for a moment before realizing he ought to look too.

Perhaps the fall had addled him somewhat.

"Here it is," she sang out. He saw it near the gnarled roots of the tree poking above the ground. Harry stepped toward it, bending at the same moment as Miss Ames, and promptly knocked into her head.

"Oh," she gasped, leaning away and raising her hand to the spot. Harry hissed a pained breath from between his teeth and reflexively reached out. His hand covered hers at her temple.

"Miss Ames, I'm dreadfully sorry." She sank back on her heels and lowered herself to the grass, then leaned back against the tree. He kept his hand on hers, following her every movement. It occurred to him he was hindering rather than helping and he dropped his hand away and curled the offending fingers into his palm.

She closed the eye nearest where their heads had collided and peered at him with the one that remained open. "Mr. Devon, I am not certain how the two of us have bungled this cat rescue so terribly, but I think we ought to cease engaging in such endeavors for the foreseeable future." Though she delivered her pronouncement with a serious tone, something about the dimple appearing in her right cheek lightened her words considerably.

§

Daisy watched Mr. Devon sit back, his position on the ground less than elegant.

"That was something of an adventure," he said, then groaned as he rose to his feet. He offered her his hand, taking his turn in assisting her to her feet. Daisy accepted the help, gripping her shawl tightly in one hand with the other in his.

"I feel quite terrible about this," she said. He looked about after releasing her, then reached down for his coat.

A splatter of mud covered its back, as it had landed in a damp patch of earth. And when he turned the garment around to inspect it further, she saw the lining on the inside bore several haphazard tears from the cat's claws.

"Oh. Oh, I'm terribly sorry." She reached for the coat while her cheeks warmed with still more embarrassment.

He pulled it away from her and folded the clothing, draping it over one arm. "Do not trouble yourself, Miss Ames. I'm certain it is repairable."

Daisy bit her lip, mortified at the damage her reprehensible pet had done him, and all the difficulties it had led to.

Mr. Devon reached down again, finally retrieving the troublesome hat. He conducted a quick inspection, then put it on his head at a slightly rakish angle. "There we are. All is restored to order."

She glanced about them, seeing nothing else out of place. "I suppose it is."

"Miss Ames, I must thank you for making my return to the neighborhood interesting." He put one hand to his back and bent to one side, wincing.

"Your return?" she asked, that wording piquing her interest. "Are you here for a visit, Mr. Devon, or do you intend to take up residence at Whitewood Manor?" The local gossips hadn't breathed a word about the return of one of the neighborhood's most eligible bachelors.

"I am not yet certain," he said with an easy shrug. "For now, it's only a visit to my sister."

"Oh." She took in his appearance again, noting the expensive cut of his clothing, the fine linen of his shirt, and boots that looked of higher quality than any she'd ever seen. Rumors of the Devon fortune had long circulated in the neighborhood, but as the late Mr. Devon had rarely mingled with the neighborhood, much less opened his house to visitors, none could say with certainty just how wealthy the man had been.

Given that his son stood before her dressed as well as the earl, and had been known to have taken a tour of Europe, she guessed the rumors were true.

"Will you be at your home, or hers?" she asked, then hurried to add, "I will need to let my father know. I am certain he will wish to see you during your stay."

He crossed his arms over his chest and regarded her with one raised eyebrow and a smile as charming as it was good humored. "Will he? And will you be joining him?"

"Me?" she asked, perplexed. "I suppose I could, though he prefers to make parish visits alone most of the time." When his lips curled into an expression of amusement, she frowned at him. Then the realization came. *He is flirting with me.* She wasn't certain if she ought to be flattered or not.

"I will be at my sister's home." He cast a glance in the direction of the vicarage, though a slight rise in the ground hid it from view. "How is Mr. Ames? The last time I saw him was years ago."

"He is well enough." Daisy wrapped her arms around her waist, looking up to see clouds moving across the sky. "It looks as though it is to rain, Mr. Devon."

He spared a glance to the sky, frowning. "May I escort you home, Miss Ames?" he asked, then gave her another charming grin.

Daisy took a step back, looking over her shoulder toward home. "Not just now, I should think. Father isn't home, and it is a short walk. You should return to the Gilberts' before those clouds burst. It was good to see you again, Mr. Devon." She curtsied, ready to take her leave of him. Perhaps he'd taken her friendliness as an invitation to flirt, and it certainly was not that. She hardly knew the man, after all.

"Yes, of course. Thank you, Miss Ames." He didn't sound disappointed, though she caught the puzzled look on his face. Perhaps he wasn't used to young ladies turning down his company. "I hope to see you again soon, Miss Ames." He turned a teasing smile on her.

Daisy answered in a neighborly way. "Thank you, Mr. Devon." She curtsied again. "Good day, sir." Then she turned and walked toward home, at a brisk pace. Before she crested the hill, she glanced over her shoulder.

He stood there still, coat in his hands, watching her retreat.

Chapter Four

Harry sat in the pew with the Gilberts, staring across the church at a dark blue bonnet. The vicar sat next to his daughter. A younger man—a curate, his sister had informed him—read the sermon. Several days had passed since Harry's encounter with Miss Ames, yet he kept thinking on it and the way she'd nearly fled from him.

Most young ladies of his acquaintance enjoyed his company, and she'd certainly seemed amiable enough given her teasing about her identity.

"Mama will question you after the service," little Charles whispered next to him. Harry looked down in some surprise, but the boy was staring at him with wide eyes. "To make sure you pay attention," he added helpfully.

As Charles was already eight years old, he accompanied the adults to church while his younger siblings remained behind with their nursemaid.

Harry winked at the boy. "Then we'd best stop daydreaming."

Charles grinned at him before facing forward again, his expression changing to one of intense concentration. "It'd be easier if Mr. Haskett didn't talk so much."

Harry masked his chuckle as a cough, covering his mouth with his fist. Christine, seated on the other side of him, leaned closer.

"You aren't being a poor example to my son, are you?" she asked in a soft whisper.

"Of course not." Harry looked down at her, pleased to see her teasing smile. "The lad is keeping me in check."

He tried to concentrate on the sermon, but the next distraction came when a young woman in the next row glanced back at him, fluttering her eyelashes in a pretty manner. Harry hadn't the slightest idea who she was, so he hardly dared offer more than a polite nod before pointedly turning his eyes away.

Perhaps attending church wasn't the best idea. Every match-making mother in the county will soon know I'm here. While he generally didn't mind attention from ladies, with his present concerns, he wasn't certain he wanted the distraction. He had a life to plan, after all.

The meeting ended and his nephew rushed from the pew without a backward glance, escaping outside with several other small boys. Christine watched him go with a rueful smile, her arm through Thomas's as they joined the other parishioners in the aisle.

Harry's attention went back to the front of the room in time to catch Miss Ames turning around. He waited, watching her eyes sweep the room, until she saw him. Then he deliberately grinned in her direction and nodded. The woman raised her eyebrows and immediately engaged in conversation with someone standing at her side, showing him her back again.

Perhaps Harry had done something to upset her, though he could not think what. *Or maybe she is only embarrassed by the absurdity of the cat's rescue.* If her sensibilities were delicate enough, he could understand how that entire interlude could be viewed as awkward. If the opportunity arose, he determined to find out how to rectify the situation.

"Mr. Devon?" a feminine voice said.

The young lady who had stolen glances at him all through services stepped into his pew, her expression one of charm and welcome. He noted the woman standing near her, likely her mother, did not appear nearly so happy to see him.

He bowed. "Good morning, Miss...?"

She colored and raised a gloved hand to her cheek. "Oh, you do not remember me? I suppose that is natural. I was only a girl the last time we met."

She didn't look as though she was much more than a girl at present, either. She couldn't be more than seventeen or eighteen, at the most.

She curtsied. "I am Miss Amelia Robin."

"Ah. Miss Robin. Of course." He vaguely recalled that their family had taken a lease on another house in the neighborhood the same year his father passed away. "Did you enjoy the sermon today?" From the corner of his vision, he could see the dark blue bonnet Miss Ames wore making its way down the aisle, slowly.

"Most assuredly." She cast her eyes downward. "I wonder, Mr. Devon, how long you might be in the neighborhood? There is to be a public ball soon, you see, and I wanted to make certain you knew of it."

The matron behind her frowned more deeply. He ought to say something to her, greet her properly, but Miss Ames's approach took up more of his attention than the conversation at hand.

"A ball, you say?" Harry asked, distracted. "I have no plans to quit the neighborhood at present. I will be certain to attend, should circumstances permit."

"Oh, that is wonderful. It will be a perfect opportunity to reacquaint yourself with the neighborhood." She stepped out into the aisle, nearly in front of Miss Ames, her frowning mother nudging her along. "I do hope I see you again soon, Mr. Devon."

"Miss Robin." He barely remembered to bid her goodbye with a deep nod before giving greeting to the woman who'd somehow held his attention even while he spoke to another.

Harry moved to block her progress, though Miss Ames had stopped of her own volition to speak to a woman who held the hand of a little girl. Harry couldn't help but overhear the conversation.

"Mrs. Sutterfield, Miss Rachel, how good to see you both. But where are your other charming children today, Mrs. Sutterfield?

I hope everyone is well," Miss Ames said, her voice a mixture of concern and cheer.

"Well enough, Miss Ames," the woman answered, real warmth in her words. "Thank you for asking. Frederick and Robert have colds and stayed behind to rest. It's the turn in the weather, of course."

The Sutterfields, he vaguely recalled, owned land on the other side of Annesbury Village.

"I do hope they feel better soon." Miss Ames bid the woman good day, then turned to Harry with an air of expectancy to her posture.

"Mr. Devon, it is good to see you again. I hope you have sufficiently recovered from our last meeting." Though her smile remained polite, Harry saw the hesitancy in her gray eyes.

"I have, thank you. Has Bell found herself up any more trees?" he asked, sharing what he hoped was a reassuring smile. "If need be, you may call on me to rescue her again."

Her cheeks turned a little pink. "I hope that will not be necessary, Mr. Devon, though I thank you for the offer of your services. At present, I have a different request to make. I told my father you returned to the neighborhood. He wished me to extend an invitation to you to dine with us, this evening if convenient."

"This evening?" Harry stood taller. His memories of her father were nothing spectacular. He had sat through the man's sermons when he attended church with his sisters but had no distinct memories good or bad. His father, on the other hand, had never had anything good to say about the vicar. That alone made Harry disposed to like the man.

"Or perhaps another time," she said when he hesitated too long. "When your family can spare you."

Harry hurried to reassure her. "This evening would be perfect, actually. I look forward to seeing you both."

Miss Ames offered him another polite, slightly bland smile, then gave him the time for dinner and took her leave. He watched her retreating form with curiosity, but only for a moment. Another old neighbor greeted him, and by the time he looked up again she was gone. Harry finally made his way out of the church to find Christine and Thomas, conversing with their neighbors in the churchyard.

"We are delighted to have my brother with us," Christine was saying to three different women gathered near her, their bonnets bobbing up and down as she spoke. "Though I cannot say how long he will remain. Young gentlemen tend to be restless, I suppose."

That's one word for it. Harry didn't feel so much restless as aimless. He steeled himself to enter the conversation, prepared for curious mothers and tittering ladies to attempt filling his social schedule. As much as he disliked London, one of its benefits would be relative anonymity. At home, everyone knew his name, even if they didn't truly know *him.*

Harry stepped forward, fixing his most amiable smile in place.

§

"The Devon boy. I must confess feeling a measure of curiosity over the sort of man he's grown into." Daisy's father spoke in his usual ponderous manner, the words coming from him slowly, as though coated in molasses. His voice, deep and soothing, had grown a little rougher with his age. Knowing his habits as she did, Daisy hummed in agreement as she tidied his study. They employed a manservant, housekeeper, cook, maid of all work, and a kitchen maid, but Daisy knew her father liked his study organized a certain way and made it part of her own work. There had been other servants in the past, before her sisters married and her father decided to use part of his income to hire a curate.

"His father, God rest him, wasn't a pleasant person for all that he was an important one," Mr. Ames continued, stuffing his pipe with tobacco. He settled more deeply into his chair. "Do stop fussing, Augusta. It is the Sabbath."

She straightened the letters on his desk. "I like to have busy hands, Father."

"One of your virtues, I'll grant you, but you would be better occupied to pass the time in quiet reflection."

Reflecting on any point of her life seemed a rather useless way to spend her time. For two years, she'd been her father's only child at home. Six years previous, she lost her mother to influenza. Lily married shortly after and left for India. Gabriella went away with her Naval officer. It fell to Daisy to care for Father, home, and the parish charitable duties. And still, she tended to her personal dreams of the school.

She came to sit in the chair beside her father's. "What did you think of the sermon today, Father?"

He puffed on his pipe, its rich scent wafting through the room. Mother had always disliked when he smoked indoors and limited the recreation to the study. Despite all the years since her loss he never took the pipe out of the room. Though her parents had never been overly demonstrative in their affection for one another, it was comforting to know he honored her memory in such a simple way.

"Mr. Haskett did well," her father said, sounding thoughtful. "I am not entirely in favor of the way he creates his own sermons so often. There are more than enough good texts in the world to read from. Greater minds than his, and mine, have already written the finest of speeches regarding the state of mortal man."

Her father's views didn't surprise her at all. He'd read many of the most famous sermons over the years, relying on texts his bishop recommended to him, and their library was evidence in his favor that more than enough had been published on every moral topic imaginable.

"I think it shows a desire to meet the people's present needs," Daisy ventured to say.

"Perhaps. You did always like creative sorts, being one yourself." The tone he used to say those words was speculative, not pleased. Her father was the sort of man who believed if one method worked, you needn't waste energy trying anything new or different.

I'm not certain I would call Mr. Haskett creative, she thought to herself, affecting an expression one might wear during quiet reflection. His sermons are nearly as dry as those read from books.

A knock on the door brought her attention away from her thoughts and the maid appeared, a cheerful smile on her face. "Mr. Devon has arrived for dinner, Mr. Ames."

"Ah. A punctual young man. That is a mark in his favor." Father pushed himself up from his chair. "Let us go meet him, my dear." He held his arm out for Daisy, and once she took it, he led them out of the room.

Mr. Devon stood in their small entryway, his hat already removed, studying a pastoral painting which hung near the door. When they approached, he turned to fully face them, and bowed most respectfully.

"Mr. Ames, it is a pleasure to see you again. Miss Ames, thank you for having me to dinner." His voice was warm, genuine.

"You are most welcome, sir." Father answered for the both of them. "Won't you come into the dining room?" Her father gestured, with Daisy still on his arm. "With only the two of us at home, we are not often formal, though we do appreciate your company."

They made their way through the dining room door, to a table large enough to sit eight people comfortably. Places were laid only at the head of the table, where her father sat, with a setting on his left for her and on the right for their guest. Father helped her into her chair while Mr. Devon, his eyes taking in the room with interest, found his way into his own.

The housekeeper brought dishes from the sideboard, putting everything necessary on the table before disappearing back into the kitchens. The meal was a simple one, but Daisy knew everything would taste wonderfully.

"I must say, Mr. Devon, that the neighborhood is most curious about your return here. You cannot be unaware of that fact," her father said, while Daisy gave attention to her potatoes.

Harry's voice, more a tenor than a baritone, was laced with amusement when he spoke. "I am exceptionally well aware of it, Mr. Ames. While our neighborhood isn't small, it is a very close community."

"It is, indeed. Tell me, sir, how have you spent these last years? I was given to understand you finished your university studies two or three years ago." Mr. Ames sliced his roast chicken into smaller pieces as he spoke, his slower speech giving Mr. Devon ample time to sample his own food before being required to make his answer.

Daisy lifted her eyes from her plate, interested in this herself. She'd been away, at school, when the late Mr. Devon passed away. The present Mr. Devon hadn't returned to the neighborhood much since that time, and certainly never long enough for her to catch a glimpse of him. She wasn't particularly friendly with his sister, as their friends were in different circles, but she'd caught snatches of rumors about how he spent his time.

Mr. Devon's lips quirked upward, as though the whole world existed for his amusement. "I spent some of the time in London, on occasion, and in Bath with my sister. Most of the time, I was in Italy. My brother-in-law, the Earl of Ivyford, has family there and they were kind enough to host me."

"Interesting," her father said, in a tone Daisy recognized at once as one of disapproval.

Hoping Mr. Devon hadn't picked up on the tone, Daisy spoke quickly. "How wonderful, to spend time in Italy. What did you do while you were there?" she asked.

"What do people do anywhere?" he asked, lightness in his voice and a sparkle in his eye. "I kept company with the family, attended balls and recitals, museums when I visited the cities."

Daisy darted a look at her father, seeing his frown deepen. She could almost hear his thoughts, as he'd expressed them many times over the years when discussing members of the gentry. *A life of idleness, pursing only pleasure, is ill-spent.*

"Much as one would do here," Daisy said before her father could speak. "And why did that come to an end, Mr. Devon?"

"My very question," he father said, already scowling. "What are your future plans, sir?"

34

With an almost careless shrug, Harry met Daisy's eyes. "I am not certain, though I have already had an adventure or two since returning."

"Not certain?" Father asked, sitting straighter. "A young man such as yourself, with all the world at his feet, a fine home in the country and family all about him, and you are *not certain* what you will do next? I should think it obvious, even to a man of your years, that there are duties to be seen to."

Daisy closed her eyes and took a deep breath, willing away her blush on her father's behalf. Sometimes, he thought because he was a vicar he had a right to call even strangers to account. From his lectern in the church it may have been acceptable, but in the privacy of a dining room it made her—and everyone else— most uncomfortable.

"Duties, Mr. Ames?" the younger man asked, sounding genuinely curious rather than affronted. "Of what sort, sir? The family steward keeps the estate running in my absence, and I receive regular reports from him on the state of things. My solicitor sees to all legal concerns regarding my father's various investments and properties, and I have an accountant to handle matters of finance. All is watched over."

Oh dear. Daisy didn't sense any malice or pride in Mr. Devon's words, but her father would likely conclude the gentleman possessed both, as his father had before him. She stumbled in her thoughts for a moment, knowing she needed to speak if the evening was going to end without Mr. Devon being given offense.

"Mr. Devon," she blurted with such haste that both men startled and turned to face her. She ignored the heat that remained in her cheeks and tried to call to mind something that would appease her father and explain to the gentleman before her what was meant. "My father would perhaps wish you to remember the parable of the hirelings."

"The hirelings?" the young man asked, his brow furrowing.

As a vicar's daughter, Daisy had more than the usual amount of scriptural knowledge a lady might boast of. "Indeed, sir. It is a parable about shepherds and sheep-herders. Two different sorts of things, you see."

He sat back and regarded her with raised eyebrows, perhaps thinking her overly pious. Yet she had begun the conversation and must see it through, whatever he thought of her.

"Shepherds, you see, are the actual owners of their flock. Owners who tend to their sheep personally. By doing so, they are always at hand when a lamb is sick, or lost, or threatened by a predator. Whereas sheep-herders are hirelings. They are paid by the owner to look after things, and so they are not personally invested. They do not care as much when a lamb is sick, because it is their master's lamb. They do not care if one is lost if it does not hinder their ability to be paid. And if a predator attacks, the hirelings think first of their own safety and not that of the animal."

"Well said," her father proclaimed, eyeing her with real approval this time. "Perhaps you ought to have married the missionary, Augusta."

Mr. Devon considered her with a frown, and she prepared herself for his dismissal, or a change of subject. When he spoke, it was with a contemplative sort of tone. "You are suggesting then, Miss Ames, that I have employed sheep-herders to look after my property and they cannot do the job so well as I can."

"Isn't that what she said?" her father asked, bestowing Mr. Devon with continued disapproval. "No one will care about your household so much as you, sir." He shook his head, and Daisy knew he was mentally bemoaning the state of the world they lived in, as he often did aloud.

"I understand the truth in that." Mr. Devon sat taller again, his eyes meeting hers. "It is something I will think on. Thank you, Miss Ames, for sharing that perspective." At least he did not say those words dismissively, but he gave real weight to each one, as though he meant it.

Daisy nodded and pointedly gave her attention to her plate, willing the men to change the subject so she needn't smooth anymore ruffled feathers. As handsome as Harry Devon had grown since her childhood, he really didn't seem all that different from other gentlemen she'd met. He flirted, he charmed, and he didn't pay much attention to the more important matters of life.

He is kind, she amended her thoughts, feeling a prick of guilt for judging him with such haste. *He rescued Bell from the tree, he accepted our very humble invitation.* The only reasonable thing for her to do was withhold her opinion until she knew him better or he went away again. Considering what she'd learned thus far, she thought the latter the more likely outcome.

Chapter Five

After his morning ride, Harry went in search of Thomas. His brother-in-law would be going over the accounts and letters in regard to his horse farm, which was thriving from all that Harry could tell. Thomas Gilbert had grown his stables from a few mares into a veritable herd of fine-blooded animals. A horse from his stables had sold for five hundred pounds at Tattersall's, or so Harry had heard from a friend. If anyone could give Harry the advice he sought, it was Thomas. Apart from being successful in his chosen path, Thomas was also a level-headed gentleman. Sometimes, Harry wondered how his somewhat exuberant sister had fallen in love with a man so much her opposite.

"Tom?" he said, poking his head around the doorframe.

His brother-in-law looked up from a desk covered in neat stacks of books and carefully arranged papers. "Harry, good morning. Did you enjoy your ride? Which beast did you take out today?"

Though he had a horse of his own, gifted to him upon completion of his studies by Thomas and Christine, Harry enjoyed trying as many of the mounts as possible when visiting. "I'm not sure I can say the name aloud and consider it respectable," Harry said, not even trying to hide his grin. "Who in your family thought naming a hunter of that size Little Rosie?"

Thomas chuckled and stood, stretching. He'd obviously been at work for some time, given the way he relished getting out of his chair. "A daughter of one of the grooms. Her father brought her in for the birth four years ago and, in his elation, asked her what she would name the animal. I was there, and you've never seen such big blue eyes. I couldn't tell her the filly would be called anything else."

"You have a great weakness for young ladies who enjoy horses," Harry said, dropping into a chair near the fire. "Am I disturbing you, Tom?"

"Not at all. I welcome the distraction. What brings you to my study this morning?" Thomas came to the fireplace and leaned against the mantel.

After leaving the vicar's home the evening before, Harry had turned over Miss Ames's words to him several times. They had built upon what Christine had spoken to him of the day he arrived for his visit. People seemed to think he needed to give more attention to his holdings. He supposed he understood, but would it really change anything if he received his steward's reports living at Whitewood instead of in a letter?

"I have been thinking about the estate," he said at last. "But for all my thoughts, I am no closer to a decision."

"You are still considering leasing it." Thomas said, his eyebrows raised.

"Not just yet." Harry sat back, crossing his arms over his chest. "I think Christine is right, that I ought to look into matters further before allowing strangers to move into the home. It may not be the best course of action, or there may be things I must see to before taking such a step."

"Then what sort of decision are you speaking of, if it is not the matter of the lease?" Thomas asked, his brow wrinkling with perplexity.

"I suppose I am talking of the largest decision. The one that encompasses everything else; the house, my position in society, the investments my father made." Harry tilted his head back against the chair and raised his eyes to the ceiling, a cream-colored expanse that revealed no answer to him. "I must decide what to do with my life, and determine what sort of shepherd I am."

There was a moment of silence, then Thomas asked, somewhat incredulously, "Are you taking up sheep farming?"

Harry's smile appeared without effort, as it usually did. "No. I apologize. I had an interesting conversation with the vicar and his daughter last evening."

"Ah. Yes. That explains...nothing." Thomas crossed the room and sat in the chair nearest Harry's. "But you are speaking of your path in life, I think."

Harry gave only the slightest nod to confirm his brother-in-law's words. "For the past several years, my way was clear. Finish schooling. Travel, spend time with my family. I've come home and there isn't a route mapped for me. There is no list of things to accomplish. What am I to do *now?* I am twenty-four years old and I haven't a plan of any sort."

Thomas made a humming sound before speaking. "Haven't you anything you *want* to do?"

"Not really." Harry sat up straight again. "Father always said he would train me up, make me a suitable apprentice in managing his business investments. That hardly seems necessary, given that I have a steward and solicitor, and an accountant as well."

"I can see why you might think that," Thomas said slowly, regarding Harry with raised eyebrows. "But your accountant could sail to the West Indies tomorrow, or your solicitor found to be a swindler, or your steward could retire. What would you do if even one of those men disappeared before they trained a replacement?"

Harry blinked at the older man, his mind unable to produce an answer. "I hadn't thought of that." He was even more woefully lost than he'd thought.

"Having those men train *you* would mean that you would have an understanding of how things work and be capable of confronting any problems that arise yourself." Thomas laced his hands together and leaned forward, elbows on the arms of the chair. "There. You have something to add to your list, or the map for your path. Whichever method you prefer."

"A list might be just the thing." Harry considered the thought, liking it more as he did. "That is where I will start. I will make a list and learn as much as I can from the men who are running things in my stead."

Thomas reached out and clapped Harry on the shoulder. "There you are. A decision made. You will find that the more you make, the more comfortable you will become."

"Let us hope so." Harry's unease had already lessened with the pronouncement. He imagined Miss Augusta Ames sitting before him, her gray eyes serious even while a smile tugged at her lips. She'd surprised him by being something of a contradiction, all friendly smiles one moment and the quiet vicar's daughter another. What would she think of his decision to inspect the work of the hirelings?

Harry grinned to himself. I must thank her for putting the thought into my head.

Although he wasn't sure how long this first step could take, after spending years in studies at Oxford he ought to be able to learn all there was to know from his employees with little effort.

Chapter Six

Pulling her sunshine-yellow shawl around her shoulders, Daisy slipped out the rear door of the vicarage at nearly the precise moment Mr. Haskett knocked on the front. She'd seen him from an upstairs window, approaching from down the lane. If he'd come to see her father, she would be required to attend them with refreshments and then perhaps be expected to sit while they discussed the ponderous aspects of Psalms.

She let a puff of air escape her, her back against the brick of the vicarage. *I am hardly a dutiful daughter, running off like this.*

The afternoon sunlight filtered through the trees from the lane, bathing the road in gold everywhere the blue shadows didn't touch. The brisk fall air wrapped its coolness around her and she pushed away from the house's shadows into the light. She'd hoped to take a long, rambling sort of walk today but chores had kept her indoors.

Thrilled to finally be outside, Daisy let the day take her, quite forgetting she didn't wear her bonnet as she should. The blue sky beckoned her to hurry, and so she would.

Once on the lane, her house safely disappearing behind the trees, the weight of her duties fell away from her shoulders. She would necessarily take them up again when she returned home, but for the moment she enjoyed the sense of freedom in her breast.

Was this always how Harry Devon felt? The man seemed to have no cares, no concerns, given his interactions with her thus far. But why would he? If rumors were to be believed, he was richer than Midas.

Had he even given thought about their dinner conversation after he'd left the vicarage? That had been a fortnight ago, and she hadn't seen him since, except for a short glimpse after services, when he'd been surrounded by young ladies.

Gossip inevitably made its way to her ears as she visited people in the parish, though she certainly didn't seek it out. She'd heard he had begun making his neighborly visits to gentlemen all about the neighborhood, but no young ladies yet boasted of a similar honor.

"Their mothers must be beside themselves," she said out loud, kicking a pebble from the road. How did a young man like him fill his days? Did he ever find himself afflicted with boredom?

Two children turned into the lane ahead of her. Daisy narrowed her eyes and studied their figures in an attempt to discern who they were. They seemed to see her at the same moment she recognized them.

"Miss Ames, good afternoon," said the older of the two, Lucy Reeves. She was ten years old, fair-haired and freckled.

Janie Chandler added her enthusiastic wave to her greeting. "Miss Ames, hello!" Janie's curls escaped the twist beneath her bonnet, and the strings were knotted untidily. The nine-year-old was forever smiling.

Putting away the thought of Harry Devon, Daisy quickened her step to catch up to the girls. They were the best of friends, nearly always in each other's company. Lucy was the daughter of the local butcher and Janie's grandmother was the town's talented seamstress.

"What are you two doing this fine afternoon?" Daisy asked when she drew near enough she didn't have to shout the question.

"Berry hunting," Janie said, holding up the basket she'd been holding. "Lucy says it's too late to find any, but I'm sure there must be some hiding about somewhere."

"Are you after anything particular?" Daisy asked, looking from one little face to the other. "I happen to be an expert forager when it comes to berries. My sisters and I used to walk every lane in search of the best."

Lucy's eyes brightened. "Really? Will we find much in October?"

"We have had a very warm summer, and the weather has stayed fine. If the birds haven't found all the berries yet, I'm certain I can help you find a few." Daisy leaned closer to them, sharing a secretive smile. "I happen to know the very best place for wild strawberries is the Ensley farm, just along the road, or we could find hawthorn berries down by the Milton's mill."

The girls exchanged a wide-eyed look.

"Which do we want?" Janie asked, excitement creeping into her whisper.

The older girl narrowed her eyes as she thought. "Wild strawberries are tart. And hawthorn doesn't make very good pies."

"Is it pies you're after?" Daisy straightened. "Why then, you must have my favorite. Blackberries." She pointed down the lane. "The absolute best patch of blackberries, in the very whole county, is less than half a mile from here."

"It is? Really?" Janie asked, gripping the handle of her basket tighter. "Where?"

"At Whitewood," Daisy answered, immediately reminded of Harry Devon again. "Along the hedgerow."

"Whitewood?" Lucy asked, starting to frown. "Do you think anyone will mind?"

"No one lives there," Janie said quickly. "My granny told me. The owner came back, but he's staying at the Gilberts'."

Even the children were gossiping about Harry Devon. Daisy resisted the desire to sigh. "I don't think anyone will mind if we go pick a few berries."

Janie gasped and clapped her hands, her basket swinging from her arm. "You will come with us, Miss Ames?"

That idea gave both girls enough confidence that they turned and started down the lane at once, chattering between themselves about the pie they would make.

Daisy followed, barely listening to their debate of what sort of crust would be best. She admired their easy friendship.

Outside of the local aristocracy and gentry, the girls before her were the best educated in the neighborhood. Janie's grandmother taught Janie to read and do sums while she herself worked on clothing commissioned by wealthier members of their neighborhood. Lucy's father had done the same for his daughter, as her mother had been lost several years previous to illness and he intended for his children to assist in the family business.

There was a school in the neighborhood for little boys, started by her father and now run by Mr. Haskett. Four days a week, for a few hours at a time, Mr. Haskett met with any boy who sought more knowledge for apprenticeships or positions their parents couldn't prepare them for. Some parents could teach their children to read and do simple sums, but more knowledge was rarely bestowed, and even that little amount rarely given.

Janie and Lucy's steps slowed as they came within sight of the Devon property, marked well along the road by white pillars where carriages would turn in. Daisy skipped forward, snatching up Janie's hand as she went.

"Just ahead here," she sang out as the girls hurried to keep up with her. "Keep your eyes open, watch for the birds. They very well might lead us to the best patch."

Lucy giggled and started searching the tops of the hedgerow.

Daisy couldn't help but smile at the girls. They were intelligent and sweet. It was a shame more children didn't have access to what they and Daisy had been given. If she could but generate enough interest in the school she planned, she could amend that for all the little girls in the village.

Not many saw the value in a servant who could read or a farmer's wife who could do complicated sums. But knowledge begat wisdom, and didn't every man wish for a wife who could raise his children to be wise?

Janie spotted the first bird and pointed, pulling Daisy from her thoughts. "There, I see one!"

Amid the girls' excited giggles, the three of them hurried off the path and to the hedges, peering into the leaves. Several little brown birds took off from the bushes as they approached, and Lucy ran ahead to peer between the branches.

"I've found some, I've found some," she shouted. Her hands shot into the branches.

"Save some for me to pick." Janie released Daisy's hand and hurried down the little incline.

Daisy slowed her steps, watching the girls gather berry after berry, their fingers quick. Several berries found their way into the girls' stomachs instead of their baskets, but that was usually the way of berry-picking. Daisy wandered in the opposite direction from the two of them, trailing her hand along the tips of the leaves, mindful of the bush's thorns.

Daisy paused when she found a particularly fat berry dangling within easy reach. She plucked it and put it in her mouth. Savoring its delicious taste, Daisy remained still for a moment, before she kept idly walking, wondering if there would be more berries on the other side of the hedge, inside the Devon property.

Not that she would ever step inside there without permission, of course.

She absently plucked another berry and ate it, wincing at the tartness of an unripe prize. She gave greater attention to the bush, looking for more of the large, sweet blackberries to get the unwanted taste from her mouth.

A very ripe berry dangled a few inches inside the bush. It looked nearly ready to fall. It had grown to such perfection due to its placement, obviously. She could see several wicked-looking thorns surrounding it.

Daisy reached inside the bush, grateful she wasn't wearing gloves to snag against any branches. She had every confidence she could retrieve the berry, and her fingertip brushed it—

"Good day, Miss Ames." She jumped, her hand scraping against several thorns at once. She hissed out a breath and tried to withdraw, but her wrist-length sleeve had caught on a bramble thorn.

Looking over her shoulder, Daisy saw none other than Harry Devon standing on the road. He watched her, a crooked grin on his lips, though his eyebrows were furrowed.

"What are you doing here?" he asked, coming closer.

Daisy turned to study her predicament, the hook of the thorn holding onto her dress. She reached in with her other hand to try and undo the fabric without causing it injury, but was immediately pierced by another thorn, causing her to emit a somewhat unladylike yip of pain.

Mr. Devon came hurrying up beside her and suddenly his hands, encased in leather gloves, were reaching around her and into the bushes. Her breath stilled as her shoulder made contact with his chest. He wrapped one hand around the one she'd gotten stuck in the branches, protecting it from being brushed by thorns. The fingers of his other hand worked to free her sleeve. Before she could protest his nearness, he had guided her hands out of the brambles.

"Thank you, Mr. Devon," she said, her voice thick and her mouth dry. Feathers tickled her from the inside, and heat climbed up her neck and into her cheeks. He stepped away, but only enough to better inspect her hands, still held in his. He turned them over, but rather than see what damage the thorns had caused, Daisy kept her eyes on his face.

It was a very *nice* face. She'd thought him handsome before. At present, there was more to it than that. He stood close, close enough for her to see flecks of green in his blue eyes. His lips were turned down in a frown as he studied her hands, and his forehead was creased. He had the tiniest scar through one dark eyebrow.

"These scratches," he said, startling her out of her study, "aren't very deep. Though this one is still bleeding." Daisy looked at last at the damage. The hand she'd used to attempt to rescue the other was bleeding, the bright red a stark contrast to her fair skin.

Henry kept hold of that hand in his left, then reached into his jacket with his right and drew out a handkerchief. "Here, this is clean. We will bind it up."

She tried to protest. "Oh. Please. I don't wish to spoil the cloth—"

"It's cloth, Miss Ames. It will wash." And he released her only long enough to take his gloves off, dropping them to the ground. Then Mr. Devon wrapped the handkerchief around her palm. The warmth of his hand brushing against hers made those feathers blow about inside her again.

"Thank you," she whispered.

"Miss Ames?" little Janie's voice asked. "Miss Ames, is something wrong?"

The gentleman glanced up. His confused expression rapidly changed to a friendly one, with a big grin on his handsome face. "Your Miss Ames was attacked by an especially ferocious bramble. I am tending to her battle wounds."

Janie had come closer, Lucy just behind her, their faces full of concern.

Daisy forced a light-hearted tone, trying to match Mr. Devon's ease with the situation. "It is a good thing Mr. Devon was here. He seems to have some experience in field-dressing injuries."

He chuckled and released her hand at last, then bent to pick up his discarded gloves. "Any gentleman who goes about rescuing fair maidens ought to have a basic knowledge of such things." He looked to the girls and gave them a wink. Janie giggled while Lucy's eyebrows rose to hide beneath the brim of her bonnet, then the two of them exchanged a secretive sort of look.

The sudden risk of the situation hit Daisy like a fallen tree branch. Harry Devon had treated her with great familiarity, before witnesses. Her mind stretched about for ways to salvage the situation, to keep her name from being crossed with his in the local gossips' tales.

"Mr. Devon is an old friend," she said quickly. "I am afraid he's rescued me, and my sisters, many times from difficulties we made ourselves."

He looked askance at her, then to the girls. "Indeed. As I said, I make it something of a habit to rescue people. Do either of you young ladies need rescuing at present?" he asked, bowing to them.

"No," Lucy said at once. Janie tucked her chin down shyly and shook her head.

"That is a shame."

"Oh dear. Where are my manners? Mr. Devon, may I present Miss Lucy Reeves and Miss Janie Chandler? They were in search of berries this morning and I thought of your fine patch here."

"Ah, of course. The finest blackberries in the county grow here." He nodded, affecting a serious frown. "Have you ladies found enough berries to fill your baskets?" he asked.

Janie held out her basket, which held maybe two dozen berries. "Not yet, Mr. Devon."

"Then you ought to step through to the other side. I came down to inspect the bushes myself, you see, when I heard you young ladies and thought to see who had the same idea as I did, at precisely the same time." He gestured back to the break in the hedges, the entry to his property. "Won't you come in? There are many more berries on the other side. I am afraid they've been terribly neglected of late. I used to pick them myself, but I have been away a very long time."

Two sets of eyes in upturned faces met Daisy's, pleading and cautious. They wouldn't go inside without her, she well knew, but they had baskets to fill. Sending them home happy, with full baskets, might be the best way to avoid them telling too many tales about Mr. Devon's *rescue.*

"It would simply be bad manners to say no to your kindness, Mr. Devon. Come along, girls. Let us fill your baskets." She waved back to the estate entrance. Janie squealed while Lucy took off at a run, her basket swinging in her hand. Both girls rapidly disappeared from sight.

Daisy clasped her hands behind her back and looked up at Mr. Devon, fingering his handkerchief around her palm. "You are very kind, Mr. Devon."

He offered his arm to her. "Thank you, Miss Ames. Shall we join the young ladies?" She wrapped her hand around his arm, allowing his charm—for once—to make her smile.

§

The measure of accomplishment he felt in Miss Ames's acceptance of his invitation was greater than Harry expected it would be. He didn't stop to examine the triumph, brushing it aside as a normal reaction to a lovely woman.

Harry followed after the girls, Miss Ames on his arm, at a more sedate pace than the children favored. The story he'd told them of hearing their happy chatter and investigating had been true. But the blackberry bushes hadn't drawn him to that portion of his property. He'd been briskly walking the perimeter of the landscaped grounds, grumbling to himself about his own ignorance. The laughter of children had drawn him, most pleasantly, from his sour mood. The distraction of Miss Ames on his arm further soothed his disgruntled attitude.

"Thank you for sharing your bushes with us," she said, pulling him away from the edge of his mental precipice once more.

"It is entirely my pleasure to be of service to you." They rounded the entrance to the property and walked alongside the hedge. "I wonder, Miss Ames, if you could explain something to me."

Her expression remained neutral and polite. Was she to be *that* version of herself today? The lady with the placid exterior and lack of warmth? The lady who made him feel, when he really thought on it, like a spoiled little boy begging for more sweets?

"Of course, Mr. Devon."

"What has become of your gloves? Or a bonnet?" He nodded to the top of her head and put a gloved hand over her fingers on his sleeve. "Have we left them behind? I would be happy to go and fetch them for you."

"Oh." Pink seeped into her cheeks, she turned hastily away. "No. I did not—that is to say, I went out quite without them. I hadn't meant to go far from my own garden. I—"

Harry stopped walking, and she did as well. "Miss Ames, I am sorry. I should not tease you. But as I have three older sisters, it often comes far too naturally. Please, forgive me."

For the barest moment she stared at him with her mouth hanging open. Then a twinkle appeared in her eye, followed closely by a faint smile. "It is quite all right, Mr. Devon. You are forgiven." Then she withdrew her hand to pull her shawl tighter around herself. "It isn't the best example to those girls, the vicar's daughter wandering about without gloves and hat."

He looked ahead, where the misses in question were darting to and fro along the hedge, gathering berries. "I doubt they have even noticed."

"I suppose not. Though they likely noticed your familiarity with me."

He turned swiftly at the regretful tone of her voice, in time to see Miss Ames's wince. "I beg your pardon?" he asked, tilting his head to the side. "Familiarity, Miss Ames? I hope I did what any gentleman would in coming to your aid. Unless the title has come to mean something else in these parts." He raised his eyebrows theatrically, though he thought over his conduct to be certain he hadn't done anything ill-mannered. Had he stood too near? Admired her features overlong?

"Oh, no. That is not what I meant." Her cheeks had darkened from a pale pink to a dusky rose color. "It is only—only that you are recently come back, and people are already speaking of you. I mean, that is to say—" She broke off, forehead wrinkling in her distress.

Harry considered her for a moment before he realized what she was trying to verbalize. In the time he'd been in the neighborhood, Harry had become creative in wriggling free from invitations extended by the neighbors. Truthfully, he had little time for entertainment since engaging himself to learn about managing his affairs. He'd thought a day with each of the three men principally in charge of things would be enough. But he'd yet to even fully grasp everything his steward had imparted to him, in a two-week span of time.

Hoping to put Miss Ames at ease, he took a step back from her. "Miss Ames, it's quite all right. I understand. Having your name bandied about with mine would cause quite the sensation." He lowered his eyes to the ground. The idea didn't offend him. *But why does she object to me so much?*

She stepped closer, putting her hand on his arm. "Mr. Devon, I have no wish to offend you. I do not like gossip, sir. I strive to avoid being a subject of it. That is all. The excitement surrounding your return makes you a particularly sought-after subject. Those two sweet girls there," she nodded in their direction, "one is the granddaughter of the seamstress, who is kind but very talkative with all who seek her services. The other girl is daughter to the butcher, who speaks with representatives of every household in the neighborhood."

He regarded the children, realization creeping into his thoughts. "Anything those two girls tells their families is likely to be told to the whole town," he said, somewhat awed by the power the two children unknowingly held.

Miss Ames nodded, her hand slipping away from his arm again. "And once rumors begin, they spread quickly, and as often as not change in the telling."

"Then we had better make certain the young ladies know exactly what to tell people. You, Miss Ames, take your ease on that bit of grass there and leave it to me." He gave her his most confident grin, the kind his sister Rebecca said portended mischief, and strode confidently to the two girls picking berries.

"Have you found enough yet? Oh, no. That paltry amount will not suffice. We must fill your baskets to the brims. Come, there is a trick to it." He took off his gloves after making a show of inspecting their harvest. Then he took off his hat. It wasn't one of his finest, but it was tall enough to rival the carrying capacity of their baskets.

"I will fill my hat, which you can see is very empty, as fast as I can. Try to fill your baskets before I can do that, won't you? We will have a race."

Both girls seemed delighted by the idea and hurried to get an even larger lead on him. Harry looked over his shoulder to see

Miss Ames staring after him, openly wearing her shock. He waved at her, then made good on his challenge to the girls.

His only advantage was his higher reach, as he could get berries above their heads. The girls giggled and laughed and encouraged each other to go faster and faster. He laughed with them and teased as much as he could, not allowing them to look into his hat to view his progress.

The smaller one, whose name had eluded him until the older called it out, finished her basket first. "Look, look!" She rushed over to him and held it out for his inspection. Then she sat the basket down. "Now I shall help Lucy and we will win the race." She turned and spun, the ribbons of her bonnet flying up behind her.

Harry called after her, "I shall still win, Miss Janie!" His hat wasn't even half full.

Miss Ames had followed his suggestion to sit on the grass, watching the display.

"Miss Ames," he called, "you didn't tell me they were champion foragers. This hardly seems a fair race."

She laughed, the sound bright and happy as a spring morning. "Mr. Devon, you ought to have studied the situation more keenly. You have none to blame but yourself." But the smile she bestowed on him, one that was relieved and grateful, indicated she knew well enough what he was about.

Harry didn't speak to her again, though he continued calling out to his competition. He'd given himself a thorough distraction, and hopefully gave the girls something to talk about other than his assistance to Miss Ames.

At last the older of the two declared her basket filled, and Harry admitted defeat dramatically. Then he offered his escort to the young ladies, at least partway down the lane, where the road branched.

Miss Ames followed behind them by several steps until they came to the turn-off that led to the village. The girls went on their way with waves and smiles. After they'd turned their backs, Miss Ames came to stand at his side.

"Well done, Mr. Devon. I believe those girls nearly forgot my presence." He studied her from the corner of his eye, noting the way she tilted her head to the side when amused. Her shoulders rose and fell with a deep sigh. "Thank you for understanding the situation."

Harry waved her thanks away easily. "I have sisters, Miss Ames. I know what a woman's reputation means to her. I wouldn't want yours to be questioned." He turned to face the direction of the vicarage. "I find myself wanting to walk in this direction, Miss Ames. Might I assume you are going the same way?"

With his back to her, he couldn't see her expression. Had he made peace enough with her to bring back the smiling, cheerful woman he'd met the day he saved the cat?

"You assume correctly. This time." She stepped up beside him. "I suppose you would like a travel companion for the arduous journey ahead of you?" she asked, and when he cut a glance at her, he saw her lips twitching upward.

The knots inside Harry loosened and he bowed, his hat still in hand. "I would appreciate that, yes. And would the lady care to share my provisions for the duration of our sojourn?"

She laughed and peered inside his misused head-covering. "You have quite ruined your hat, Mr. Devon. Those berry stains will not come out. I cannot think your valet will thank you."

"I currently do not employ a valet." Harry peered into the hat as well and studied the splotches of purple berry juice. "But as all the stains will be on the inside, I cannot see there being any difficulty in wearing the hat again." He withdrew a few and popped the berries into his mouth.

"No valet?" she asked, looking him over with obvious skepticism. "I find that difficult to believe, with a gentleman of your standing."

"I make do. The Gilberts' footman saw to assisting me today. There is usually someone about if I need help." He withdrew some berries and held them out to her, realizing belatedly he'd never put his gloves back on.

Miss Ames regarded him with puzzlement, but then took the berries, her fingertips not even brushing against his palm. But his skin remembered the feel of hers anyway, from bandaging her scrape. Her hand, warm and soft, marred by the brambles, had been delightful to hold for even a short amount of time.

With a sudden need to say something to her, to repair the opinion she had of him, he blurted out, "I have been meeting with the estate's steward."

She started at his rush of words, her lips parted with a berry hovering just before them. She cleared her throat and lowered the fruit. "I recall you said you wished to do something of the sort." She waited, politely, for him to continue.

Harry, without much direction of thought, began talking to cover his embarrassment. "I thought a single meeting would be enough to determine how the estate ought to be managed, but it has been twelve days and I feel more confused than when we began. There is much to take into account in running a property the size of Whitewood, things I never considered. Did you know there is a dam on the property? And twelve families are tenants. *Twelve*. And there is a household staff, the gardeners, the groomsmen, the gamekeeper, and likely a flock of other people I have yet to hear about."

While he spoke, her expression changed from confusion to amusement. "You didn't know how many people depend upon your estate for their livelihood? Was that information not in the regular reports your steward sent you?" She plunked a berry into her mouth, her eyes laughing at him even if her lips were pressed together.

Harry fished more berries from his hat. Their progression down the road was slow, they were barely nearer the vicarage than when they'd begun. Miss Ames showed no impatience to be on her way. Perhaps she wanted to know more about the situation, and given her view of gossip she was likely a safe confidant.

"A lot of information was not in the reports." Harry huffed. "There are things I am learning of that I find important, like knowing the number of children running about on my lands, that my father apparently never cared for. The steward has been sending me reports of a nature that would be sufficient for Mr. Charles Devon but are entirely lacking for me."

Miss Ames reached out and brushed her fingers against his knuckles, arresting his attention to the spot where she touched at once. He realized he'd taken hold of the brim of his hat and started twisting it in his frustration. He immediately relaxed his grip.

"You do not wish to spoil your hat even more," she said, her voice gentle and almost teasing. "Mr. Devon, you seem rather vexed. Why? You have found a problem, but I am certain you will find a solution as well."

He raised his eyes slowly to meet hers, his heart thrumming quite pleasantly to find her so near.

One would think I have never been in close proximity to a pretty girl before. Harry cleared his throat and tucked his hat beneath his arm, berries still inside. "I am not certain I am the right person for this, Miss Ames," he said. "My father had a good head for business. He managed things in a certain style, in a particular manner, and I haven't been trained up in his way. I am giving serious thought to leasing the house."

She tucked her hands behind her back, regarding him with a frank expression. "Mr. Devon, that will only delay the inevitable. You have already started your garden, you may as well finish and see what sort of harvest you reap." She nodded once, firmly, then began walking again. She'd made it several steps before he rushed to follow.

"Garden? Miss Ames, I have only just begun to understand shepherds and sheep. Please, no more metaphors."

"Parables, Mr. Devon." She gave him a disapproving frown. "But very well. I think, sir, that you are troubled by the idea of walking away more so than you are by the idea of staying put. What I cannot understand is why you would consider leaving in the first place. Whitewood estate is stunning in its entirety. The people of Annesbury village are kind. The neighborhood charming. Why not remain here and build your life? Especially considering all the good you might do."

He drew up, his mind sorting through her words and latching on to a horrid idea. "All the things I might do because of my money?" he asked, then clamped his mouth shut. One did not discuss one's income in such a manner, with a near-stranger. Why had his tongue been so loose?

She shook her head. "Because of your influence. Because of the people who depend upon you. Your standing in this community could be of nearly as much importance as that of the Earl of Annesbury. You own nearly as much land in this county as he does. Yes, you have wealth, but it means nothing to the people here if they never see any of it." She spoke as if the money meant nothing, and he supposed she might be free with it when it did not belong to her.

"I have no influence here, Miss Ames," he said. It seemed the smiling Miss Ames was gone and in her place was the sermonizing vicar's daughter once more.

"You could change that." She regarded him with a more cautious expression. Perhaps she sensed the withdrawal of his more charming nature. "You could be an example of kindness, of gentility, to this neighborhood. The earl is a good man, but he is often gone to other properties and to London. It would be good to have another to look to when he is away. Someone to be a voice of respect and reason."

"I would think your father would fill that position readily enough." Harry didn't exactly sound bitter, but he knew he didn't sound pleasant either.

Her eyes grew distant and she turned away. "My father does his best, but the people are not particularly close to him." She sighed. "And the curate is still too new to have much trust."

"I'm as new as Mr. Haskett." Harry bit his tongue. Why was he continuing this conversation? He ought to bid her good day and have done with all of it. Especially given his mounting frustration. It would be easier to leave again. Much easier than accepting the responsibility she put upon him with her words.

"Not really." She appeared focused on the ground before her feet, stepping lightly around the larger stones and pebbles. "Your name is familiar, your sisters well-liked, and your reputation somewhat established. There is far more in your favor than against it."

Harry tamped down his frustration, turning his hat over as they walked, spilling the last few berries, leaves, and twigs onto the road.

"What is against it, Miss Ames?" He didn't look at her as he fixed his hat back upon his head. "Besides my lack of caring for my responsibilities."

Her head turned sharply in his direction, her eyes narrowing at him. "Mr. Devon, I have obviously offended you with my observations. Perhaps it is best that we leave this conversation where it is." They were nearly to the vicarage gate. He could easily do as she asked.

Except now that they had come to this point, the conversation irritated him as surely as a pebble in his shoe might.

"Miss Ames." He stopped, and she did as well, straightening her shawl. "I cannot say the idea of settling permanently in the neighborhood appeals to me, but you are not the first to suggest it. If I am to consider such a thing, I should like to have facts laid out before me. You have given me a great many things to think about in regard to the way I can help this community. But then you imply there are things not in my favor. What are those things?"

His long hours working with his steward gave him every reason to wish to bolt, to take up a life of leisure in Brighton, Bath, London, anywhere but this country village. Yet learning how ignorant he truly was of what it meant to be a landowner stung his pride.

She studied him, her gray eyes taking in his expression, reading him. Did she see his earnestness, or did she only see a presumptuous man who had no right to prod her in such a manner?

"Here I thought you a most incorrigible gentleman," she said at last. "But you really wish to know these things?"

"I do. Yes."

She regarded him with the same sort of interest one might a mathematics problem. Searching for an answer yet not entirely willing to work one out.

"The thing you have most against you is not of your doing," she said at last. "Your father's reputation has cast something of a shadow. People wonder just how alike you are to him."

Harry's blood ran cold. He turned away from her, clenching his jaw. "That is all?" he asked at last, the light tone obviously false. "Of course. The apple doesn't fall far from the tree, after all. Thank you for your information, Miss Ames. I hope you have a good day." He bowed and took his leave of her, not meeting her eyes again.

While she said *people* wondered such a thing, he could hear the question in her voice. She wondered, too, if he was as miserly and selfish as the late Mr. Devon.

Miss Ames's conjecture irked him. Hadn't he been invited to meet any number of gentlemen in their homes?

Of course, there had been some interesting lines of conversation in those instances. Especially in regards to his desire to settle at Whitewood. Harry had assumed people were merely curious, looking for gossip to share with friends. But—no. Thinking on it now, there had been at least two instances when the men he spoke to encouraged him to go back to London. One had said, *London is a fine place for bachelor's such as yourself.* Harry had laughed and agreed, though he abhorred the town, in an attempt to be polite.

Furthermore, he certainly hadn't been invited to anyone's dinner table since his arrival, with the exception of the vicar. The young ladies he had met at the church had seemed eager enough to reacquaint themselves with him. Their parents, less so.

Having done everything in his power to avoid being like his father, the thought smarted. A whole village of people silently questioned his character.

Brighton would be lovely. No one knows the Devon name there. I think.

Working against the reputation of a dead man, to earn the esteem of neighbors he barely knew, didn't appeal to him in the slightest. His father's history loomed over him, casting a long shadow indeed, and overcoming it would take more time and energy than he wished to give.

He'd never particularly wanted to come back for that very reason.

Harry's steps slowed as he approached his family's estate, the thought taking hold of him.

I never wished to confront all that my father left behind.

Miss Ames's words came back to him. "You could be an example of kindness, of gentility, to this neighborhood."

His thoughts spun and his heart ached. All he wanted was to find some purpose, find his place in the world.

Why did it have to be here?

Chapter Seven

D aisy's Father leaned on his walking stick in the doorway, watching for Mr. Haskett and the Gooches. Mr. and Mrs. Gooch had a little farm and were near neighbors to the Ameses, so when they offered to give the vicar and Daisy a ride to the assembly ball, Daisy had thought nothing of accepting their kind invitation. After she said yes, Mrs. Gooch informed her they were to bring the curate as well. Five people in a carriage, for such a short ride, would normally be no inconvenience. Knowing Mr. Haskett would be one of the party, however, caused Daisy to feel terribly crowded even before the conveyance arrived.

"Being tardy to a ball is hardly a matter to worry over," her father said, misinterpreting the way she fidgeted with her gloves.

Daisy peered out the doorway again. "Yes, Father. I know."

"Are you anxious about something else?" he asked, studying her with his thick brows furrowed. A tall, thin man, he'd never exactly been an imposing figure. Perhaps that was why he took great pains to speak slowly and in such a forward manner. Daisy had often privately thought so.

"Not at all." She managed a tight-lipped smile. "Merely looking forward to dancing."

He nodded sagely and opened his mouth to say something— when the sound of hooves and wheels on gravel came to their ears. The carriage had come, and in another moment they were finding their seats inside.

Thankfully, Daisy was given a seat between Mr. and Mrs. Gooch while her father and the curate sat across from her on the forward-facing seat. The Gooches were terribly respectful to clergy.

"My dear Miss Ames, you look quite pretty this evening," Mrs. Gooch said. "Isn't it wonderful to be on our way to a ball? Mr. Gooch so enjoys dancing."

Mr. Gooch chuckled and bent toward Daisy. "It is very true, Miss Ames. If possible, I will dance every set this evening. Some say it is not seemly for one of my age, but the young ladies never seem to mind."

"Especially if there is a lack of unmarried men to ask them." Mrs. Gooch tutted. "Of course, with Mr. Haskett added to our numbers, and now Mr. Devon as well, we will see many of our girls cheerfully engaged in dancing this evening."

Heat rose in Daisy's cheeks. She'd been trying, and failing, not to think about the possibility of Mr. Devon attending the ball. After their last meeting she'd known they parted in less than favorable circumstances. Something about their conversation had put him out of humor with her, which she regretted terribly. He had behaved so kindly toward the girls, and to her. His handkerchief, cleaned and pressed, sat on her dressing table reminding her every day of his gallantry.

"Will he be in attendance?" Mr. Haskett asked. "I do look forward to making his acquaintance. We have not yet been introduced, and I have not had the opportunity of paying my respects to him."

Daisy raised her eyebrows without thought. *He has been here more than two weeks. I thought everyone had called upon him.*

"Several young misses have taken the opportunity to be certain of his attendance," Mrs. Gooch said, a knowing sort of humor in her words. "I believe quite a few new gowns will be seen tonight."

Daisy's eyes lowered to her lap. The carriage was too dark to make out the simple lines of her best evening gown. It was hardly more elegant than the dresses she wore to church, with few frills and a less-than-daring neckline. She'd worn the gown several times in the past year, but had nothing more appropriate for the evening. Her very best dress she kept back for special occasions, such as the earl's Christmas ball.

I should not wish to wear it tonight, she thought for the tenth time at least. People would notice and certainly think it had something to do with either Mr. Devon's arrival or the curate's incidental escort.

Father took up another line of conversation with Mr. Gooch, as they were of a similar age. Mrs. Gooch took the opportunity to lean in closer to whisper to Daisy.

"He really is a fine young man, Mr. Devon. He came to the house last week and spoke to my husband for some time. What do you guess it was about?" she asked, sounding delighted.

Daisy swallowed and kept her eyes down upon her lap. Heat filled her cheeks, which was ridiculous. Thankfully, no one could see her in the dark to guess at the reason behind her embarrassment.

"I cannot imagine," she said, trying to sound polite without sounding interested.

"Tenant rents."

Daisy's head came up and she tried to make out Mrs. Gooch's expression through the shadows. Surely, she hadn't heard the woman correctly. "Rents? That is an odd topic of conversation, I suppose." She clamped her lips shut. She would not participate in gossip or conjecture. It was unbecoming of a vicar's daughter to do so.

Mrs. Gooch didn't require further encouragement, however. "Indeed. He said he had been asking several of the gentlemen about in order to determine the fairness of what his tenants are paying. My husband says that the late Mr. Devon was too hard on his tenants. He says—"

The curate's voice interrupted Mrs. Gooch's whispering. "Mrs. Gooch, I understand you are one of the women who assists in the organization of the fall harvest celebration held in the village. Will you have need of any assistance from me, madam?"

Daisy realized the men likely had stumbled onto that subject in their own conversation. Mrs. Gooch didn't seem to mind being interrupted in the least.

"I would be most happy, Mr. Haskett, to have your help. We make something of a fair out of it. There are pie tastings, and weighing of the pigs and such. Perhaps you could be one of our judges." She started speaking with great animation, describing the past harvest celebrations with delight.

Daisy didn't pay much attention. She was rather busy puzzling over Mr. Devon's sudden concern for the local cost of rent. Though he'd told her of his time spent with the steward, she hadn't realized he had extended his education to other landowners. She admitted, if only to herself, the knowledge impressed her.

It is only right a man take such an interest in his responsibilities. I shouldn't be surprised. Mr. Devon is doing what he ought to have done all along.

His charming smile appeared before her mind's eye, his hat full of blackberries teasing at her memory. Nothing about him, so far as she could tell, was selfish or unkind. Her thoughts remained on Mr. Devon for the duration of the carriage ride, much to her annoyance. A man who had no relation to her daily activities ought not to hold such a place in her mind. Turning her thoughts more resolutely to the evening ahead didn't take him far enough away. She wondered who he would dance with, considering several of her peers would likely attempt to secure a set with him. Certainly, the whole neighborhood would be watching Mr. Devon with interest.

Well. She wouldn't. She'd keep her attention where it belonged. On her friends, her neighbors, and her dance partners.

The carriage rolled to a stop before the village's largest building, the Sword and Shield Inn. The lower rooms on the ground floor would be set apart for gentlemen to play cards, while the larger room on the first floor would be given over wholly to dancing.

Daisy accepted Mr. Gooch's hand out of the carriage, then took her father's arm to enter the building. She could already hear music coming from the windows. The public ball occurred the first full moon before harvest, every year. She smiled freely, happily anticipating the hours before her.

"Miss Ames," the curate's voice called before she and her father had made it many steps.

Father paused and turned, releasing her arm as he did so. His expression was solemn in the torchlight.

Daisy bit back a sigh and gave Mr. Haskett her attention. "Yes, Mr. Haskett?"

"Might I have the pleasure of requesting your first dance this evening?" he asked, bowing.

She could give only one answer, as was expected of her. "Of course, Mr. Haskett."

Her father took her arm again and swept her away. He bent slightly, once they were inside the inn, and murmured in her ear, "He is a good man, Augusta."

She nodded her agreement, but her heart clenched. Her father hadn't shown any interest in marrying her off to anyone. He hadn't done much to encourage his elder daughters to wed, either, though he approved of both of their husbands. She hoped, most fervently, he wasn't about to start matchmaking.

Daisy wasn't ready to wed. One and twenty wasn't quite the age for her to worry over such things. Not when she was still a help to her father.

I needn't think about marriage. Not yet. I have other plans, after all. She entered the upper rooms, music swelling as the current dance came to an end. *And Mr. Haskett certainly doesn't fit into any of those plans.*

§

Harry spent the first quarter of an hour going about the hall introducing himself to the people he had not yet met. Gentlemen who had politely presented their wives, daughters, and sisters, but rarely with enthusiasm. He bowed from one end of the room to the other, paying compliments as sincerely and efficiently as possible.

He finally found himself back at his sister's side, where she remained on the arm of her husband.

"Hello again, Harry," she said, smirking up at him. "Why aren't you dancing yet? I think every young lady in the room is waiting for you to take the floor."

"I wouldn't be surprised if wagers had been laid," Thomas said, earning an amused glance from his wife.

"I find the whole thing terrifying," Harry said at last, his voice lowered and his eyes sweeping the room. Several women were looking in his direction, but the one he searched for had yet to appear. "I cannot dance with anyone without giving insult to everyone else."

"Only when it comes to the first." Thomas remained cheerful as ever, pointing out the obvious. "And do not dance with anyone more than a set."

"Christine, will you dance with me?" Harry asked, at a loss for what else to do. "No one can dislike me for dancing with my sister."

She chuckled. "You wish to be universally liked? I never thought you cared much for popularity."

He scowled. "I didn't. But that was before it mattered so much." And it did matter. When he'd been in London, in Bath visiting Julia, and in Italy, no one cared who he danced with because he wasn't a permanent fixture. He came and went as he liked. But here, if he remained at Whitewood, he needed the good opinion of his neighbors. Giving offense with so simple a thing as standing up with the wrong girl wouldn't be wise.

Of course, he hadn't exactly decided to stay yet. But the option, and thus the concern, remained before him.

"Very well," Christine said at last, releasing her husband's arm to take her brother's. "I will dance with you. But that will not entirely solve your problem."

"Thank you." He escorted her to the floor where the second dance in the set was forming. They stepped into position and

Harry looked down the line, searching for a particular blonde head.

The music started and Harry entered into the steps with ease. Christine followed the figures well, and spoke more often to the other ladies near her than to him. Because he needn't give his sister his full attention, Harry's mind wandered.

Miss Ames wasn't in attendance this evening. Not yet, anyway. Augusta Ames confused him. The day before, he'd bandaged her wound, guarded her reputation, seen her laugh, and then felt the sting of her censure. The only thing more confounding than her complexities was his inability to banish her from his thoughts.

The music concluded, and the next dance was called, another that required more energy than thought. Christine gave Harry a firm shake of the head, dashing his hopes she would continue with him for another moment. He took her hand and turned to escort her from the floor—

Miss Ames approached on the arm of the curate, drifting over the floor with ease in a gown of periwinkle blue. Harry nearly stopped to speak to her, but Christine gave his arm a fierce tug, pulling him out of the way.

The vicar's daughter didn't meet his gaze, but the way her lips tightened when she passed let him know she'd seen him. And chose not to look at him.

"You cannot ask her to dance when she is already on her way to the floor," Christine whispered. "Where are your manners, Harry?"

Harry scoffed, albeit quietly. "I had no intention of asking her." Not at the moment, anyway. But now that she had turned up, somehow prettier than she had been the day before, and obviously upset with him, he reconsidered.

Christine cut him a look of supreme skepticism, complete with narrowed eyes and pursed lips. "Did you plan to simply bar her way?"

"No." Harry sped up their walk around the edges of the room in an attempt to outrun the tips of his ears turning red. Since they were attached to him, he failed. But at least Christine hadn't seemed to notice. "I barely know Miss Ames. Why would I wish to dance with her?"

"I haven't any idea." Christine stopped, making it necessary for him to do the same. "Have we a goal with our quick-march, General, or is this merely a drill?" She adjusted her gloves as she spoke.

"I apologize, Chrissy." Harry tucked his hands behind his back. In as nonchalant a manner as he could manage, he turned his head to look out of the room to the couples dancing. It took him a moment to find Miss Ames's blonde coiffure, as she wasn't of a great height. He found the tall, thin curate first and deduced her position from his.

"At least you have managed to skip this dance. Entering it now would be ridiculous." She stood on her toes. "Do you see Thomas?"

Harry shook his head, still observing the progress of Miss Ames down the line of the dance. "I am certain he will find you. He always does."

"Yes. Isn't it marvelous?" she asked, happiness coloring her words.

Harry didn't miss her tone, and when he glanced at her expression he saw softness rest upon her features. His vivacious and outspoken sister wore the mantel of wife and mother quite well. Gratitude eased his heart, not for the first time, in knowing that she'd found Thomas. Somehow, all three of his sisters had obtained happiness, despite his late father's determination to put finances above family and lucre before love.

Christine caught him staring from the corner of her eye and raised her eyebrows. "What is it? Have I grown an extra nose?"

He started to laugh but covered the sound with a cough, raising his fist to his lips. "No. Merely observing that you have grown short, Chrissy."

"Short? You know that it is you who has grown abominably tall, you terrible boy." She took his arm. "Come. Several matrons are glaring in our direction. We must do our duty and at least introduce you to their daughters."

It took a great deal of will to avoid groaning, but Harry managed. He cast one last look over his shoulder to find Miss Ames halfway through the required steps of the dance.

"You may ask her in a moment, Harry, but attend to me in the interim." Christine's words were accompanied by a knowing grin.

He tried to protest. "I wasn't—"

"Yes, you most certainly were." Christine lowered her voice as they approached a woman dreadfully surrounded by young ladies. "Miss Ames will be here all evening, Harry."

Harry fixed his most charming smile in place, bowed to the woman and her four daughters, and tried to remember their names. They were a family newly come to the neighborhood through an inheritance, which made it more difficult to remember them. But he gave it every effort.

While Christine facilitated conversation, Harry kept one ear on the musicians. Somehow, with a few sly questions on the part of the mother, Harry found himself engaged to dance with one of her daughters for the very next dance. Only Christine's gentle squeeze of his arm kept him from running away.

He went to the floor as the young lady's escort, and realized soon after that Miss Ames wasn't dancing. There were more ladies than gentlemen present, but it surprised him someone wouldn't have asked her. Harry tried to concentrate on his partner, returning her smiles and putting some energy into the steps.

Before long, he was escorting her back to her mother. Christine had disappeared, and he had every intention of doing the same before he could be tricked into another dance.

But somehow, he'd only taken his leave of Mrs. Raleigh and her four daughters when a Mrs. Quinsy appeared with a niece, and as the girl looked rather terrified of her aunt's attempts to push them onto the floor, Harry asked her to stand up with him.

An hour passed from the time Harry saw Miss Ames first enter the room, and four partners had come and gone with him onto the floor. The room had grown unbearably hot and Harry's temples thrummed with the beginnings of a headache. He returned his latest partner to her father's side and hurried away as fast as politeness allowed.

His desire to see Miss Ames, when she absolutely must be upset with him, warred with his pride. Why seek her out? He did hope to obtain some measure of forgiveness. He hadn't exactly spoken to her as a gentleman. She hadn't been offensive. Not truly. And certainly not purposefully.

He went to the windows, hoping to find one open enough to snatch a breath of cool night air. But Harry had only made it a few steps that direction when a ripple of periwinkle blue caught his eye.

Changing course, Harry made for Miss Ames's place near the door.

She cannot be leaving already. He quickened his step. There must still be an hour left to the ball.

The curate stood near her, bent in half to speak almost directly into her ear. Was the man on more familiar terms with her than friendship?

Harry scowled but hurriedly smoothed his expression when Miss Ames turned. She saw him coming and stilled, her face betraying nothing of her thoughts.

"Miss Ames," he said when he came within an easy distance. "Tell me you are not leaving. We have yet to dance."

If she was confused by his words, the woman did a fine job of not showing it. "Mr. Devon, good evening." She curtsied, reminding him of his rudeness. He hastily bowed. "We are not leaving yet."

We? Did she mean her father and herself, or the curate? Harry turned to look at the fellow, taking in the man's somber attire and solemn countenance. He certainly wore a more humble appearance than Harry. Did that give him greater favor in Miss Ames's eyes?

Why did it matter?

"I do not believe we have been introduced," Harry said, then cleared his throat. He'd sounded less than amiable. Hopefully no one else noticed his tone. Or thought he only spoke firmly to be heard over the sounds over the room. Or—

70

"Oh, forgive me." Miss Ames gestured to the man at her side. "Mr. Devon, might I present Mr. Haskett, our curate. He has been assisting my father with his duties for several months now."

"Six." Mr. Haskett bowed. "A pleasure to at last make your acquaintance, Mr. Devon. The people of Annesbury village and Kettering speak most highly of your family."

Harry raised his eyebrows. "Thank you, Mr. Haskett." He tried to remember the man's last sermon, to find something to speak upon, and failed. *Oh well. Best get to the point.* "I hope you will not think less of the family when I ask to steal Miss Ames away. If she will have me, I would like to secure her hand for the next set."

Miss Ames blinked once, as though surprised, but then nodded with more enthusiasm than he'd hoped for. "Yes, of course, Mr. Devon. Thank you."

He barely glanced at Haskett as he reached for her hand. It was the same hand she'd injured that she laid in his. They started threading their way to a starting position for the dance. "How is the injury?" he asked, lowering his voice so as not to be overheard.

Her fingers tightened around his briefly, and her chin dipped low. "Much better, thank you." She stepped into the line for the dance, several feet across from him. "You have been dancing all evening, Mr. Devon. I hope you are not too tired for this."

Harry listened to the starting lines of the music. "I am not even certain which dance this is."

To his surprise, this elicited a laugh from her. The gentleman at his right heard the comment and gave him a look of commiseration. "They do all blend together, don't they? It's a reel, reel of six," he said.

"Thank you," Harry said, nodding to him. "I am in your debt, sir."

"Robert Ellsworth." The man nodded back, then stepped forward to take his partner's hand. Harry turned back to Miss Ames, waiting another measure before doing the same.

"Mr. Ellsworth rescued you, it would seem," she said as they stepped around in a circle, her amusement still in her eyes. "You would ask a lady to dance without knowing what it requires of you?"

Harry didn't bother to hide his grin as he retook his place. "Do the steps really matter so long as I engage the partner of my choice?" Her eyebrows lifted and she turned away, walking around Mr. Ellsworth's partner to take his hand briefly. When they had the ability to speak again, as he promenaded a few steps down the line with her, she finally answered.

"I cannot make you out, Mr. Devon. Are you flirting with me?"

He felt the tips of his ears growing warm again. "Do you find the idea offensive, Miss Ames?"

She narrowed her eyes at him and stood still, waiting for her turn to move again. "No, I find it unnecessary."

His heart sunk, but he forced himself to smile. "Can we not be friends?" He stepped forward and took her hand, leading her to bow to another couple, then back to their places.

Although she didn't deny his request outright, her brow furrowed and the corners of her mouth turned downward. "Friends?"

It is an absurd request. What gentleman asks friendship of a young woman he barely knows? Apparently, gentlemen such as Harry did so. He wanted, very much, to understand Augusta Ames. She was kind and clever. She didn't care for his wealth, so far as he could tell, and spoke to him with such a candid manner he never quite knew what she would say next. Her thoughtful gray eyes were at odds with her bright smiles.

He'd enjoy flirting with her, of that there was no question, but perhaps befriending her would satisfy his curiosity. For a time.

After they'd moved through another round of stepping around couples, changing partners, and stood facing each other again, she finally spoke.

"I suppose friendship is well and good. But no more flirting, Mr. Devon." She fixed him with a stern expression, her eyes dark as thunderclouds.

"Agreed. Of course." Harry nodded solemnly and they joined hands again. The moment felt like the first victory of a war, with the promise of more skirmishes to come. He oddly looked forward to more such battles.

The music closed and Harry waited with her for the next song to begin. When he heard the first strains of music pronouncing the dance a waltz, satisfaction suffused him that he'd secured Miss Ames for the entire set. He grinned at her, and she narrowed her eyes at him.

At least he could claim innocence in choosing a set with a waltz.

Chapter Eight

Though a week had passed since the assembly ball, Daisy still found herself humming the strains of the waltz she'd danced with Mr. Devon. The incorrigible man had fought a smile through every step, which amused and annoyed her in equal parts. Why he insisted on a relationship of any sort with her, she could not understand.

Today she had risen early to get as much work done as she could. Though she wasn't a fine lady, she still kept a day each week set aside for receiving visitors. Many of the parishioners would come by for a short time, paying their respects to her due to her father's position.

There would hopefully be a few among them who would listen to her plans for the local school she wished to provide for the girls of the village and farm. While she was capable of beginning the school with nothing more than her wits, it would be better to provide slates and writing implements for the children, and a book or two more than she had. Not to mention the support she would need within the community to help encourage parents to send their children to learn.

"The only book those girls need to worry about learning from is the Bible," her father had said. "There will be little enough cause for them to read or understand other texts."

Although Daisy disagreed with her father, she refrained from arguing with him. Hopefully, there were others among the village who would feel similarly to her.

Before the guests arrived, she helped Mrs. Worth put the finishing touches on sweets and she tidied the parlor. Humming as she dusted, and stepping around the furniture as though around couples in a row of dancers, Daisy smirked at her own silliness, then executed a twirl just to feel her skirts lift from her ankles.

Mr. Devon might be a little odd, but he was also kind. *Perhaps he is lonely and only wants a friend.* She could well imagine it so. Though he had his sister and her family nearby, he hadn't spent enough time in the area to have formed many close acquaintances of his own age. *He may even be restless, staying in one place for so long.*

After finishing with her dusting, Daisy went in search of a basket, garden sheers, and her gloves. Fixing a broad-brimmed straw hat to her head, she went out the front door in search of any wayward blooms or greenery that might decorate her table.

There were flowers near the lane. Her mother had planted asters and dahlias years ago. The showy dahlias were in bright bloom, but Daisy much preferred the little purple asters with a few sprigs of waving grasses. They didn't last very long indoors, but they would do for the day.

Daisy started clipping what she needed, her back to the lane. Until she heard horse hooves clopping along at a fast pace. She straightened and glanced down the path, seeing a gentleman on a tall horse the color of wheat.

It was Mr. Devon. Had they not been near neighbors, she would question the number of times they crossed each other's paths.

She waited, wondering if he would ride by or stop to speak to her. She wasn't at all surprised when he reined in his mount a few feet from where she stood and dismounted.

"Miss Ames," he said, his smile somewhat cautious. "Good morning."

"Mr. Devon." She curtsied. "It is a lovely morning, isn't it?"

He nodded and lowered his head, twisting the horse's lead. It seemed if the man wasn't permitted to flirt, he didn't entirely know what to say. Daisy took pity on him by speaking next.

"Are you riding for pleasure or purpose this morning, Mr. Devon?"

He looked up at her, then at his horse. "A little of both, I suppose. My solicitor is coming to meet with me today. I felt it would be a good idea to exercise before being locked away for hours in the library with him."

He really is trying to learn about his estate. Daisy studied him with greater interest, noting the dark smudges beneath his eyes and the way his smile didn't grow as it had when she'd first seen him. "You are working with great dedication of late, aren't you?"

He let out a puff of air and tilted his head back. "I find the way to learn a thing is to devote oneself to the subject, and as I have a lot of time to make up, my devotion to accounts, tenants, and the like borders on religious."

Daisy bit her bottom lip to keep from laughing. "Sir, you forget yourself. I'm the vicar's daughter and that was near blasphemous."

Mr. Devon's eyes widened and he gestured with one hand, in a supplicating manner. "I beg your—" He stopped when he saw her expression. "Oh, that wasn't kind, Miss Ames. Feigning insult."

Daisy shrugged and laid her sheers in her basket, not bothering to hide her smile. Her father would likely lower his eyes in disapproval of her playful tease. And teasing was akin to flirting. It would be best to speak in a more business-like manner. "Where will your solicitor stay while he is here?"

"At the inn. My sister's house is rather full." He narrowed his eyes at her, as though suspicious of the change in topic.

"Poor man. While the Sword and Shield is a perfectly respectable place to lay one's head, they haven't the best of food." She let the basket handle rest in the crook of her arm. "Why don't you stay at Whitewood while you are here?" She asked the question with a tilt of her head and honest curiosity.

The gentleman shrugged and looked away. "It is too large a house for one man."

Daisy watched him, her new theory of his loneliness, of his need for friends, keeping her on the alert. What was the duty of a friend in a case such as this? Was it to let him speak the lie or beg the truth from him?

"I suppose that's true. I sometimes feel our house is grown too large, with my sisters away." She gestured to the vicarage, which was small and humble compared to his grand house. "But I imagine your staff is happy to have you returned, even if for only part of the day."

His forehead wrinkled. "The staff? I suppose so." Of course. As a man used to being waited upon, he likely wouldn't think on the feelings of the people doing the waiting.

"Mm. Whitewood, as one of the larger estates, employs quite a few people even when no one is at home. I think the staff was greatly reduced after your father passed away." In fact, she knew it had been cut by more than half. Several young maids had lost positions, footmen returned to their families hoping the references in their pockets would be enough to find work outside of tenant fields.

The whole economy of their little village had changed for a time. Eventually, adjustments were made and life continued forward.

Mr. Devon appeared to be considering her words, perhaps understanding all she did not say. "I haven't given it very much thought. That does explain why my steward was pleased with himself when he told me all economies were taken in my absence." He groaned and took off his hat. "Can we speak of something else? I am trying to escape thinking of my duties for a few moments."

Although tempted to say he'd escaped them for several years, Daisy bit her tongue. It wasn't her place to goad him on more than she already had. Every time she spoke to him of his duties it didn't seem to end well for either of them.

Though they had grown up not far from one another, they had limited things in common. This made settling upon another topic for conversation difficult.

"What have you enjoyed about your return to Kettering?" she asked at last, studying his handsome face. He didn't look very much like his sister, Mrs. Gilbert, except for his coloring.

"The ball was diverting," he said, his lips quirking upward. "Though I think my favorite thing about these past weeks has been being back in the country. It's beautiful here, as the seasons change."

Daisy readily agreed on that opinion. "It is as though nature gives one last glorious effort before going to sleep for the winter." She held her basket out as evidence. "The flowers will be gone soon, but aren't they pretty in the meanwhile?"

"Asters," he said, recognizing the blossoms. "I always liked them. They look like daisies—" He broke off suddenly. "Daisies. That's what you were called years ago." He stood back, his eyebrows shooting upward. "I knew Augusta didn't seem quite right. Your sisters always called you Daisy."

A bewildering sort of warmth spread within her chest as he regarded her. Daisy lowered her head, avoiding his eyes. Why did he disconcert her so much? He'd only remembered her childhood nickname, yet she felt oddly exposed. Or pleased? She couldn't be certain which, given the odd twitch in her chest.

"So they did." She adjusted her hold on the basket of the traitorous flowers. "But I am too grown up for such pet names now."

He spoke as though he had not heard her. "You do strike me as more of a Daisy than an Augusta." He tilted his head back and crossed his arms, affecting a somewhat triumphant pose that was entirely unwarranted. The horse apparently objected to the tug on its lead as it abruptly nudged his shoulder with its nose.

Daisy laughed as he cast the horse an insulted look. When Mr. Devon turned back to her, she tempered her amusement into an apologetic smile. "It serves you right, speaking my Christian name so casually. I didn't give you leave to use it, after all."

"It was merely an observation." Mr. Devon didn't appear the least repentant. "And as one who was Christened with an equally unsuitable name, I am uniquely qualified to make that observation. My father insisted I be named after his. Horace." He shuddered a touch dramatically.

"It isn't all that dreadful," she said. "I'm certain it must be quite respectable. It sounds distinguished." Although she certainly thought it a very somber sort of name to give to a little boy. "And your family calls you Harry."

"Thankfully." He grinned at her. "And I refuse to outgrow it. No one calls me Horace, except for my sister Rebecca. She does that when she wishes to annoy me."

"Does it work?" Daisy asked, raising her eyebrows at him. "Because I might try the trick if it does."

He considered her with narrowed eyes. "Why does the idea of annoying me amuse you so? I thought vicars' daughters were supposed to be sweet, unassuming, and meek?"

Daisy spoke without thought, his challenge lightening her mood. "The first two daughters are required to fulfill those qualifications. Subsequent daughters may do as they like." She tossed her chin, affecting a flippant expression.

"Then if they like, they can be called by childhood names. Like Daisy." He grinned most impertinently and tipped his hat to her. "Good day, Miss Daisy."

She gasped and lowered her hands to her side. "Mr. Devon, you must call me Miss Ames." That is what she got for being familiar with him. What was it about the man that brought out the childishness in her? Why must she return each of his remarks with something clever of her own?

He mounted his horse, his broad smile still in place. "Such a shame. Miss Daisy really does suit you better." Then the man had the audacity to wink at her before putting his heels to his horse and setting off once more.

Watching him go, Daisy wasn't certain if she wanted to be amused. She knew she ought to be insulted. At least in part. But there had been something refreshing in hearing another say the name written in her heart.

The truth was, she would much rather be Daisy than Augusta. Daisy was a happy, cheerful girl who laughed whenever she wished. Augusta was more proper and worked to fulfill the role others had set for her. She looked down at the purple petals of the asters.

"You need water before you wilt. I suppose we flowers must look after each other." She hid her smile when entering the vicarage, her basket tucked close to her side.

Chapter Nine

Daisy walked with purpose, her chin thrust forward and her shoulders straight. Down the road she went, kicking up yellow and orange leaves in her path. Her mind tumbled with conflict. Three days previous she'd brought up her idea of a school to everyone who paid her a visit, only to be laughed at and dismissed by three matrons and their daughters.

The day before, she'd paid some of her own calls to other women of esteem. Their responses to her idea of a school for farmers' and merchants' daughters had been varied, and none of them what she hoped.

"Those girls in school? What use would knowing the kings of England do a woman whose only job is to cook and clean for her family?"

"They would take on airs and never amount to anything."

"You ruin people like that with education. They start expecting more than they can have."

"I doubt many of them have the brains for schooling. Poor breeding, you know."

Daisy's fists clenched as she walked. Her father had put up with her brooding, but after a time her morose thoughts gave way to her temper.

"You will either damage yourself or my belongings if this keeps up," he'd said when she'd forcefully shelved some of his books. "Take your frustration out of doors, Augusta. Return when you have hold of yourself."

He'd glared down his nose at her, but she'd caught the gleam of concern in his eyes. Then he'd added, most unhelpfully, "Not everyone is as receptive to new ideas as you are, my dear."

It wasn't really a *new* idea, to educate children who otherwise might not receive schooling. She'd heard of a countess in Suffolk who held a Sunday seminary for girls, teaching them the Bible, and morals, and etiquette befitting a servant. There were schools in London, too, for the poor children. Ragged schools, they were called.

Some of Daisy's frustration escaped her in a puff of air. Perhaps her plans were rather ambitious, but they were well meant and she could carry them out with success. If only people would listen and give her a chance.

Daisy left the main road, entering the property of the Gilbert family. She'd decided to make her walk useful by returning Harry Devon's handkerchief. Hopefully, he would be at Whitewood working matters out with his solicitor, or steward, or whoever else he intended to speak to in regard to his estate. If she could speak to Mrs. Gilbert, she felt certain the woman would not make much fuss over the return of her brother's personal belonging. Christine Gilbert wasn't known for being overly conservative, after all.

Daisy knocked on the front door nearly the same instant it was opened. She lowered her eyes to see the eldest Gilbert child standing there, looking up at her with wide brown eyes.

"Miss Ames," he said, his face lighting up. "Did you bring any sweets?"

"Charles," his mother said from behind him, obviously exasperated as she bustled through the entryway toward him. "If you are going to open the door to a guest, please greet them politely." Her eyes twinkled merrily and she raised her eyebrows at her son, prompting him to sigh in a put-upon manner.

"Good morning, Miss Ames. Please come inside." He stepped aside, pulling the door all the way open.

Daisy's humor improved a margin as she stepped inside. "Thank you, Charles. I am afraid I haven't any sweets this time, but I remember you favorite is molasses candy. If you will come say hello to me after services on Sunday, I will be sure to have one for you."

His grin reappeared. "Thank you, Miss Ames."

"Off you go," Mrs. Gilbert said, waving him out the front door. "You need to attend to your riding lesson."

He bowed to his mother and Daisy, then the boy was off as quickly as the colts his father raised.

"Excuse us, Miss Ames." Mrs. Gilbert extended her hand to indicate a side parlor. "Please, come inside. It has been an age since we have visited together."

Daisy followed the woman inside, not removing her bonnet or jacket. She had no intention of staying long.

Once seated across form her, Mrs. Gilbert folded her hands in her lap. "It is lovely to see you today. I am sorry we didn't have the opportunity to visit at the ball. Did you enjoy that evening?"

As it was nearly a week past, and Daisy's thoughts had been on her present disappointment, it took her a moment to answer. "The ball? It was most enjoyable. I always look forward to dancing."

"I believe you danced a set with Harry?" Mrs. Gilbert said, her tone nothing but cordial.

"Yes, he is a talented dancer. I believe many young ladies enjoyed his partnership that evening." Daisy shifted in her seat, adjusting the ribbons of her purse. "I think he may become something of a favorite in the neighborhood."

"He might indeed. I have had one or two ladies call upon me with the obvious hope of meeting him while they visited." The woman's eyes twinkled merrily, as though the visits were a matter to be laughed at.

Daisy smiled, too, though she wondered that Mrs. Gilbert wasn't irritated by visits of that nature. Daisy certainly would be. "I understand he has been very busy with his estate's business." She opened her reticule. "In fact, I have come hoping he would not be present. I have an article of his to return, and I did not wish to disturb him." She took out the handkerchief. "Could you see that he receives this?"

Mrs. Gilbert's eyebrows came down as she accepted the white linen, studying it with interest. "It is his. I recognize the pattern. Our sister, Mrs. Hastings, gave Harry a whole box full of embroidered handkerchiefs." She placed the folded square in her lap and fixed Daisy with a look of curiosity. "May I ask how you came by it?"

"He came upon me picking blackberries, and I am afraid I caught my hand on a thorn. Mr. Devon offered his handkerchief as a bandage." There. She managed to speak the whole of it without stammering or, thankfully, blushing. Daisy relaxed, pleased to have the errand and explanation over with.

"It seems you two have been seeing a great deal of each other," Mrs. Gilbert said, eyebrows arching while one corner of her mouth pulled to the side.

Daisy blinked, the tension immediately returning to her shoulders. "Only in passing, I assure you, Mrs. Gilbert." Heat bloomed in her cheeks. "No more than I see any other neighbors."

Mrs. Gilbert's eyes crinkled at the corners. "Really? I hope Harry is proving himself a good neighbor. It is always useful to have a kind gentleman willing to offer aid to a young lady." She glanced away, her fingers tracing the edge of the handkerchief. "He has spoken highly of you, Miss Ames. Mr. Gilbert and I believe that you gave him some very good advice about his estate."

"Me?" Daisy asked, surprise startling the word from her. "I am afraid I cannot claim such a thing. We have barely spoken."

"Yet you have given Harry a great deal to think about." Mrs. Gilbert lowered her chin to fix Daisy with a solemn stare. "Harry is a good man. Intelligent and kind. But I am afraid he hasn't had much in the way of direction the past few years. He has three sisters rather than a mother or father to guide him, and we have busied ourselves with our husbands and children. Harry credits you with the idea for him to learn from the men who have looked after things for him. His steward, his solicitor."

Daisy's blush refused to dissipate. "I am happy to have helped in any way, of course, but I am certain Mr. Devon would have come to such a decision on his own."

"Eventually, perhaps." Mrs. Gilbert tilted her head to the side. Daisy attempted not to fidget while under the scrutiny of the older woman. "You seem out of sorts, Miss Ames. Is there anything the matter?"

It would be easy, and perhaps the politest thing, to simply deny any difficulties and be on her way. But, as she had told herself earlier, Daisy knew Mrs. Gilbert wasn't one to always behave in a traditional manner. People knew she ran the horse farm alongside her husband, and that she spoke her mind more often than not. Daisy had always rather admired Mrs. Gilbert for those things.

"There is something bothering me, Mrs. Gilbert. I am not certain you wish to hear of it. It is only a dream of mine that I am afraid may never come to pass." Her voice cracked awfully on the last word. Daisy blinked rapidly, forcing away the tears before they dared fall. "I apologize, I ought—"

"Nonsense," Mrs. Gilbert said, moving from her chair to sit beside Daisy on the couch. "Dreams are important things. If you are comfortable speaking of it, please know you can confide in me."

"It isn't a secret." Daisy tried to laugh, but the sound was rather strangled. "I have spoken to several ladies of my plans this very week. I am attempting to—that is, I would like—" She broke off again and shook her head.

"Oh, dear." Christine handed her the handkerchief she'd only just returned.

"I cannot take this," she said, opening her reticule and shuffling her things around only to find she'd somehow forgotten to put a handkerchief of her own inside. With a sigh of frustration, she took Harry's and used it to dry her eyes.

"Miss Ames, would you like something to drink?" Mrs. Gilbert sounded gentler than Daisy had ever heard her, and she laid a kind, sisterly arm around Daisy's shoulders.

"No. I am sorry. This is ridiculous. It has been a trying week. You see, I wish to start a school in the village. Not a boarding school, but a school for the daughters of farmers and merchants, for tenants' daughters." She didn't look up to Mrs. Gilbert's eyes.

Daisy didn't think she could face more criticism or laughter. Yet she continued speaking, worrying the linen cloth in her hands. "I wish to provide them with enough of an education to better their lives, no matter what they choose to do. A woman who can read, who is trained to practice intelligence, would be a boon to any family, poor or rich. I am prepared to teach only a few hours every day, so the girls can fulfill their family duties.

"I wish to lease a room in the village, large enough and with a stove for warmth, to have at least ten students at a time. I need more books, and slates. Just a few things, really, but they would help me to start. I have enough saved to lease the room above Mrs. Chandler's shop for four months. I am hoping to secure more time with help from our neighbors."

"That doesn't sound unreasonable," Mrs. Gilbert said slowly. "You were soliciting funds?"

Daisy nodded. "And support. I would need people in the community to help, to encourage parents to send their daughters to me. But everyone I have spoken to thus far has seemed to think the whole idea a jest."

Mrs. Gilbert patted Daisy gently on the shoulder. "Did they say why?" she asked quietly.

"Yes." Daisy took in a deep breath before listing everything that had already been said to her, about the general ignorance of children from lower classes, about the uselessness of the plan, and every other remark meant to discourage her. Finally, she gulped back her tears, dried her face with the handkerchief, and fell silent. She didn't look at Mrs. Gilbert, though the woman had removed her arm.

"I am sorry to trouble you with this, Mrs. Gilbert," she said after the silence had stretched for several moments.

"What troubles me," Mrs. Gilbert said, "is that you have not received more support. I find your idea to have real merit."

Nothing could have surprised Daisy more. She lifted her eyes from her lap at last, seeing Mrs. Gilbert's concerned frown. "Really?"

"Yes. I can think of a dozen ways an education would aid a family. To be honest with you, Miss Ames, I have thought at times that I wished to do more for people like the Thatchers. They have beautiful children, their mother is an angel on earth, but not one of them knows how to read. They will have trouble enough finding positions for all their children. They would be suitable for more trades, more sorts of employment, with a little education." Mrs. Gilbert nodded to herself. "I would like to help you, Miss Ames."

Daisy risked turning into a watering pot again, this time from being treated with honest interest. "That is wonderful, Mrs. Gilbert."

"I can think of a few other ladies who might be more receptive to your idea," Mrs. Gilbert added. "Starting with Lady Annesbury."

Daisy hadn't even dared to think of approaching the earl's wife. But Mrs. Gilbert and Lady Annesbury were cousins; if Mrs. Gilbert thought it a good idea, Daisy must approach the countess.

Mrs. Gilbert went to a small desk in the room. For another quarter of an hour, Mrs. Gilbert wrote down names and ideas for Daisy, speaking all the while of the ways in which a school for the girls of Annesbury village would raise the entire community's standards. The woman spoke with an enthusiasm that lifted Daisy's spirits considerably, and by the time she walked out the door with the paper in her hands, her dream had righted itself.

Her original purpose had been quite forgotten until she opened her reticule at home and saw she'd stuffed Harry Devon's handkerchief back inside. Taking it out, Daisy shook her head at herself. She would need to launder it all over again, and make another attempt at returning it.

Daisy hummed a waltz to herself as she laid the handkerchief upon her dressing table, along with Mrs. Gilbert's notes.

§

Slumping into a chair in the parlor, Harry folded his arms over his chest and glared into the hearth. "I need a new steward." The realization had been building for some time, but had finally settled firmly that very day. The steward had proudly shown Harry how he had saved money by giving the servants second-hand gifts on boxing day, two years running.

Christine looked up from the book she had been reading. Her husband was stretched out upon a couch, both eyes closed, but he spoke first. "I knew you would come to that conclusion."

"The steward is too set in his ways—ways Father approved of, but I cannot think are wise. His only concern is the money coming into the estate. He never thinks about the tenants, the servants, or the community." Harry sunk further down in his seat. "He appears to be an honest man, but not a kind one."

"What will you do with him?" Christine asked, laying a ribbon in her book before closing its covers. "Is he old enough for a pension?"

Harry considered for a moment, then nodded. "I think so. I can offer that, but if he wishes to keep working I can give him a good reference." He groaned and pushed himself into a more dignified posture. "I will need to find a new steward immediately."

"It shouldn't be too difficult," Thomas said, still unmoving. "Advertise, check references. Perhaps write to Christian, he may know of someone to fill the position. Or Lucas."

Asking for help from his brother-in-law, or cousin-in-law, wasn't entirely appealing. Would he forever be dependent on his relatives? Of course, they were both earls, with seats in the House of Lords, which made them extremely well-connected.

"That would probably be the best thing to do." Harry folded his arms over his chest. "Do you oversee all your own finances, Thomas?"

His brother-in-law opened one eye and smirked. "Father helps with the household management at this time, though I have been considering finding a steward. But Christine and I handle all the finances related to the horses."

Harry looked to his sister with some surprise. "Really? I thought you only concerned yourself with bloodlines."

Christine's smirk appeared and she shook her book at him. "That is because you never knew how well I do with sums. It isn't a talent I bandy-about."

"Why ever not? I could ask you to be my steward." Harry chuckled and tilted his head back against the chair. "I admire the way the two of you work together so well. Your horses have given you a great deal of success."

"They have," Thomas admitted, his eyes both closed again. "And though it has been a great deal of work, it has been worth every moment to reach this point."

"Achieving a dream is most fulfilling." Christine rose and went to the couch, lightly tapping her husband's knee until he moved his legs onto the floor. He sat up and opened an arm for her to snuggle against his side. Harry watched with a fascinated sort of envy. The two of them seemed to have everything they needed to be content. They had their home, their horses, their children, and each other. Christine and Thomas knew where they belonged, and with whom. They had plans as settled and sure as the foundation of their house.

What would it take for him to find such happiness?

"And as we are on the subject of dreams," Christine continued, oblivious to Harry's internal musings. "Miss Ames was here earlier today."

Harry's attention immediately jumped to his sister. "She was?" he blurted loudly, without thinking. "What was Miss Ames doing here?"

Christine turned toward him, her brow creased. "She came to return your handkerchief. Then we discussed her plans for a girls' school."

"I am sorry I missed her visit," Harry said, deflating slightly. Had she asked after him? She likely guessed he would be at Whitewood, since he told her that's where he spent his days. Daisy, for he could hardly think of her as anything else, had purposefully come when he would not be present. Had he offended her again somehow?

His sister was staring at him with a peculiar, tight-lipped expression. Harry swiftly latched on to the latter part of her explanation. "A girls' school?"

"Mm." Christine regarded him a moment longer, looking as though she meant to puzzle him out. "She wishes to open a school for the village girls, to give them a basic education in reading, writing, arithmetic, etiquette. To help better them and their future prospects for employment and families. I think it is a marvelous idea."

"It sounds forward-thinking of her." Thomas tipped his head to study his wife. "Although I imagine such an undertaking would require a bit of work on her part."

"Yes. She was quite discouraged when she first spoke of the idea." Christine went on to describe the difficulties Daisy had faced in the doubt and amusement of some of their neighbors, then said, "I told her she had my support. I will happily contribute funds and whatever influence I can to her cause. But there are women with more influence than I have who might help. Like Cousin Virginia."

Harry listened with real interest but said nothing. Daisy dreamt of opening a school for girls, a school that sounded as though it would be more of a charitable organization than one based on payments received. It was a noble plan, showing her kindness and practicality in a way he could not help but admire.

I wonder if there is anything I might do to help? The coffers his father had built up over the years were substantial. If he could manage to find a steward to his liking, a portion of his money could be appointed toward good causes, such as the school.

"Have you decided what to do about the estate yet?" Thomas asked, interrupting Harry's thoughts. The abrupt change in conversation gave him pause.

Whitewood. It had hardly been home during his school years. There were few warm memories of his parents there, though he could readily picture his sisters in the gardens and rooms. He'd hardly done more than enter the study since he'd returned. He met with the men under his employment and was gone again before dinner.

Daisy's words came back to him, about the servants' happiness to have him there. "I am thinking, more and more, that perhaps I should reopen the house," he said slowly.

Christine jolted forward, eyes large and mouth falling open. "Really, Harry? You might stay?"

"I might. For a time." He could not imagine his affairs coming into order speedily. Though he'd now spent three weeks working through ledgers, books, and interviews with farmers on the side of the road, he felt he had yet to attain more than a primary education on what it meant to have holdings such as his father left him.

"We would be delighted to have you in the neighborhood." Thomas's expression remained somewhat neutral as he spoke. "Though I caution you against raising the hopes of people round about. A man with your amount of lands and finances would be considered an important one, should you stay, and that would extend your responsibility in other ways. People would watch you, Harry."

Harry wanted to groan and say it had been nothing but a wild thought, not an actual decision. But Daisy's low soprano voice, the expectant tilt of her head when she spoke to him of sheep and shepherds, entered his mind again.

"Then I had better make very few mistakes." Harry forced a smile. "I will begin preparations to move back into the house. I will tell the staff tomorrow. I imagine they will want to take on a few more servants."

Christine moved to the edge of the couch, her hands clutched before her in something like glee. "The fair. It is next week. Your housekeeper and butler can hire anyone they need. The groundsmen, too. And there are to be carriage-makers. It is the perfect time for you to set up house."

Thomas, still leaning back in his corner of the couch, appeared to be admiring his wife's enthusiasm. "The house is set up, Chrissy. It just needs filling." He redirected his grin to Harry. "And with more than servants. If you intend to stay, every young woman in the county not spoken for will set their hopes on you."

Though he laughed at the teasing, Harry's heart picked up speed. If Thomas's prediction included a certain vicar's daughter, Harry found he did not mind the idea of husband hunters as much as he otherwise might.

A month ago, he hadn't a thought about courting anyone. Yet Daisy's presence in his thoughts, her opinion growing in importance to him, bent his thoughts in that direction. He'd secured her friendship. What would it be like, and would it even be possible, to secure her heart?

And did he want to?

Chapter Ten

The image of Miss Ames's indignant frown when Harry called her by her childhood name stayed with him, amusing him throughout the day. A time or two, he had nearly thought of her as *Augusta,* but the name did not suit her. Not so well as Daisy.

He needed that picture in his mind to get him through the day. His solicitor, Mr. Carew, had brought a box full of paperwork. There were contracts from every investment his father had made, lists of people who owed Mr. Devon money, and reports from overseas where his father had invested heavily in the West Indies and Americas. The sums were enormous, the variation in schemes too much for Harry to understand the reasoning behind all of them.

Trying to organize his thoughts on his estate and his father's investments had left him with something of a headache. After days of sorting through numbers and percentages, Mr. Carew and Harry agreed to meet at the inn to speak of which investments could be dropped and which maintained.

A new steward needed to materialize quickly. Harry couldn't continue managing everything on his own.

Clouds hung heavily in the sky when Harry prepared for his trip to the village. He ordered the old family coach to avoid coming home in the rain. But, once in Annesbury village, Harry thought of other errands he might see to before meeting with his solicitor.

"Simmons," he addressed his coachman. "I have a few things to see to today. Why don't you take an hour to visit with your sister? She lives nearby, does she not?"

The coachman's eyes widened. "She does at that, sir. Thank you." Then he glanced up at the sky. "Though it looks like rain might be falling soon."

"Better make it two hours, then." Harry grinned and waved the man along. "I'll be at the inn if the sky starts to fall." He turned on his heel and strode away before the surprised Simmons could utter another word of thanks. Though it was happening slowly, Harry learned more about his servants with each passing day. It was time to show them they were worth more than second-hand boxing gifts and a minimal salary.

The first place he visited in Annesbury was the seamstress. Mrs. Chandler was known throughout the county as a talented designer. He'd heard of her being called away to wait on entire families. As her work usually consisted of gowns for the gentry and nobility, he hoped his request would not be seen as a slight.

He entered her shop, a bell jingling merrily above him, and saw the woman herself sitting on a settee with notebook and pencil in hand. A girl sat on the floor near her, playing with a doll. He instantly recognized Janie from the bramble adventure and winked at her when she smiled at him.

"Mr. Devon," the seamstress said, coming to her feet. "Good afternoon, sir." She curtsied and he quickly bowed.

"Mrs. Chandler, good afternoon. How are you this cloudy day?"

She did not smile, though he offered up a broad grin of his own. She clasped her hands before her and pressed her lips together a moment before answering. "I am tolerably well, sir. To what do I owe the pleasure of your visit?"

One would almost think she did not like him standing there, in her shop. Ignoring the slight frost in her tone, Harry went on cheerily. "I have come with an odd sort of request, Mrs. Chandler. My sisters have spoken highly of your work for years. They say your dresses are finer than any that can be found in London." It was flattery, but his sisters really had said such things about the woman.

94

"Most kind of them," she said, her eyes growing wary behind her spectacles. "They are lovely ladies. I am happy to be thought of when they need something new."

"It is because of your great talent that I thought to enlist your help with a particularly unique project. I hope you will not see it as an insult, but rather understand I am attempting to pay a compliment to your skills." Harry took a step closer, but stilled when her frosty expression returned. "You see, I have discovered that the household staff, the women in particular, have been woefully neglected in my absence. Their salaries have remained stagnant, and their uniforms cheaply made. I would not presume to ask you to outfit an entire household, of course, but I am wondering if I might commission you to make aprons for them. Serviceable, yet lovely. If you would consent to this, I would want them to be prepared so they may be given as Boxing Day gifts."

Her nostrils flared and her chin came up. The lines around her mouth, though they appeared to have been created from years of smiles, deepened with her frown. "You wish for me to create garments for your *servants*? I think you would find Mr. Harper's shop the better place to obtain such things."

Heat flew up his neck and into his ears. "I beg your pardon, Mrs. Chandler. I promise I meant no offense, but rather to pay a high compliment to the servants. You see, last year they received second-hand gloves. The year before, paper fans. I only wanted to make up for their neglect by offering a gift of true value. Everyone knows your handiwork is the finest in the county." He bowed again, deeper than before. "But I have misunderstood what such a commission would mean. I apologize. Please, forgive me for wasting your time."

When he looked up again, contrite and kicking himself for not asking Christine if his idea had merit, the woman's expression appeared less affronted and more curious.

"Not at all, Mr. Devon," she said at last. "I suppose I can understand the gesture."

He bowed again. "You are most gracious, Mrs. Chandler. Thank you. Good day. And good day to you, Miss Janie." At least the child's name had returned to him in time to bid her goodbye.

The little girl, who was frowning up at her grandmother, turned to smile and wave goodbye to him. Harry left with a tip of his hat and the bell ringing mockingly behind him. He hadn't realized making aprons would be such an affront, but he supposed one did not ask such things of women who had created gowns for countesses.

He went, as she suggested, to the shop owned by Mr. Harper. No bell clanged above the door when he stepped inside, but Mr. Harper and his daughter were at the counter. Behind them on shelves were bolts of cloth, most of somber colors meant to be serviceable rather than eye-catching, Harry imagined.

Miss Harper was a girl of perhaps fifteen. She stepped up to the counter before Harry, her eyebrows raised and an expectant smile appearing on her face. He relaxed somewhat and opened his mouth to greet her, but her father's voice spoke first.

"Betsy, go on back and inventory the thread. I need to send to London for more black, I think."

The girl's smile vanished and she looked to her father with consternation. "Yes, Papa." She cast a look over her shoulder at Harry, who offered her one last smile, and disappeared behind a curtain into a back room.

Harry turned his attention to Mr. Harper, a tall, reedy man with more gray hair than brown. "Good afternoon, Mr. Harper. I have come today to inquire about the possibility of commissioning aprons for my household servants." Best to get to the point this time, Harry decided.

"Aprons?" the man asked. "Usually your housekeeper orders the cloth necessary and I deliver it to her. The maids do their own work. It's cheaper that way." His eyebrows drew downward and he folded his arms over his chest. "Would you like me to ask the missus what sort of fabric the maids will need for aprons?"

Why such a simple idea for a gift had spiraled into such a complex situation, Harry couldn't understand. Had he gone about everything wrong? Was the housekeeper supposed to supply the family's gifts to the servants? It didn't seem right.

"No," Harry answered, his spirits drooping. "I suppose I should consult her myself. I had hoped to secure the aprons as boxing day gifts. But perhaps that was impractical. Thank you, Mr. Harper. Good day to you." Harry bowed, which seemed to take the man by surprise, but he didn't wait to see if the gesture was returned.

Here he had thought the people of the village would leap at the chance to have his funds, whatever he asked. Obviously, he had been sorely mistaken. His plan to obtain new grooming kits, the finest he could find, for the male members of the household had also withered away to nothing. When he returned to the Gilbert house, he would apply to Christine for better ideas. Boxing Day was weeks and weeks away. There was time to think of something else. Maybe he ought to just give everyone especially large bonuses.

Hopefully, Mr. Carew wouldn't mind Harry turning up early for their meeting. There was nothing else he could accomplish in the village today, it seemed.

§

Rain came at the most inappropriate moments, of that Daisy felt certain. She stood in the doorway of the inn watching the torrent of water fall from the sky. In her arms she clutched a parcel delivered to the inn with her father's name upon it. The hand was firm and dark, and she knew it must be from her sister Lily and her husband. All she wanted was to get home swiftly and open it with her father. The thunder rolling overhead mocked her wish most cruelly.

Mr. Ellsworth, a gentleman only a few years older than Daisy, stood at her side. His arms were crossed and he glared at the rain, too. "If I had my carriage," he said to her, "I would see you home, Miss Ames. But blast it, I rode to the village today."

"Language, Mr. Ellsworth." Daisy raised her eyebrows and shook her head at him, but she smiled before he could make an apology. "You must simply be in debt to me another time. As we are both rather stuck today, I will forgive you this once."

He chuckled and looked behind them at the inn's common room, where there were a handful of patrons scattered among little square tables. Some drank, others smoked. Daisy had several acquaintances among them. A few were fathers to girls she hoped to one day teach. That thought kept her from wishing to converse with them. It would only make her heart ache, to keep back her dreams still longer. She wouldn't speak of her desire for a school to the people who needed it most. Not with things so uncertain still.

"How is your family, Mr. Ellsworth?" she asked, attempting to be a good companion.

"Well enough. My younger brother wishes to start at Oxford soon." He sighed and fiddled with the hat in his hands. Robert Ellsworth was a steady gentleman, his family in reduced circumstances. He was the second son, which meant he had a decent education but no property of his own.

"That would be exciting." Daisy looked back at a table near where they stood. It was unoccupied. "Would you care to sit, Mr. Ellsworth?"

"Oh. I beg your pardon. I should have offered to get you a chair." He turned and helped her into a seat at the table, then sat across from her. "I am afraid I am rather preoccupied. You see, I rode here today to the apothecary. My father hasn't felt well of late." Mr. Ellsworth gave her a tight-lipped smile.

Daisy well knew the rumors surrounding his father's health. Mr. Ellsworth's father had been poorly for some time. The old gentleman had three sons, and as they'd lost their mother young they were devoted to their father. The eldest ran the estate, though there was no longer much to it, and Mr. Robert Ellsworth shifted about as best he could. The youngest son possessed a studious nature and dreamt of the life of a bachelor academic.

"I am very sorry to hear he is unwell. I will tell my father. He will wish to visit." She knew all too well how difficult it was to watch a parent struggle with ill health. Her mother had been sick for some time before passing away. "Is there anything I might do to assist your family, Mr. Ellsworth?"

He shook his head and tapped his fingers against the tabletop. "I am afraid not, Miss Ames. Unless you can find me a position in the village that will assist with my family's situation." He grimaced. "Forgive me. I ought not to burden you."

"I am the vicar's daughter," she said, leaning slightly across the table. "Who better to speak to, besides the vicar himself? I will speak to him on your behalf, and I will not share your business with others. You are looking for a position of employment?"

Mr. Ellsworth tapped his fingers again. "I am. But this is a small village, a humble neighborhood. There will not be a place for me that someone's brother or uncle or nephew will not hear of first." He looked to the window again. "Blast the rain."

She smiled at his mild curse and cast her eyes about the room again, looking for another topic of conversation.

Two men were coming down the steps from the second floor, and she sat taller when she recognized one of them as Harry. Mr. Devon. Blast. It was difficult to think of him as Mr. Devon when every time she saw him they committed some sort of social impropriety.

Harry appeared every bit as handsome and charming as usual, dressed well with hair that looked to have been carefully tousled. His expression was certainly earnest as he spoke to the other man, who must be at least twice Harry's age. The stranger wasn't dressed as finely either, though he appeared respectable.

His solicitor, Daisy remembered. Though she couldn't recall the man's name. When they came to the bottom of the stairs, the two shook hands and the solicitor turned and went back up the steps. Harry turned to the door, but stopped when his eyes met hers.

An infectious grin spread across his face and she found herself answering it with a smile and a wave, almost without thought. He came directly toward her, then his eyes fell to Mr. Ellsworth and Harry froze a moment.

Daisy supposed he wouldn't remember meeting the man at the ball, even though he'd practically run over Mr. Ellsworth and his dance partner.

She stood to make the introductions again, and Harry took the final steps to the table as Mr. Ellsworth stood politely.

"Mr. Devon, it is good to see you this afternoon. You remember Mr. Ellsworth, from the assembly ball? Will you join us for a moment? We are waiting out the rain." Daisy gestured to an empty chair at the table. Harry's conversation, while at times unusual, was at least always diverting. Truthfully, Daisy enjoyed his company.

"I do not wish to intrude." Harry looked from her to Mr. Ellsworth again.

"Do, please, Mr. Devon." Mr. Ellsworth bowed before retaking his seat. "I have yet to speak with you since your return, which is a shame." He turned to Daisy. "After meeting him again at the ball, I recalled a time from our childhood when we went fishing together."

Harry spoke slowly, as though the memory came upon him in that very moment. "Even though we were mortal enemies," Harry added, sitting down slowly. "Yes. I recall now. I was a Harrow lad, and Ellsworth was Eaton."

"I think we fished together more out of a desire to best each other than anything." Mr. Ellsworth sat back, amusement lighting his eyes. "But occasionally we forgot ourselves, and the rivalry, to compare bait and stories about school."

"That is true." Harry seemed to relax, his eyes crinkling at the corners.

Daisy looked between the gentlemen with some interest. They had all grown up near one another, yet she had never known Mr. Ellsworth and Harry had spent time together. Of course, being a girl meant she didn't spend much time in any boy's company.

"What brings you back to the neighborhood?" Mr. Ellsworth asked. "Rumor has it both that you have come to settle down or come to sell the estate for a finer one north of London."

Harry chuckled. "The rumors are more interesting than the truth. I have been trying to take stock of my estate and holdings in order to actually make a decision." Yet the way his eyes slid to the side as he spoke made Daisy raise her eyebrows.

"Ah. Mr. Keyes still keeping the books for your estate?" Mr. Ellsworth raised his eyebrows a touch skeptically. "If you will excuse me for saying so, Mr. Devon, I have always been less than impressed with his business practices. There are not many with a kind word to say about him."

Daisy gulped and tried to ascertain if this offended Harry, wondering if she ought to say something, to divert the conversation.

Sighing deeply, Harry turned to face her. She saw a sort of pained acceptance in his expression rather than any kind of upset. "I haven't much to say of the man's charitable nature. If he has one. I wish I had a steward with all the intelligence of Mr. Keyes and more heart."

Mr. Ellsworth nodded as though such a desire made perfect sense to him. Daisy looked between the men somewhat incredulously. Could they not see the solution to both their difficulties lay in each other? Mr. Ellsworth said nothing of his search for employment. Perhaps he only though it presumptuous to say anything, given his lack of personal connection to Harry. It would be the very height of impropriety for her to enter into a discourse of business with them, yet perhaps—like the Biblical queen she was named for—she was sitting between them in order to facilitate this very thing.

"Why not ask Mr. Ellsworth if he would take the position?" she said at last, steeling herself against a look of rebuke from one or the other of the gentlemen. "As a local man, he understands the neighborhood and its inhabitants, and I believe his Oxford education makes him well-equipped for the position. Not to mention, he wishes to stay near family."

Mr. Ellsworth spoke quickly, but without censure. "Miss Ames is too kind. I wouldn't presume to press myself upon you, Mr. Devon." Mr. Ellsworth's cheeks pinked.

Harry looked between them again, his eyebrows drawn tightly down. "Are you looking for a position, Mr. Ellsworth? Would you be interested in being a steward?"

"Go on, Mr. Ellsworth," Daisy said before the man could protest. "You were telling me a moment ago that you wished that very thing." She turned to Harry. "It would not hurt anything to discuss the possibility, would it? Or to allow Mr. Ellsworth to look over the books, to determine if the position is one he could improve upon?"

Harry's lips pressed together, but she could easily see he was resisting a smile rather than a grimace. Mr. Ellsworth had control over his blush and wore instead an earnest sort of frown.

"If you wish to fill the position, Mr. Devon, I would like to put my hat in the ring, as it were." The hat in question was being bent at the brim in his hands. Daisy tried not to feel pleased with herself. Though she had facilitated the conversation between the men, it would all rest on Mr. Ellsworth's capabilities and Harry's decision. But she had rather a good feeling about the situation.

She turned her attention to the rain outside the window, listening with only half an ear as the men set up an appointment to discuss the possibilities later, at Whitewood. The rain had eased somewhat by the time the details were settled, with few enough drops falling that Daisy was of a mind to return home. She waited for an opportunity to speak.

"Gentlemen, it was very good to see you both today. I believe I am ready to brave the elements and return home now, if you will both excuse me." She stood, tucking her parcel beneath her arm.

Both men came to their feet.

"Very good, Miss Ames," Mr. Ellsworth said. "Do you wish me to accompany you?"

Harry Devon spoke before she could, as though in a rush to get his words out. "But you are going in the opposite direction, Mr. Ellsworth. Miss Ames and I must travel the same way. I will be happy to see her safely home."

Daisy raised her eyebrows. "Really, it isn't necessary—"

"Nonsense. I am on my way home anyway." Harry offered her his arm. "We can share the road for a time."

Mr. Ellsworth bowed to them both. "A practical suggestion, Mr. Devon. I look forward to our meeting tomorrow. Good day, Miss Ames."

Rather surprised to be on Harry's arm, Daisy made her goodbye before he whisked her out of the inn and into the light mist that had taken the rain's place.

"Did you walk to the Shield and Sword today, Mr. Devon?" she asked when they had left the inn's yard.

"No, I took my carriage since I had rather important documents to give to my solicitor." An impish gleam appeared in his eye.

"Your carriage?" Daisy tried to halt, but Harry kept walking down the lane. "Shouldn't you retrieve it?"

"The driver is visiting his sister. He will not mind the extra time with her. At any rate, I couldn't escort you if we had the carriage." He tilted his head back to regard her. "It wouldn't be seemly to ride without a chaperone."

Daisy couldn't help the laugh that escaped her. "You make it sound as though I have improper intentions toward you, Mr. Devon."

"Do you not, Miss Daisy?" he asked, sounding most doubtful.

"Most certainly not." Daisy tried to sound as affronted as she ought to, though it was a difficult farce. "As you well know. And you mustn't call me that. I haven't given you leave—"

"I suppose not. You could, though. And if you let me call you Daisy, I will allow you to call me Harry." He held himself magnanimously, as though bestowing a knighthood upon her.

She laughed again, this time without trying to stop the sound up. "You are perfectly incorrigible, Mr. Devon. It wouldn't be right."

"Only when we are not in company, Miss Ames. I promise no one would think us too familiar with one another." He took on the expression of a piteous puppy, all large eyes and sad frown. "Please?" Their walk slowed nearly to a halt.

"Does wearing that expression usually get you what you want?" she asked. When a boy had three older sisters at home she imagined he must be creative in order to get his way. *Incorrigible. That is the only word for him.*

"More often than not." He kept the pleading expression on another moment before releasing a rather dramatic sigh.

"However, I do find that I encounter difficulty with the hard-hearted."

Daisy tossed her head. "Is that what you are accusing me of, sir?" What was it about him that made her feel playful? When she spoke with other gentlemen, she could remain staid and polite, but it seemed as soon as Harry opened his mouth, she was capable of meeting jest for jest. That sort of openness from her was usually reserved for the children of her acquaintance.

Harry's expression sobered as he regarded her, and he stopped walking to stare down into her face. The mist had turned his hair a trifle damp where it peeked out from under his hat, causing it to curl beneath the brim. That detail made the sudden seriousness of his expression all the more unexpected.

"I have it on good authority you are a woman in possession of great kindness and compassion." He looked down at the road a moment. "My sister told me of your desire to start a school for the local children." His voice had changed timbre as well in his solemnity, deepening enough to send a shiver through her.

Here she had thought him a playful sort of person and he immediately contradicted that idea by turning considerate.

"It is nothing but a dream at present," she said, shifting the parcel in her arm.

Harry mutely held out his hand and she handed the package over to him without a thought. He tucked it beneath his other arm and then continued down the lane.

"Christine told me of your difficulties. You need more support, from the people. If there is anything I might do to help, Miss Ames, I hope you will tell me." The sincerity with which he spoke touched her heart.

"Really, you must call me Daisy," she said quietly, staring down the road rather than see his reaction, though she did feel his arm tighten beneath her hand. "And I thank you for your kind offer." Why did she give in to his request so easily? Her Christian name was said by almost no one. Her childhood name never even heard anymore.

Perhaps that was why she granted him that familiarity. She missed the sound of her name.

When he spoke again, it was as though nothing of significance had passed between them.

And nothing has, she told herself firmly.

"I am most adamant that you allow me to help. Once I have a greater understanding of how such things are done, I would be pleased to make a donation to the cause."

Somehow, that disappointed her. When a man had funds readily at his disposal, and Harry Devon undoubtedly did, giving money to a cause could not really count for much in his heart. Not that she was concerned about Harry's heart.

Daisy frowned at the trees stretching above them, leaves turning from yellow to brown. "Thank you," she said at last. "That is a generous offer, Mr. Devon."

"Harry," he corrected. "And what have I done wrong this time?"

Her eyes sought his with surprise. His brows were drawn together, his lips thin, and the lines of his jaw hard. His perplexity was as genuine as his playfulness.

"Nothing," she answered quickly. "You have been most kind."

"I can see it, Daisy." He faced forward again, still leading them down the path one step after another. "Your nose wrinkled, your gray eyes went dark, and it was as though your whole body wished to be away from me. I upset you."

Again, he startled her. Despite his lively nature, the man was most observant.

"I am grateful for your offer," she said, but when he cast her an incredulous glance she hurried her words. "It was only a silly thought, Harry." His name fell a trifle reluctantly from her tongue. "I am less worried about the funds than I am about the support of people in other ways. What I wish for is encouragement, for myself and the families who would benefit most from this. I wish for people to take an interest that goes beyond handing me a purse and bidding me good luck." She closed her lips over the last word and winced.

She certainly didn't sound grateful, even to her own ears.

Harry said nothing for several steps, and he kept his gaze before them. Daisy did her best to bite her tongue, but the misty weather wasn't the only thing dampening her spirits.

"I am sorry," she whispered at last. "I should not have said anything. I am ridiculous."

"No, Daisy." His arm drew her closer to him. "I am the ridiculous one. It is as you said, about the way I have managed things thus far in my life. I hand my money over and trust a good job will be done with it, rather than put any effort along with it. I see that now."

Despite her earlier thoughts, Daisy's estimation of his character rose. "Do you? What has changed?" When she'd met him, after all, he'd seemed to have few plans and even less direction. He had heaps of money but little regard for what such a blessing meant.

"You helped me to understand my responsibilities to the people under my care, as servants and tenants. My duty to the community. I will not say I have a course of action decided just yet, but learning all I have—" He broke off, shaking his head while that perplexed expression returned to his face. "I cannot say all that I intend to do, or to change, because I am not certain. But I have a good feeling about Mr. Ellsworth. Perhaps he can assist in more than just ordering the estate's finances."

Daisy bit her bottom lip and said nothing, though her heart lightened considerably to hear him speak with real intent. Truly, it wasn't her place to say more. Or was it? They had agreed to friendship, after all.

"I am impressed." The compliment, though it was simple in nature, seemed to settle upon him like a warm blanket. His whole being relaxed and his smile reappeared. He glanced down at her, a gentle look in his eye.

"Thank you. That means a great deal coming from you." He nodded to the side. "Here is the vicarage." He released her arm. "And here is your parcel."

She accepted it, hugging the brown papered box to her chest. "Thank you. For seeing me home."

106

He regarded her in silence, one corner of his mouth slightly higher than the other. He opened his mouth to speak, but a boom of thunder above interrupted him.

Daisy peeked up at the clouds. "You had better hurry home." She lowered her eyes to his, catching a strange emotion in them that was gone before she could identify it.

"I suppose so. This rain had better stop soon, or the fair will be rained out. Good day, Daisy." He touched the brim of his hat.

"Good day, Harry." She turned and hurried up the path to the front door of the vicarage. She looked back with her hand on the door handle. He waved at her one more time before turning and going on his way.

Slipping inside, Daisy closed the door behind her and leaned against it. Though she had obtained the safety and warmth of her home, her heart beat a hasty rhythm within her breast. As though she were afraid, or anxious, or excited—

"Augusta? Is that you?" her father called, halting her examination of her feelings.

"Yes, Father." She pushed away from the door. "And I have something from Lily." She tugged off her damp shawl just as the maid appeared to help her with her bonnet.

Daisy attempted to put Harry from her mind, but his infectious grin and serious blue eyes were not easily dismissed.

Chapter Eleven

H ave you heard, miss?" Katie, the maid of all work, helped Daisy in the kitchen. They were putting the finishing touches on pies for the fair. "They're hirin' on at Whitewood again. My sister, Betty, she's goin' to try for a position during the fair. Folk will have to go to the house to try for it."

Daisy had been brushing the tops of the pie crusts with egg whites, an essential step to make them glisten, and she stilled, her hand hovering over a spiced apple pie.

"Whitewood? Mr. Devon's property?" She studied the girl's hopeful expression, wondering how Katie had come upon the news before Daisy had.

"It's true enough. I have heard it from more than one source." Mrs. Bramston, the housekeeper, was sitting at the table tying ribbons to little parcels of soap. She spoke with authority, as she usually did. The soaps were one of her specialties, and she'd always done well selling them during the larger fairs. Annesbury had only two, one in spring and another in autumn. Everything from ribbons to oxen were sold and traded, and even the great houses would bring out wares to sell. The first day was devoted to the selling of cattle and sheep, then other wares, and the final day was for hiring farm workers. The larger houses would advertise if there were positions to be filled, too.

"Do you think that means Mr. Devon intends to stay?" Katie asked, cutting out another leaf from the pie dough.

"I do not know." Daisy clutched the brush tighter, remembered what she was doing, and hastily used her apron to clean the table. Several large drops of clear liquid from her brush had fallen during her inattentive moment. She tried to concentrate on the pie again.

Cook came over to take the completed pies to the oven. "I'm not so sure I'd trust that kind of position. That old steward, the second the young gentleman's back is turned, will send everyone packing."

"Mr. Devon is hiring a new steward," Daisy said without thinking, then bit her bottom lip when three sets of eyes looked up at her.

"How did you come by that news, Miss Ames?" Mrs. Bramston asked, her eyes curious beneath the lace cap she wore. "You aren't usually given to spread rumors, so it must be true."

"I hope it is," Cook said, wiping her hands on her apron as she returned to the table. "I've got a nephew who'd like his chance as a gardener at a big house."

Daisy put the brush down in the bowl and handed the last pie to her cook. They'd cut out leaves to cover the tops of every variety. It had become something like a signature on Cook's masterpieces. On fair days, everything from their kitchen was covered in leaves. Already, an entire tray of shortbread baked in the shape of oak leaves sat to one side of the table. With the pies, it made for quite an impressive spread.

"I am afraid that is all I can do for the day. I am to visit the countess this afternoon and must clean up." Daisy ran her hands down her apron, then reached up to check that her hair was still in its pins.

"You go on, miss," Cook said with a wave. "And thank you for all your help."

"I will be up shortly to help you dress," Mrs. Bramston added. "I have but three more soaps to tie."

Daisy nearly bolted from the room, the need to hurry away from her own servants unaccountably strong. She had been startled by the maid's revelation, but it was more disconcerting to have it confirmed by both housekeeper and cook. When had Harry decided to hire more servants? He hadn't said anything to her on their walk home after the storm.

Not that she expected him to share all of his business dealings with her.

But if he is to take on more servants, he must be planning to stay.

Though she originally hoped for such a thing, the idea now caused some anxiety. How had she allowed herself to grow so familiar with him in such a short time? The man called her by her childhood nickname, for goodness' sake.

Calm down. She went to the basin of water in her room and washed her hands, then her face. She started to undress. I wanted him to stay, to take his place in the community. Knowing that he will should not change anything about our regard for each other as friends.

She turned her mind more firmly toward her visit with the countess, thinking on how she might present her plan to the lady in a convincing manner. By the time Mrs. Bramston appeared, Daisy had settled her nerves enough to discuss the fair with enthusiasm.

Once dressed, she found her father in his study, kissed him goodbye, and stepped out the door. She walked to Annesbury Park, the home of Lord and Lady Annesbury. It was the countess's at-home day. Daisy rarely visited the great estate due to her status being far beneath Lady Annesbury's. Not that the countess had ever made Daisy feel unwelcome in the past. Daisy simply couldn't imagine they had enough in common to form anything more than a neighborly sort of acquaintance.

The leaves and gravel crunched beneath her half-boots at a steady rhythm. Daisy kept rehearsing her explanation of her school and how best to bring it into conversation without sounding as though she was hoping for money. It would be the height of rudeness to go visiting on such an errand. The purpose of this visit was to obtain the countess's interest in the project, perhaps gain some support through her approval of the school.

Daisy bit her bottom lip when she came within sight of the large house atop its hill. It lazed about in the afternoon sun, stretched out, comfortable and old. The great big trees lining the path from road to house had all turned yellow, some tipped with brown leaves. Doubtless the gardeners would be coming through to rake up those that had fallen very soon.

She paused long enough to pick up a yellow leaf, newly fallen, and twirled it between her fingers. She tucked it in her reticule on an impulse. If all went well, the leaf would be a memento of the day.

The butler showed Daisy to an upstairs parlor and announced her to the room. Daisy entered just behind him and curtsied to Lady Annesbury. Thankfully, Daisy appeared to be the only caller at the moment.

"Miss Ames, how delightful to see you." Virginia Calvert, the Countess of Annesbury, carried herself with the poise and grace one would expect of a princess. It often startled people to find out she had six children, ranging in age from twenty down to three years old.

"Thank you, my lady. It has been some time since I visited." Daisy took the chair Lady Annesbury gestured to, prepared to begin her conversation with speaking of the fair. That was the topic most on people's lips at the moment, after all.

Lady Annesbury spoke first. "I have not been to the vicarage of late, either, but I was planning to send word to you this very day and ask for a visit." Her deep green eyes sparkled and she leaned forward, almost with excitement. "My cousin, Mrs. Gilbert, came yesterday and told me about your plans for a school. The idea has taken a strong hold on me, and I am terribly envious I did not have it first. I hope you will let me help you."

It was as though a vice binding her heart loosened with those words. Daisy stared at her ladyship for a long moment, too startled to speak. Finally, she found her voice again. "You think it a good idea?" she asked at last, her question nearly a squeak. Her whole plan for the conversation dissipated. "Oh, I am so relieved, my lady. I have spent the entirety of the last two days trying to decide how to speak to you about the school."

"Leave it to Christine Gilbert to take the business of others in hand," the countess said with a gleam in her eye. "My cousin devotes herself to people and causes, and as you have given her both she wasted no time in championing you. If you tell me what

I can do to help, I will do it. May I have your permission to speak to others of the idea? I have several friends in the neighborhood who will likely be interested, too."

Daisy had to clasp her hands together firmly in her lap to keep them from fluttering about like excited birds. "Of course, my lady. Allow me to tell you the particulars of my plan." She stayed longer than the quarter of an hour expected of guests, and the countess asked several questions. She even retrieved a sheet of paper and pencil to take some notes, making certain she understood the manner in which the girls would be taught and what would be considered essential skills.

"I am impressed by you, Miss Ames." The countess put the pencil down in her lap and regarded Daisy carefully, her eyebrows raised and her expression most cheerful. "Most young women your age are not thoughtful of the less fortunate. I have but one concern for the whole venture. What will happen to the school when you marry?"

As her own father had voiced this worry, Daisy had an answer. "I have no intention of marrying at present, my lady. If I should change my mind one day, a great deal would depend upon the gentleman." For some reason, Harry Devon's crooked grin came to mind.

Daisy tried to put thoughts of him away, but the memory of him holding her injured hand and binding it with his handkerchief added itself to her thoughts.

"Your own children will take precedence over the daughters of others." The countess rose to return her paper and pencil to the little desk in the corner of the room. She stood still for a moment, elegantly framed by a tall window. "As you say, you have no present plans. If anything changes in that regard, please let me know. I will speak to my friends, and perhaps we could hold a meeting in a fortnight with those who are interested in assisting. When do you hope to start?"

"January," Daisy answered firmly. "Many of the girls will have nothing to do at home and their brothers will be attending the National School run by Mr. Haskett."

"It is a shame they cannot all be educated together." The countess returned to her seat with a sigh. "The old Sunday Schools started out with boys only, but they allowed girls in after a time. I kept hoping our local school would do the same."

Daisy twisted the strings of her reticule. "Thank you for your time today, my lady."

"The pleasure was sincerely mine." Lady Annesbury rose and gestured to the door. "Do you intend to enjoy the fair this year, Miss Ames? My husband has already promised to take our children to look at everything each day. I am not certain who will tire of the arrangement first."

Daisy laughed. "I remember extracting similar promises from my father. Yes, I hope to spend a little time enjoying the general excitement of the event. It is so important to our farmers and community. Good day, my lady."

"Good day, Miss Ames."

After taking her leave, Daisy exited the house with the bounce returned to her step. She took out the leaf she had claimed and twirled it between her fingers again, this time unable to hold back her grin of delight. She would press the leaf between the pages of her journal at home. The day was one to be remembered happily.

When she stepped onto the lane, beginning her walk home, Daisy listened for horse-hooves on the road. Not that she was looking for anyone in particular, but it was near the time she'd encountered Harry before. And if he wished to go anywhere in the county, he would have to start his journey on that very road.

She made it home without sight of him, but he stayed in her thoughts. Was he truly staying at Whitewood? For how long? And why did her heart's rhythm increase when she thought upon him, or heard others speak his name? It was nonsensical. It wasn't as if she cared for him—beyond friendship. Yet telling herself that, as often as she had, did nothing to decrease the tightness in her chest, the warmth in her cheeks, when she though about his kindness, the way he listened to her as if what she said was always of great interest and importance.

His esteem meant a great deal to her, his attentions lifted her spirits. At times, when they spoke alone, she wished their conversations needn't ever end. It was a selfish thought, vain and foolish.

His being here is good for the community.

That was all that mattered.

Chapter Twelve

The somewhat musty smell of sheep wool in the sunshine wasn't particularly enjoyable, but as Harry's new steward had informed him they could use more livestock on the property, he stood outside a large pen full of the bleating animals. He wasn't making the purchases himself, of course, but observed how the process went. After several ewes and a ram had been deemed good enough for his flock by an elderly shepherd, Harry paid the bill. He shook hands with the old man who had possibly more fingers than teeth.

"Thank you, Moore. I appreciate your expertise in this matter."

"Not at all, Mr. Devon. I've been keeping sheep for your family for fifty-three years. I wouldn't ever lead you astray." He tipped his cap, then lifted the crook he'd carried with him. He called to his great-grandson, a boy of twelve, who hurried to offer his shoulder for the old man to lean on.

The old shepherd had been pensioned off by Harry's father and lived with his grandson, the current man in charge of the sheep. Harry watched them go, thinking of Daisy's opinion on whether those men were sheep-herders or shepherds.

Daisy. Would she be present today? As it was a day dedicated to the buying and selling of livestock more than entertainment, he tried to put his hopes of seeing her aside. He wandered between pens full of animals, not really paying attention to where he was going, except to avoid walking into other people.

He left the animals behind for a smaller field, cleared to showcase plows and the like.

"Devon," a voice called, pulling his attention out of his thoughts. A tall blond man waved at Harry from beside a shining, low phaeton. "You are just the man to give me an opinion." It was the Earl of Annesbury, and Harry's cousin-in-law, if there was such a thing.

Harry picked up the pace to hurry to Lucas's side and made the requisite bow. "Annesbury. Good to see you. How may I be of service?"

Lucas gestured to the phaeton behind him. "I am thinking of getting Phillip his own vehicle. Just for use at home, of course, not at school. He claims all my gigs are not dashing enough."

As Harry wasn't far from the age of wanting the latest in wheeled transportation, he could well understand Lucas's stepson. "How old is he now? Nineteen?"

"Twenty, this summer." Lucas sighed, but his eyes crinkled at the corners. "And determined to finish his formal education so he can run off and be a baron. He is a good lad, but I worry if I leave the choice up to him he will select something his mother will disapprove of and then we will both be in her ladyship's black books."

"We cannot have that." Harry turned his attention to the phaeton, a low and light model of the variety, though he quickly realized it was not built with fashionable men in mind. "I believe this is a model considered suitable for ladies to drive. I am not certain the baron would appreciate that."

Lucas glared at the dark-blue paint of the equipage and sighed. "I cannot get him one of the taller monstrosities. Virginia seems to think every carriage accident involves one of those foolish things."

"Let us walk on." Harry gestured to several more carriages. "Where is the man in charge of selling these things?"

"I sent him off," Lucas admitted. "He chattered at me like a weasel. Seems not many have come by looking to purchase carriages at the last several fairs he's attended. The man is rather desperate." Lucas stopped before a two-wheeled vehicle. "What about this one? It is dashing without being deadly-looking."

Harry looked it over. "A Stanhope gig." It was painted red, which gave it an additional sort of charm he knew would appeal to a young man. "This is a better option than the phaeton." He spotted a curricle, painted a bright yellow that immediately put him in mind of Daisy's shawl from the day he'd discovered her caught in his blackberry bushes. Harry approached the vehicle with narrow-eyed interest.

"What have we here?" Lucas asked, coming up behind him. "Suggest the gig for Phillip and then find something better for yourself?"

"Something expensive, more like." Harry walked around the curricle, inspecting its wheels and axle with interest. "If I am to stay in the country for any length of time, a carriage would be more the thing than a horse. Wouldn't it?"

Lucas crossed his arms, raising his eyebrows at Harry. "I had heard rumors about you staying. I must confess, at your age, I wasn't all that interested in country life. Not until I decided to marry Abigail." Abigail was Lucas's first wife, who had died of an illness five years before he met and married Harry's cousin Virginia, who had been a widow with two young sons.

"Town life isn't all that exciting." Harry paused on the other side of the gig, crossing his arms over his chest. "If a man isn't a gambler or womanizer, what does he do in Town? I will return for a portion of the Season, of course. But as I learn about the details of running an estate, I find I am more resolved to see the thing done correctly. And I haven't an interest in going to London just to have young ladies in search of a husband thrown in my path."

"No?" Lucas mimicked Harry's stance and smirked. "Most gentlemen in your position would not mind such attentions. Unless, of course, you already have a lady who is of interest to you."

Dropping his arms back to his side, Harry pointed in the direction of the village. "Where did you say you sent the carriage man to? The inn, perhaps? I shall go and tell him we will take two vehicles off his hands." He made it a step before Lucas started laughing.

117

"Come now, Devon. I am jesting. Let me come with you." The earl came and clapped a hand on Harry's shoulder. "Although if there is a young woman on your mind, I will advise you to make your feelings known sooner rather than later. There is no use waiting for happiness." He squeezed Harry's shoulder before leading him to the inn.

After their business with the carriage-seller was complete, with promises of delivering the very vehicles the men had inspected by the fair's end, Harry and Lucas parted ways. Lucas to bring his smaller children to gawk at sheep, as he said, and Harry to peruse the market stalls in the village. It did not take him long, once on the street, to spot a familiar bonnet.

It was the same bonnet Daisy had worn home when he walked with her from the inn, last week. She was standing before a booth full of pies, arranging them from the front while another woman behind the structure laid out more.

He took two quick steps before he noticed a gentleman standing behind Daisy, apparently speaking with her. It was the curate.

I am obviously not the only man who enjoys being near her. His shoulders tensed. Harry approached in a more sedate manner, determined not to appear over-eager.

Perhaps the curate was only on friendly terms with her, like Mr. Ellsworth. Harry came near and cleared his throat when he was but a step away, in order to gain attention.

§

Mr. Haskett's long-winded explanation of the importance of vestments for members of the clergy cut off abruptly when a throat cleared behind them. Daisy, who had barely been listening to the curate, glanced up at the welcome interruption.

"Mr. Devon." She straightened and curtsied. "What a pleasure to see you at the fair today." She did not even attempt to hold back her delighted smile.

"Thank you, Miss Ames. I admit, I am glad to have found you here as well." He returned her grin, one side of his mouth rising higher than the other. "And Mr. Haskett. Good day to you, sir. I regret I must once again steal Miss Ames away. I have a matter of business to discuss with her."

The tall curate's eyebrows came down and a most disapproving frown appeared on his face. "Business? I confess, I cannot fathom what sort of business one might have with the vicar's daughter. Is it a matter regarding the church? I would be happy to discuss such with you, Mr. Devon."

"I am afraid it has nothing to do with the church." Harry offered his arm to Daisy, which she took without comment. "But if I have any need for such discussion in future, I will know who to speak to. Thank you, Mr. Haskett." After they had taken a few steps away, Harry bent his head toward her. "I hope that was not too forward of me." His voice, lowered in such a manner, caused a shiver to run down her back.

"You are a most direct gentleman, Harry." She matched his tone as best she could, watching him from the corner of her eye. The warm, spiced scent of cider floated through the air. It seemed everyone had thought food and drink would be wanted.

As though he had heard her thoughts, Harry stopped before the booth with the cider and obtained a mug for each of them. "Here you are. You look as though you might be cold."

"Thank you." She sipped at the drink, the warmth of the liquid slipping down her throat a welcome comfort. She tasted cinnamon and nutmeg on her tongue. With a sigh of delight, she threaded her arm through his again. "This is delightful."

"Indeed." He spoke with a thick voice and when she glanced at him, curiously, he hastily put the mug to his lips and drank. When at last he lowered the cup, apparently empty, he said, "Yes. Delightful."

"Did you truly have something to discuss, or were you only being heroic when you took me away from Mr. Haskett?" She sipped at her mug while he led them to a bench beneath one of the trees on the village square.

Harry allowed her to sit, then he crossed his arms and leaned his shoulder against the tree. He stared down at her, forehead wrinkled. "Did you need rescuing from the curate? He does not appear all that dangerous to me."

Daisy turned the mug around in her hands, wishing some of its warmth would seep into her fingers. The days were growing colder, and her thin summer gloves were no longer good for much besides looking pretty.

Answering Harry's question would be almost like confiding in him. As friends, she ought to be able to do so without any worry of what he would think. She considered for another moment before answering him.

"Mr. Haskett is a good man, and he takes his position as curate quite seriously." She sipped at her cup again. "But I do find, from time to time, that his conversation becomes more detailed than I wish."

The gentleman above her did not laugh, but she could see the merriment in his eyes as his posture relaxed. "I see. In that case, I am glad I came along when I did." He adjusted his position against the tree, settling his back against it. "Although I did wish to speak to you about something."

"Lovely. I have something to talk about as well. You may go first." She sat taller on the old worn bench, giving Harry her full attention. He had a rather handsome profile. His straight nose neither long nor short, his jawline pronounced just enough to appear firm. His dark hair peeked from beneath the brim of his tall black hat.

"I have obtained Mr. Ellsworth's services as my new steward." He glanced at her briefly and she nodded her approval. "And I am making numerous other changes on my estate. So many, in fact, that I thought it best to settle in more permanently. All my belongings are at Whitewood now. The staff is, as you guessed, most approving. Though I do not think caring for a bachelor will be nearly as exciting as they wish." His smile was self-deprecating. "I wanted to thank you for encouraging me to take an interest in my property and responsibilities. I am not certain I would have made such decisions without your help."

The cold in Daisy's fingertips was chased away by a satisfied, warm contentment that crept through her as Harry spoke. "Although I have been most forward in our conversations, if this is what such behavior leads to, I am not sorry for it. I am glad you will stay, Harry." Even if it meant she continued to experience the complex reactions to his presence. She had hoped they would fade with time, but knowing he would be a permanent fixture in their community did not seem to decrease the way she felt.

"Thank you. Now. What is it you wished to say?" His expression turned inquisitive.

"I wished to ask about the rumors of you staying," she admitted. "Though many people have confirmed them, I did not think it wise to believe it until I spoke directly to you."

"Ah." He looked away again, a smile teasing at his lips. "Your abhorrence of gossip and rumor. I remember."

She took in the way he stood and considered how it might appear to others in the area. They were, after all, in plain sight of anyone at the fair. But Harry seemed aloof rather than attentive, and he stood a few feet away from where she sat.

He is even now honoring my wishes. No one watching us would think us anything more than mere acquaintances.

Somehow, the thought both pleased and disappointed her. She frowned down into the remnants of her cider, which had turned cold. The leaves above her head shivered with a gust of wind, and several drifted down to land on the village green.

"How are the plans for your school coming?" he asked, watching a leaf float to the ground.

"Very well. I spoke to your cousin, Lady Annesbury, and she is a strong supporter of the project. I am most grateful for that. With ladies such as her and your sister championing the school, I think it must be a success."

At that Harry laughed, the sound low and soothing more than surprising. "The ladies I am related to are all well practiced in being champions and rescuers. We are both fortunate to have them on our side."

Daisy rose from the bench, another breeze coming by to ruffle her bonnet and hem. When she peered upward through the branches of the tree, she saw gray clouds moving to absorb the blue sky. "Oh dear. It looks as though it will rain again."

Harry glanced up as well. "May I escort you home?"

She shook her head. "I ought to help Mrs. Bramston, our housekeeper, and our cook. They will wish to pack their things and go home before the rain ruins everything."

"I will assist you. Is there a cart I could fetch?"

"Yes. In the pasture behind the inn, we tied up a little pony and dogcart. Thank you, Harry." She laid her hand on his arm, trying to give extra weight to her gratitude.

Harry briefly covered her hand with his and his eyes turned darkly serious. "Of course, Daisy. Anything for you." Then he was gone, before she could decide what he had meant by such a statement. There really was no time to consider it, either, for she still had to return the cider mugs and help her servants.

Yet, even as she ran to help pack up their wares before the rain began, Daisy knew the earnest gleam in Harry's eyes would be with her for quite some time.

Chapter Thirteen

The weather had turned from bright sunshine to darkened gray skies with a rapidity that would have discouraged Harry, had he not so much to do. The days of the fair were the last that the village enjoyed the sunshine. October was nearly over, and November would be filled with cold days and even colder nights.

Which was why he and his new steward were out on an important errand. Mr. Ellsworth drove a gig he had found in Harry's carriage house, and Harry sat up in the seat beside his employee.

"I know it isn't the best time of year for such projects," Mr. Ellsworth said, flicking the reins. "But it isn't the best time to live in a house with a patchy roof and drafts either."

"This is the sort of thing I should have looked into first." Harry tried not to grind his teeth at his own stupidity. He'd been enjoying the comfort of the study at Whitewood, taking his walks almost daily, but never once had he gone to inspect the tenant houses on his property. "Or Keyes ought to have said something."

"He has been ignoring the repairs for years." Mr. Ellsworth had only seen the problems of the housing himself the day before, when going about to interview tenants to make certain their rents were the proper amount in the books. He'd returned to Whitewood flustered and angry, and gave Harry a detailed account of what he saw.

Harry needed to go out and see for himself. He needed to understand the depth of his own neglect and his former steward's lack of care.

They stopped before a small row of cottages, all nearing a century old. The cottages were low, small buildings with thatched roofs. There were gardens in a few yards, full of the practical sorts of plants one found about cottages.

Even from his place on the road, Harry could see places where repairs had been made but appeared insubstantial. "It looks as though someone has tried to bandage up a flour sieve," he said, a weight pressing against his heart. "There are families in all of these houses?"

"Yes. Paying a rate similar to what the earl's tenants pay. But the earl's properties are in far better repair, and newer, than these." Ellsworth's disgust was apparent in the frustrated growl of his voice. "What do you want to do, Mr. Devon?"

"My father has only been dead four years," Harry said quietly, not moving from his seat. "These houses have obviously needed attention for longer than that."

The man beside him said nothing, leaving Harry to stare at the crumbling stone wall between him and the cottage in silence.

"I want to tear them all down." Harry jumped out of the gig without a backward glance and strode through the crooked white gate of the first house. He went straight for the door and banged on it, his frustration urging him on to action.

The door swung open to reveal a startled looking woman, perhaps near Harry's age, wearing an apron over a stomach swollen with child.

"Mr. Devon, sir," she half-gasped. "I'm sorry, sir, I didn't know you were comin' today. Is there somethin' you need from my mister, sir?"

Harry shook his head and lowered his eyes, the shame choking him. He met the startled stare of a little boy, holding onto the woman's skirts and staring up at Harry with wide, frightened eyes.

"Only tell him, and the others in these cottages, that there will be no rents paid this winter." It was the least he could do. But he certainly meant to do more. He touched the brim of his hat and left her staring after him, her mouth gaping at him.

He climbed back into the gig. Ellsworth spared him only a glance before taking up the reins and moving the horse along. "That was kind of you, Mr. Devon."

Harry snorted. "It was the right thing to do. The worst of it is that woman knew exactly who I am, and I could not for the world tell you who she or her husband are."

"Mr. and Mrs. Dempsy," Ellsworth supplied. "He is a tenant farmer."

"Thank you." Harry groaned and covered his eyes with a gloved hand. "We need to do more, and soon. Make inquiries. See about hiring a team of men to build new cottages. We can set them across the road from the old, so the tenants won't have far to go. When we tear down the old buildings, perhaps we can salvage the stone for something else. I don't know."

Ellsworth hesitate in speaking long enough that Harry uncovered his eyes, casting the man an expectant look. "What, Mr. Ellsworth?"

"It will be expensive, and difficult, to build at this time of year."

"I am certain I can afford it." Harry thought of Daisy, of her desire to better the lives of entire families through the somewhat simple act of educating their daughters. She saw such a thing as creating stronger families, better people. It was like—

"It's an investment," Harry said out loud, his mind wrapping around the thought with ease. "Better homes mean better tenants. Those cottages, they are falling apart, but you could see the care taken in the gardens, in the painted gates. Those people want homes they can be proud of. If we supply those houses, make the rents fair, we will have happy and loyal tenants."

"You do not need to convince me, sir." Ellsworth's tone lost some of its edge, though he remained slightly hunched in his seat. "I will make inquiries and let it be known quality and speed are of the utmost importance to the project."

"Money is the least important factor." Harry sat back, crossing his arms. "I would like to see at least some of the families settled before the snow begins falling."

Ellsworth nodded tightly and said no more. His brow was puckered, his lips turned down in an earnest frown, and Harry knew his steward was making plans. Though they had been working together for a short time, Harry knew and understood Ellsworth quite well. It spoke highly of Ellsworth's character that he would bring his concern to Harry with such speed, rather than take it for granted that Harry knew the state of those cottages.

How could my father have left property, property he ought to have taken some pride in, to rot in such a horrid manner? There were children in those dilapidated structures. Families who needed warmth in the winter and a roof to keep out rain.

Harry had never been particularly close to the elder Mr. Devon. Now, he wondered if there was anything at all he liked about the man who had fathered him. Certainly, nothing came to mind. He had never shown even a shred of affection for any of his four children. They were assets, not receptors of love. In truth, it was their mother that saved the Devon children from becoming weak, withered things. Mrs. Devon had raised her three daughters on love, and they in turn had given Harry the ability to be himself, despite the dark shadow cast by his father.

Mr. Devon senior had left behind a legacy of wealth and greed, pride and snobbery, and it was left to Harry to make things right.

Chapter Fourteen

Seeking Daisy out for a private conversation was out of the question. It would be totally inappropriate for Harry to write her a note, to request to meet with her. If he went to her home, to call upon her, that could alert her father to their less than conventional friendship. With so much weighing on his mind and heart, he found himself longing for her opinion, perhaps even her approval. Despite his attempts at creativity, he could come up with nothing better than lurking near her home in the hopes of catching a glimpse of her.

That would not do, of course.

He went to Christine.

"Would you like to invite Miss Ames for dinner one evening?" he asked. "Or to come spend an afternoon with you when Thomas is away?"

Christine, who had been standing in the middle of the nursery when Harry walked in to make his request, stared at him as if he'd escaped from Bedlam.

"What was that, Harry?" She put the tin soldier she had been holding on the floor for her sons. They had an impressive array of animals and soldiers lined up for war. She stepped over their battlefield, lifting her skirts to avoid knocking their toys about. "You wish for me to invite Miss Ames here? Why?"

"It doesn't really matter what you invite her to do," Harry said, "only that you send me with the invitation. I need to speak with her, but if I call on her directly her father may not approve."

Christine took him by the arm and pulled him from the nursery, down the hall, and into an upstairs parlor. She said nothing as she dragged him about, but acted with her usual vigor. After she placed him before a chair, and took one of her own, she finally spoke. "I can see you are upset. Is it because you need to speak to her, or do you need to speak to her because something has upset you?"

Harry tried to untangle his sister's words. Apparently, neither of them had been blessed with the ability to speak clearly when disturbed. "The latter. I think."

She regarded him most seriously, her eyebrows drawn down, an incredulous smile in place. "I see. She is someone in whom you can confide. Is that all?"

He did not need to hide his feelings from his sister, not really, except that she may take it upon herself to meddle. Christine was quite a notorious meddler. But it would be far safer if she knew exactly what was in his mind and heart rather than going about with her own suppositions.

"I have come to care for and admire Miss Ames a great deal." Harry clasped his hands before him and bent forward. "I have not, however, given her any indication of feeling more toward her than friendship. I do not think she is ready or willing to hear declarations of that sort from me. But you should know, I have every intention of asking her father's permission to court her."

Christine's expression bloomed into one of delight, her grin unrestrained. She seemed at a loss for words, which was incredibly rare for the most outspoken Devon sister.

"Say something, Chrissy," he prompted at last, though his own grin had spread. "You are making me rather nervous."

When she spoke, the pitch of her voice was high and her words came quickly. "I cannot even begin to tell you how excited I am by the very idea of you courting. Miss Ames is as close to perfect for you as anyone could be. She is kind, and sweet. Your nephews adore her. She is also intelligent enough to think for herself. The only mark against her is that ponderous father of hers, but as he is a vicar, some leniency must be given."

"I am glad you approve." Harry, despite his concerns over the matter, relaxed. "Telling someone about this is something of a relief."

"Why haven't you told her of your interest?" Christine asked, sitting back and crossing her arms. The pose wasn't exactly lady-like, but it suited his sister. "You must tell her."

Harry dropped his face into his hands, then scrubbed his fingers through his hair, likely leaving it a horrid mess. "Miss Ames has consented to being my friend only recently. I cannot say she entirely approves of me yet. I am hoping that as I make improvements to the estate, to our family's reputation, that she will see I am not the directionless fool she thought I was when I returned."

"I would say you are making tremendous strides in that endeavor." The approval in his sister's voice buoyed his spirits, but not by much.

"The other matter to consider is that I do not believe her father approves of me. That dinner with them, almost a month ago, he all but said it to my face."

"Keep working to change his mind. You are a good catch, Harry." Her eyes twinkled merrily. "Every unwed girl in the neighborhood has practically come right out and asked me if you were considering marriage. What was that book that Rebecca loved—the one that said 'a single man in possession of a large fortune must be in want of a wife.'" She chuckled. "I think some must truly believe such things."

There was not much to say to that. It was nearly the truth, after all. He wanted for nothing that money could buy. His wealth ought to be a mark in his favor, but thus far Daisy had only indicated something like disdain for his income. She rose in his estimation for that.

Christine stood and went to a writing desk in the corner of the room. "I will write her a note at once, inviting her to dinner tomorrow evening. You ought to come, too. Then I can amuse myself by watching the two of you together."

"I accept your invitation. Thank you." He tapped his foot where he sat, then rose and went to the window, standing near his sister. "Will you invite her father, too?"

"I think that would be the most sensible thing to do, especially if you think he doesn't care for you. Perhaps his opinion would soften seeing you among family." She wrote out the invitation in silence, the only sound in the room that of her pen scratching against the paper.

Harry distracted himself by looking out the window, over the grounds to the stable yard. He could see his brother-in-law in conversation with a groom. Thomas Gilbert had taken the family by surprise. Somehow, the quiet man with the dry wit was the perfect match for their adventurous Christine. Harry had seen all three of his sisters show true love and admiration for their husbands. The thought made him happy, but also a touch wistful. Memories of his mother were rare and vague, and he could not conjure an image of his parents together no matter how hard he tried. Theirs was not an amiable marriage, due to his father's cold nature.

If Harry hoped to have a union based upon more than mutual tolerance, he had to look to his sisters' examples.

"Do you think Julia and Rebecca would approve as you do?" he asked, somewhat cautiously. His old school chums would think him soft, wishing for the approval of the women in his life on such a thing. But he had no parents to please, no one to advise him, except for the sisters. All three had practically raised him, after all.

He caught Christine's gentle smile from the corner of his eye. He saw her rise, letter in hand. "We all want your happiness. Whether that is found here with Miss Ames, in London with a duke's daughter, or on the Continent with a woman who speaks not a word of English." She held the letter out to him.

"Thank you." He took the paper and turned it over in his hands, pretending to study the flourish his sister had added to *Miss Augusta Ames.* "I greatly appreciate this."

"I only hope it gives you what time you need with her."
Christine gave his arm a squeeze, then pointed to the door. "Away
with you. See to your lady love."

Harry groaned. "Chrissy, I haven't said anything to her yet.
You cannot call her that."

She laughed, then shoved him toward the door. "Go, Harry. I
will be discreet in company, never fear."

He went, with as much haste as possible, needing the person
who had spoken the most sense to him since his return to
Annesbury.

I hope she hasn't tired of me yet.

§

The door to Daisy's morning room did not often receive knocks.
Daisy only withdrew to the room when she had accomplished
household tasks and could claim time for herself. When the soft
knock came, she barely looked up from her work.

"Come in," she called out, making another notation on her
paper. She sat at a long, narrow table positioned to give her a
view out the window. A handful of children's schoolbooks were
stacked to the right side of the table, lists of supplies were at her
left elbow, and she attempted to create an account sheet for the
other things needed for her school. Her meeting at the countess's
home, where other interested parties would be gathered, was
but two days away. If she wished to make a good impression, she
must be perfectly prepared.

"I am not quite ready for tea," she said, attempting to
multiply the number of drawing pencils by children hoped for,
but not yet truly expected.

"Neither am I," said a deep voice that most certainly did not
belong to Mrs. Bramston or Katie.

Daisy dropped her pencil. She rose with some haste, lifting
one hand to check her hair was all still in place. She had worn a
cap to dust her father's shelves earlier. The cap was gone, but she
could not be certain of the mess it left behind.

"Harry," she blurted when she saw the handsome young man framed by the doorway, his blue eyes settled upon her as though he had no intention of looking away. As though he wanted to look nowhere else.

Nonsense. Daisy dropped the hand from her hair to gesture to the chairs at the center of the room. "Would you care to sit down? I confess, I was not expecting visitors. Did someone show you in?"

"Your maid," he said. "She opened the front door, told me Mrs. Bramston was out and she couldn't leave the oven to show me up here." He stepped into the room somewhat hesitantly, leaving the door behind him open. "I am not entirely sure what the girl meant."

"Oh. Cook must have gone out as well and Katie is minding the kitchen." Daisy turned back to the mess behind her, noting the plate with her half-eaten luncheon and the haphazard scattering of papers. Out of habit, she reached down to try and tidy her piles back into neat stacks.

Harry came up beside her, and her sudden awareness of him stilled her hands.

"Have I disturbed your work?" he asked.

She laughed, a trifle weakly. "No. I am only trying to order my thoughts, yet somehow I have grown more disorganized." She lifted up the sheet where she had been doing sums, showing him. "For the meeting, with the countess."

He took the paper from her, his eyes flicking from hers to the list. "At times, when something matters to me, my mind grows muddled at the mere idea of confronting the object of so much thought."

"That is exactly the same for me." She lowered herself into the chair where she had been working, fatigued by the whole thing. "And this is so very important, Harry. It is something I have dreamt of. I know, I *know*, this would be a great blessing for so many of the girls, in many ways." She rested her elbow on the table, dropping her forehead to her hand. "And so far, not many people have listened to me. Nor do they see the value in the work I wish to do."

132

"I cannot understand why." He turned about to find another chair and brought it to her table. "It is obvious you have a passion for the work, and the ability to see it done correctly. You convinced me of the importance of your school in less than a quarter of an hour." He put the sheet down and took up her pencil. His eyebrows drew down and in a moment he was scribbling at her math problem.

Daisy studied him, the serious lines of his handsome face, the fine cut of his coat upon his shoulders. His words sunk into her heart, like balm on a bruise, easing some of the tightness there. "Really? You were not merely being kind?"

The pencil paused in its scribbling and he lifted his eyes to hers, the intensity in their blue depths giving weight to his words. "I am in earnest. When someone believes in something as you believe in your school, they ought to be taken seriously. Listened to. And when the cause is just and right, it falls to those privileged enough to learn of it to lend their support."

Daisy ran her fingers along the edge of the table. She dropped her eyes to the grains of the wood, finding them safer to study than the honest emotion in Harry's eyes.

"Those are wise words, Mr. Devon. Where did you learn them?" She tried to keep her tone light, as though discussing a less weighty subject.

"My brother-in-law, Dr. Hastings." Harry gave his attention to the pencil again, allowing her to relax. "He is one of the most intelligent people I know. I spent some time at his home two summers ago."

She nodded to herself, sorting through what she knew of his family tree. "He lives in Bath. Your eldest sister married him."

"Yes." He gave his attention to the sum, finishing it at last, and laid the pencil down. "And Rebecca married the man who is now the Earl of Ivyford."

"Are they well? Your sisters, I mean." Somehow, her head had become more muddled the longer she sat doing nothing. Was it because Harry sat so near? Though she did not mind his company, he certainly had interrupted her work. Perhaps that was all it was. The desire to finish her lists. She might not be able to order her thoughts at all until she completed the task.

"They are happy, which is the most important thing." The answer was strange enough that she looked up, puzzled. "What of your sisters?" he asked, sitting back in his chair. It took her a moment, thinking of the two girls she'd looked up to and chased after, grown into women and wives, leaving her behind.

"Happy," she said, unable to stop the smile that turned her lips upward. Both of her sisters were pleased with their matches and their lives. "Lily always wanted adventure, and now she lives in India. She sent me a shawl, and my father a fine pipe made of the most beautiful stone. Gabriella lives in Brighton, but sometimes she goes away with her husband on voyages. I think her captain makes her brave." Daisy had never been much like either of her sisters. Their eyes had always turned to the horizon, while she found delight in the familiarity of the people in their village.

Harry waved a hand to the stack of things upon the table, as one might gesture to a grand vista. "And this, Daisy? Does this make you happy?"

She allowed her eyes to wander from the stacks of books to her papers, to the pencils and plans. "To bring knowledge to those little girls I have known since their infancy, to spend my days serving them, would bring me joy. I find peace in purpose." She lowered her head, unwilling to see his reaction to such a ridiculous statement. "I know it is unusual. It is how I was raised, my father and mother both teaching that a life of service and caring for others is worthwhile. This is how I give of myself in a way that brings me contentment."

His hand covered hers where it rested on the arm of her chair, the soft leather of his glove against her skin a surprisingly intimate touch. There was nothing improper in the gesture, but the familiarity of it warmed her heart.

"I admire you for knowing what it is you want to accomplish and being so sure of yourself. You are making your dream into a reality, too. I wish I was as confident as you are." Admiration colored his words, causing a tingle of delight in her chest. No one had ever paid her such compliments before. The sincerity in his voice humbled her.

"Thank you." Daisy's hand turned and grasped his, grateful for the understanding he offered. Perhaps she could find a way to return the kindness. He took such an interest in her work. Had anyone noticed all his efforts in regard to his estate? "What is it that makes you happy, Harry Devon?"

His gaze dropped to their joined hands and remained focused there. "I am trying to discover that for myself, and I think I come closer every day. I—" He cleared his throat and offered one more squeeze of her hand before gently disentangling his fingers from hers. "I have found I enjoy the duties of a landowner. There are challenges at times. I want to change things. Find new ways to use the property and the funds my father left behind. His only goals were forever to turn a profit."

"What are your goals if not to increase your funds?" she asked, folding one hand over the other in her lap. She needed to secure her hands, for certain, to avoid taking his up again. What a silly thing, to wish to hold a man's hand.

"At the moment?" A muscle in his jaw tightened. "All I want to do is the opposite of everything he did. I want to be known for my choices and decisions, build my own reputation. I have seen the expressions of people in town when they see me. The tradesmen, wondering about me. I know what I look like." He tugged at the lapels of his jacket, cut from fine cloth. "A Town dandy."

Tilting her head to the side, Daisy swept her eyes from his windblown hair to the tips of his highly polished boots. "I have never thought you a dandy. Finely dressed, perhaps, but not a flighty snob."

His eyes widened and a short laugh burst from him. "Thank you. That makes me feel marginally better."

"You have already earned some favor, merely by reopening the house and taking on more staff. People want to give you a chance, I am certain." She shuffled her papers about on the desk, not so much tidying as simply busying her hands. Daisy needed to take her eyes off Harry, too. Staring at him had started to make her stomach do unusual things. It felt as though she had swallowed a hummingbird. "As a prosperous gentleman, merely by being present you increase the prosperity of everyone else."

"Hm." Harry did not sound convinced. "Having the reputation of my father hanging over me like a specter isn't exactly helping others to see it that way."

As a vicar's daughter, she well knew what the expectations of society could be like. Because of who her father was, there was a natural belief in the neighborhood that she must carry herself above all reproach, to an even higher standard than the daughters of other gentlemen in the area. She was expected to be both holier and humbler than the average young lady of her age. If she fell short, the gossip fell heavily upon her.

"Perhaps it is time you socialized more often. I know you have devoted a great deal of time to learning about your duties."

"Someone told me I ought to be a shepherd rather than let a sheep-herder do my work." His eyes gleamed when he interrupted, but she fixed him with her best disapproving stare.

"Harry."

His grin was unrepentant. "I will never forget it. Why should I allow you to pretend it did not happen?"

She blew out an exasperated breath, narrowing her eyes at him. "As I was saying. You need to get to know the people in the village better. Form a few relationships and bonds. No one knows you as the man you are, only as the boy you were before your father passed away."

"He did not like me to visit the country." The simple statement surprised her, and Harry seemed to notice. He leaned forward again, his hands on the arms of the chair. "My father kept me away from Whitewood and in London, on the holidays from school when I had to be at home. He would make certain I was getting on well in my lessons, then he would disappear. I could go a whole week without seeing him. I actually preferred it that way."

Though he hadn't exactly spoken warmly of his father before, and certainly no one in the village ever did, she had not realized their relationship was that distant. "You and your father did not get along?" she asked, trying to gentle her tone.

"My father did not get along with anyone. Perhaps I should not tell the vicar's daughter this, but I was almost relieved when my father died." He ducked his head, and she watched his hands tighten on the arms of the chair. "He wasn't the kindest man, nor did he care for anyone or anything outside of his desires."

Although her own father was not overly demonstrative in his affections, Daisy never doubted he loved her and wanted what he thought best for her. How would it have been, to grow up with a father one always wished away?

"I am sorry to hear that," she said at last, unable to think of anything better to say.

Harry shrugged, still not meeting her eyes. "We made the best of things, my sisters and I. The truth is, while I am sorry for the way the relationship between my father and the rest of us was, I am sorrier for all my father lost by treating us as commodities rather than children." He sucked in a deep breath and let it out in a humorless laugh. "I apologize, Daisy. I did not mean to grow so melancholy. The truth is, I have wanted to speak to you for some time about something else entirely."

Daisy tried to banish the sorrow for her friend that had settled on her heart and sat taller in her chair. "Really? What about?"

"I want to make some changes to the way my estate is run," he said, some of the exuberance back in his voice. "I wish to try new things, make new investments, and be rid of my father's mistakes. One of the things I have been working toward, since learning of your idea for a school, is setting aside funds in order to patronize those doing good works. I know you wish for the support of the village, and I will do my best to help you with that, but I would also like to invest in your school."

She drew back in her chair and folded her hands in her lap. "It is a school for the lower-classes and will only meet a few times a week. We do not need a great deal in funds."

"I know. But I wrote to my brother-in-law, the Ivyford earl, and asked about school endeavors in Town and throughout the country. You probably know all this, but it is the first time I have wanted to learn such things. There is a movement for the government itself to supply schools to every village. Take over from the church, build schools where none have yet been supplied."

His eyes lit up as he talked, and he opened his hands in an expansive gesture. He looked almost as excited by the prospect as she became when she thought on the future. She had to press her lips together tightly to keep from smiling, not wishing to give away her amusement.

"What is needed is more support for the men who are proposing these changes, and the foundations supplying education at present. I will donate a modest sum to the school here, and the boys' school Mr. Haskett leads. But what I would really like to do is give support to the societies pushing for educational reform. I wished to discuss the matter with you to see what you thought and if you might have any suggestions for such an investment."

Daisy stared at him, uncomprehending for a moment. "I am not sure I understand you, Harry. You wish for me—" She placed a hand over her heart "—to do what, exactly?"

"Advise me on educational reforms and how best to support a movement that will offer education to all, no matter their station in life." He smiled, without the teasing tilt to his lips, and his eyes softened. "All you say about the education of the children in our village is true for children throughout the country. And not everyone is so fortunate as to have someone like you championing their daughters."

Warmth flooded her cheeks, straight from her heart. Had she done this to Harry? Did she inspire him to such action, or was it the cause itself? It should not matter—yet it did. She wanted him to rise to this new desire, to help others as she so longed to help them, and perhaps because it was she who first presented him with the thought. Not that she wished for credit. But she wished to be a part of his thoughts. A part of his plans.

"I would be most happy to discuss my thoughts on the matter with you, whenever you wish." She stared into his eyes, admiring the way the light from the window picked up gold flecks in his irises. He always exuded warmth and excitement, and he often left her laughing or exasperated. But this was an entirely new side to him, and it was most intriguing. He saw her as an equal, given the tone of his conversation and the desire for her advice. That did not happen often in her conversations with gentlemen.

"Thank you." The simplicity of the words did not diminish the obvious gratitude in his voice. "There is one other reason I am here today."

Daisy's heart picked up in rhythm. "Oh?" she asked, anticipation building, though she did not know why.

"Mrs. Gilbert sent me with an invitation to dinner, for you and your father." He reached into his coat and produced a folded paper, holding it out to her.

Annoyed at the way disappointment threatened, Daisy accepted the paper from his hand and unfolded it. What had she been hoping he would say?

"Should I tell her you will come? I am not certain it makes a difference, but I will be there as well."

It did make a difference. She felt her cheeks warm as she admitted that much to herself. "Yes, we accept the invitation. Of course."

Harry grinned and rose from his chair. "Wonderful. I will deliver your acceptance to Christine. Now, I had better be going. I can see how busy you are."

She stood too. "I will see you out." They started to the door, but Daisy stopped abruptly. "Oh, Harry. I still have your handkerchief. Allow me to fetch it."

For a moment he appeared puzzled, then he chuckled. "From the bramble incident? Do not trouble yourself. If you like, I can fetch it another time. Perhaps when we speak of the school next."

Daisy ought to have insisted he take it right away. She really had no business holding onto it any longer, as it was his personal property. Yet having it in her possession afforded her another opportunity to speak to him. Something she found herself anticipating most happily.

"I suppose the return of your handkerchief does afford me a proper excuse for seeing you another time." She bit her tongue at her boldness. Her ridiculousness.

They stood in the hall, at the top of the steps, when she spoke. Harry stopped walking and turned to face her. Though they were but a foot apart, Harry took a step closer.

"If you say things like that, Miss Ames, I shall think you have grown fond of me." It was almost a flirtation, but for the even tone he used, tempered with a gentle smile.

Fond of him? She swallowed, realizing there was more to it than that. "Perhaps I have," she admitted, her heart picking up speed.

"Fonder than when we rescued Bell?" he asked, his voice a trifle lower.

Every particle of Daisy's body became aware of him, his nearness, the alert way he stood and how his voice made her tingle from her toes upward. What on earth was happening to her? She lowered her eyes, trying to sort out her feelings in too hasty a manner for it to be done with any certainty.

"Yes," she answered, distracted by her strange physical response to make light of the situation or tease.

He leaned closer; she practically felt the warmth in his voice emanating from the rest of him. "Fonder than when we decided to be friends?"

Daisy's eyes darted upward and her lungs constricted. Why couldn't she breathe or move? What was happening? He stood so close. She lowered her eyes to his lips. What would it be like—? She startled herself out of the thought and took a step back.

"Thank you for coming with the invitation, Mr. Devon." Formality did not save her, because he raised his eyebrows at the use of his surname and that started a whole new flood of sensations through her. "I will see you at dinner tomorrow. Excuse me." She took another step back.

To his credit, he neither pressed the issue nor teased. He bowed, his expression almost contrite. "Until then, Miss Ames." Was he not going to call her Daisy again? Throwing the light of formality on the situation was not meant to be permanent, after all. He started down the steps and she hurried to the railing.

"Harry?" she called softly, hoping her voice would not carry to her father's study. The gentleman paused and looked up, expression curious, his eyes...hopeful? "Perhaps I could return your handkerchief the day after that? Friday. Where you rescued Bell?"

What was she thinking? Forward, presumptuous, ridiculous—

"I would like that." His grin returned. "Good day, Daisy."

"Good day." She watched him go to the entryway, collect his hat from a hall table, and disappear out the door. As it shut behind him, Daisy knew something essential within her had changed. Perhaps had been changing, all along.

She floated back to her table covered in notes and books, though she did not so much as lift a single one. She opened the invitation to dinner again, hardly taking in Mrs. Gilbert's words. Her mind remained preoccupied with one subject; what exactly were her feelings for Harry Devon? And what would become of her dreams if she gave way to them?

Examining her heart took the better part of the afternoon, and she was no closer to an answer when the room darkened around her.

Chapter Fifteen

H arry flew through his work the following morning. Mr. Ellsworth barely kept up as Harry shared his vision for the tenant cottages. "My expert from Warwickshire is arriving this afternoon. He will give the estimate on demolishing the cottages and begin looking for a place to relocate the tenants. While I understand frugality is important, the earl himself trusts this builder. Do not dicker overlong on price. The sooner we agree to the work, the sooner it can begin."

Harry marked off an item on a list he had made for himself. "Make certain he uses as many local men as possible for different aspects of the projects ahead. Then the money stays in the community."

"Yes, of course." Ellsworth closed an account book, glancing askance at Harry. "Mr. Devon, you seem anxious about something. Might I be of some assistance? That is why I am here, after all."

Harry paused in another notation and glanced up at Ellsworth, trying to conceal his agitation behind a mask of ignorance. "Anxious? Not at all. Everything is going quite well."

Ellsworth folded his arms over his chest and sat back, fixing his employer with narrowed eyes. "If there is something amiss, I should like to know. Especially if it effects my responsibilities."

"It does not," Harry said, then clamped his mouth shut. He had grown distracted and as good as admitted there was something on his mind. "Merely a personal matter."

"Ah." Ellsworth considered Harry for a moment, then sat forward and turned his attention back to the papers scattered across his desk. "A lady, then."

"What?" Harry tried to cover his surprise by clearing his throat. "What makes you say that?"

"Everything. From your recent state of distraction to your sudden overly energetic tackling of projects. If you will excuse me for saying so, Mr. Devon, you are either so lost in thought I must repeat myself to be heard or else working yourself into something of a frenzy. Now that you say it is a personal matter, I know it could only be a lady." He tapped the nib of his pen against a blank sheet of paper as he spoke. "A family matter would incur less bursts of enthusiasm, a financial matter more focus on the actual accounts."

Harry's chuckle came out somewhat stuttered. "You are an observant man, Mr. Ellsworth."

"Which makes me quite suitable for my post." Ellsworth raised his eyebrows. "It is Miss Ames, isn't it?"

Surprise overtook Harry and he dropped backward in his chair. It seemed Ellsworth needed no other confirmation, as he nodded once and went back to his notations.

"Tell me how you guessed," Harry demanded at last, wondering if he had somehow conveyed to all the world his interest in the vicar's youngest daughter.

"The consuming interest in donating funds to educational causes was a telling sign." Ellsworth shook his head, his amusement showing clearly though he kept his eyes on the paper before him. "And you may have mentioned her name a few times this past week as well. I do not believe you have spoken even once of any other young woman in our county."

Harry supposed that did make him rather transparent. "Then you are less a genius than I am obvious."

"Perhaps." Ellsworth pulled the news sheet near, looking through the columns. "But everyone knows the curate is hoping to attach himself to her. You ought not to wait too long to make your feelings known, in case he outpaces you to asking for her hand."

Harry narrowed his eyes. "The curate? I do not think she even likes him."

Ellsworth glanced up from the paper, his forehead wrinkling. "Are you certain of that, Mr. Devon?"

"I did not take you for a meddlesome matchmaker," Harry said, frustration coloring his words.

"I am your steward. I have all your best interests at heart." Ellsworth smirked and went back to his work without another word.

Continuing the conversation would be futile. Harry had already revealed too much of himself, and the bounds of employer and employee had certainly been crossed beyond salvaging. He stood. "I have some business to attend to, Mr. Ellsworth. I will check in with you again before you go home for the evening."

"Yes, sir."

Harry tried to retreat with some dignity, and Ellsworth let him.

The curate. Harry shook his head, brushing aside that worry most soundly. Daisy had been relieved when he rescued her from Mr. Haskett's conversation. She certainly held no interest for the man.

Then again, the idea of someone else expressing an interest in courtship, in exploring a greater connection to the exquisite Miss Ames, before Harry even had a chance, set his back up.

Something needed to be done. But if he moved too soon, would that ruin everything?

§

Leaves scattered out of Daisy's way, blown by the breeze and practically racing her to the church. She held one hand to her bonnet while the other clutched a basket full of fresh bread. Cook had baked enough for the vicarage and to supply the curate for at least a week. It fell to Daisy to deliver the food to the bachelor, who usually spent his Fridays overseeing the cleaning of the church.

If Daisy hurried, the women who volunteered to sweep, dust, and polish the pews would still be at their work and she would not be left alone with Mr. Haskett. She burst through the door into the vestibule, the wind putting more force into her entry than she liked. Daisy closed the door behind her and loosed the scarf around her neck and face.

Whatever the case, she had another appointment to keep. She must meet Harry on the edge of her father's property, where they had encountered each other the day he rescued Bell from the tree.

The church stood silent and still. Perhaps everyone had left.

"Hello?" Daisy called, stepping into the knave. "Mr. Haskett?" The scent of furniture polish drifted in the air, and the sharp lye used to clean the floor mingled with it. The women had come and gone, it would seem.

Footsteps brought her attention to the vestry, and Mr. Haskett stepped through the doorway. Her heart sank. Their last few interactions had been filled with his pointed attentions toward her. Though Mr. Haskett was a kind man, and somewhat attractive in appearance, she could not work up any more enthusiasm for him than she did for any man of her acquaintance. Excepting Harry, who stirred an unusual amount of excitement in her feelings.

"Miss Ames," the curate said, his tone surprised. "How good it is to see you this afternoon." He approached, his shoes clapping against the stone floor with haste. "To what do I owe this pleasure?"

Daisy held the basket out to him with both hands, using it has a barrier between them. But rather than stretch his arms out to take the offering, Mr. Haskett stepped around it to her side.

"Cook wished me to deliver your bread to you," Daisy said, somewhat belatedly.

"Ah, thank you. She is a marvelous woman. Please extend to her my deepest appreciation for her efforts on my behalf." He took the basket from her, his eyes never leaving her face. His eyebrows were raised, almost expectantly. "I am grateful you came when you did, Miss Ames. The ladies who generously give of their time to clean the knave have only just departed. Perhaps, if you will allow me to make a bold request, you would give me a moment of your time for a private conversation?"

How is it that one man can turn the simplest of requests into an entire oration?

Daisy forced a smile. "I am at your service, Mr. Haskett. What is it you wish to speak to me about?"

His whole expression brightened, his lips turning up and his eyes gleaming. Guilt smote her. She had been avoiding him, avoiding the opportunity for him to speak to her alone. It had simply become impossible to feel at ease in his presence.

"A most serious matter. Please, will you not sit down?" He walked into the knave and put the basket down, then sat on another pew and gestured for her to sit next to him. Daisy hesitated, but there was nothing inappropriate in sitting in a church, with a man of God. She took care to keep some distance between them on the pew, however.

Seated on the edge of the pew, Daisy kept her hands still in her lap. "What is this serious matter, sir?" Surely it could not be anything that would disturb her. Surely, he was not about to say anything that would be unbearable to hear.

The rather grave look he fixed upon her suggested otherwise. "Miss Ames, I have been giving a great deal of thought to your situation of late." He paused, expectantly.

"My situation? I am not sure what you mean."

"You are the youngest of your father's daughters, and at twenty-one you are yet unmarried."

Those were facts. Not a situation. "Yes, Mr. Haskett."

"And you are a servant to the parish, always giving of yourself to the people. I wish to tell you how much I admire your selfless character and kindness." He spoke gently, and most sincerely, but it still struck Daisy as an odd sort of way to pay a compliment. "Your desire to educate the daughters of the parish also says a great deal about your compassionate heart."

146

If it had been anyone else saying such things to her, Daisy may have blushed. But his compliments were only paving the way to the true subject of the conversation. This left her rather impatient, yet dreading the point which he would soon reach. "Thank you. I hope others feel as I do in support of the school." Would her matter-of-fact tone put him off at all?

No. It seemed he determined in his course, sliding a few inches closer to her.

"I am certain when they see the efforts you have gone through, all will be most moved, as I have been, by your good works. I have been most deeply moved by *you*, Miss Ames. Augusta."

Every hair on the back of Daisy's neck stood up on end and her stomach shrunk.

"That is supremely kind to say." She moved back the same distance he had moved toward her. Was there no way to escape this conversation and save face? Glancing behind her at the door, she realized bolting out the way she had come in would be far too graceless.

"I speak the truth. And there is more, Augusta. Your gentleness and compassion are the very reasons I wish to speak with you today. I would ask if you might consider doing me the great honor of allowing me to pay court to you." He reached for a hand she had let fall to the lip of the pew, but the instant he touched it she drew away.

"Mr. Haskett," she said in what she sincerely hoped was a firm tone. "I have not given you leave to call me by my Christian name." And every time he said it, she liked the name even less. "And while I do understand the honor you are bestowing on me with your request, I must decline."

He drew back, almost as though she had done something as shocking as bit him, and considered her with wide eyes. "I—I understand that I am not in the best position to take a wife. A curate's income is a mere pittance, after all. But I am hoping to obtain a living not far from here, in perhaps a year's time. If you could wait—you could begin your school and we may come to know one another better."

Daisy started to shake her head. "That is most considerate of you, Mr. Haskett, but—"

"I am not proposing marriage yet," he interrupted, his expression turned somewhat pleading. "I know this must be something of a surprise to you." It really wasn't, though she had hoped to put off this moment a great deal longer. "I have admired you almost since the moment of my arrival in this parish. Will you at least consider a courtship? To be sure, I must merit some thought rather than a hasty answer." Though his tone had grown somewhat sad, she sensed a demand in his words.

Daisy stood, having no wish to draw out the conversation. She had never been attracted to Mr. Haskett, though she recognized him as a good man of high moral conduct. Not once had her mind imagined him in the position of admirer or husband. He had never entered her daydreams, never crossed her fancy, and she could not allow him to think there was hope for any of that to change.

"It is not a hasty answer, sir. I am afraid I have not been oblivious to your attentions." She spoke gently, hoping to ease whatever sting her words would give. "I have never thought of you in any way save as my father's curate. I admire the work you do, but I am not interested in having a connection with you that is any different than your relationship with any of the parishioners. I thank you for your interest, but my answer will not change."

He stared at her, his face rather pale. His voice sounded as empty as the knave when he spoke. "Is there someone else who has claimed your interest?"

Harry's charming grin came to mind, but Daisy brushed that away. "Whether there is or is not, I am afraid it is not your concern." She was less gentle and more firm. "I am afraid you must excuse me. I have another appointment. Good day, Mr. Haskett."

He did not return the farewell, and Daisy did not wait for him to rise from his seat. She turned and left the church at a fast clip, determined to put as much distance between her and the curate as swiftly as possible. When she broke from the building into the biting autumn wind, she inhaled deeply.

Cold air filled her lungs and brought vigor back to her body. She shuddered and pulled her jacket tighter about her. Her cloak would have to be brought out if she was to be walking about in such weather.

Distressed and chilled, Daisy checked the watch she kept in her reticule. There wasn't enough time for her to return home for warmer clothing, if she meant to be punctual when she met Harry beneath the tree. With his handkerchief tucked securely in the same purse as the watch, she set off to see him at least long enough to return the square of fabric.

After the curate's attention, she hardly felt fit for much else. Why had he felt the need to address her today, of all days? Had he spoken to her father first? That made the whole situation that much more humiliating for him and uncomfortable for her. Especially given that her father had seemed less disapproving of Harry at dinner the night before.

Dinner with the Gilberts had been a comfortable, quiet affair. Her father and Thomas Gilbert had done most of the talking, though she caught Christine Gilbert smiling into her napkin a time or two. Harry, seated directly next to her, hadn't said much to anyone, but certainly sent quite a few knowing looks her way.

And he *did* speak of his improvements to the management of his estate, his desire to be an active part of the community. Daisy's father had nodded in his ponderous way, approving of the younger man's efforts. It had felt rather like a triumph to end the evening without having to be a buffer between her father and anyone else. She had missed the easy conversation between herself and Harry, as had become their habit. She looked forward all the more to seeing him in a more private manner.

Daisy tried to put Mr. Haskett's unwelcome request from her mind and walked faster toward the old tree.

Toward *Harry*.

Chapter Sixteen

H arry waited beneath the tree, staring up into its bare branches. Weeks had passed since he saved the ungrateful cat, yet he could recall that day with perfect clarity. Meeting Daisy again, seeing her for the first time as a woman instead of the girl always following her elder sisters about, had become a memory he relived again and again. Somehow, most of their meetings seemed to have ended in misadventure, whether it was affront, a fall from a tree, or rain. Would they ever have one pleasant interaction not immediately followed by a minor catastrophe?

He leaned against the tree, the bark rough against his overcoat. The weather had teased at autumn that day, now here he stood in thick gloves and scarf hoping winter would wait a while longer to make its appearance. Not for his own sake, but to ensure his tenants were well prepared. His eyes swept from the bushes concealing the road to the hill concealing the vicar's house. He couldn't be certain from which direction Daisy would come. He had arrived early, intent upon seeing her again. Being near her, though it often reminded him of all his failings and faults, also inspired him. Daisy expected more of him than anyone had before, pointing out his duties and stating what must be done. She had such a straightforward way of speaking, though she had never been unkind.

A bonnet with a wide blue ribbon above its brim appeared at the corner of his eye. Harry turned, took two steps forward in his excitement, then waited as Daisy drew near. She had come from the opposite direction of the vicarage, not quite where he had been looking. She wore a Spencer to match the ribbon, both a jewel-toned blue. Wisps of hair that may have once been curls brushed against her cheeks, rosy from the cold wind. As she neared, he saw her eyebrows were pulled together and her lips formed a straight line.

The excitement building in his breast stuttered, wavering like a candle left near a window.

Had he done something wrong? Could she be upset with him? But she had proposed this meeting, hadn't she? His mind flew through the possible causes of her less than cheerful expression, each one more unlikely than the last.

Then she raised her eyes from the grassy path she followed and met his stare. Everything in her expression changed, just as sunlight bursting through clouds transformed a dreary landscape into a gleaming vista full of adventure and possibility. She hastened her step and put a hand to her bonnet while the other lifted her skirts.

"Am I late?" she called out as she ran.

Harry wouldn't have minded waiting hours more for her appearance, had he known it would make him feel as giddy as it did. His heart tripped along inside his chest like it was stumbling down a hill, falling ever faster in love with her.

Love? He had never felt romantic love for anyone before.

"You're not—" Harry stopped and cleared his throat, his voice having come out slightly hoarse. "You are not late. I came early. No gentleman ought to ever keep a lady waiting."

"How very mannerly of you." Her steps slowed, her eyes took him in. "I have your handkerchief, as promised." She made no move to produce the article, but stopped walking when she stood a pace from him.

"That is wonderful news, since that is the entire reason we are meeting." He tried to tease, tried to keep his words light, but her gray eyes held him still and kept his words soft.

Love. The word crept into every corner of his heart and continued to spread into the rest of his being. He'd always found her attractive, but he had found any number of young ladies pretty. This was different. Everything about being near Daisy made him long to be more, to be worthy of her friendship and esteem.

Something of his thoughts must have leaked through to his expression. Daisy's smile faded, she leaned toward him and put her hand on his arm. The sensations that simple touch caused, through layers of fabric, sent his tumbling heart careening down the side of a cliff.

"Is something wrong, Harry? You look—well, I am not certain how you look. But it is somewhat unsettling to be stared at like that."

Say something. Something witty. Harry tried to grin, tried to laugh, but the sound he emitted—anxious and strangled—made her appear more concerned. "Forgive me," he said at last. "It has been a trying day." It hadn't. Not until that moment, when all rational thought abandoned him, skipping gleefully away before he could grasp even a word that might save him.

She pressed her lips together, turning to look out over the fields behind him. "I can certainly understand such a thing. I am afraid my day took a turn I was not entirely expecting." She brushed her hair back behind her ear. "I do hope your day will get better, Harry."

It was marvelously better, yet torturous. Somehow, his faint interest in Daisy had grown into an admiration and respect, then a deep regard, and now—now he did not quite know what to do.

"I hope yours will, too." His head full of wool, nothing wittier came to mind than to return her sentiments. The conversation would not last long if all he did was echo her words back to her. "Would you care to walk?" he asked, gesturing to the tall bushes hiding the road from view. "It would be good to keep moving in this cold weather."

"That is a very good idea." She folded her arms against her middle and took a step. Harry fell in with her, the two of them walking together at an easy pace. They went to the bushes and Harry reached out to pull the branches aside for her.

"Let us stay on this side," she said quickly. "I have no wish to encounter anyone on the road today."

"Ah, yes. Avoiding gossip." He let the branch fall, and with it some of his enthusiasm. Would it really be so terrible for her name to be linked to his? If she thought so, his heart had little chance of finding happiness with hers.

Then she erased his momentary disappointment. "Not at all. I am avoiding a certain person who may walk by on his way to the village." She kept walking along the side of the bushes, at a slower pace than before.

"I see." He tried to think who it might be she hoped to avoid, but gave up on that line of thinking. If she evaded the man, whoever he was, that man posed no threat to Harry's hopes. He kept to her slow pace, hands tucked behind his back though he longed to reach for her.

The wind rustled by, stirring up the scent of wet leaves and cold earth. There would not be many more times when he might meet Daisy out of doors, whether accidentally or contrived. It grew too cold, and people throughout the country huddled closer to their fires rather than take a step outside.

"How is your estate business? Have you and Mr. Ellsworth made a great deal of progress?" Daisy kept her eyes on the path in front of them.

"I feel I learn one thing only to discover my ignorance in several other directions," Harry admitted, watching her from the corner of his eye. "But I am determined to get the management of my property correct."

He must do so, for Daisy would never approve of him otherwise. Kind-hearted, intelligent, forward-thinking Daisy Ames deserved nothing less than his best efforts.

"That is wonderful to hear. I am glad you will stay in the neighborhood for a time."

"Perhaps forever." He spoke softly, not even certain she heard him. But he meant the words. If he wished to be linked to Daisy, her dedication to the school must be considered. If she wanted to teach and see to the education of the local girls, he could not take her away from that.

Daisy's expression turned inward, her eyes dimming as she lost herself in thought. Harry did not mind studying her from the corner of his eye, watching the play of emotions on her lovely face. What must she be thinking? Had she any idea of how he felt? Did she wrestle with her own emotions as he did?

It would be arrogant to presume so, yet he hoped she did.

"I need to visit London," he said, ending the comfortable silence between them. "I will be away for a week."

"Oh?" She kept her eyes ahead, but he quite easily saw her frown. "Only a week?"

"Yes. I do not wish to be gone from here any longer." He did not speak his true sentiments. He did not wish to be gone from *her* any longer. Their meetings were few enough as it was.

"I hope everything goes well." She stopped walking and looked up at him, her gray eyes a reflection of the sky above them. "I will miss you."

He stared at her, thoughtfully, taking in the pink of her cheeks, the slight part of her lips, the confusion in her eyes. Had she not meant to make such an admission?

"You will?" he asked, somewhat surprised by the bold statement. But he did not try to keep from saying what he felt. "I will miss you. I fear if I am gone you will put me from your mind completely."

Her blush deepened and turned her face away. "One does not forget one's friends."

"Ah. Friends." Her words did not mean what he hoped. His plans to ask her if he might court her, might try to build something beyond friendship with her, drifted back to the forefront of his mind. Realizing he already felt more than friendship made the question of courtship more important. More fraught with danger to his heart.

Their steps, hers lighter and his heavier, crunched a few leaves and twigs fallen from the bushes and trees.

It might be wiser to wait until he returned to bring up the subject. Yet—he did not want to wait. Would it not be best to speak right away and face possible heartbreak than live in fear of her denial?

"Daisy," he said, hazarding a glance in her direction. Her expression was solemn, her profile reminding him of a Greek statue. "Before I leave, there is something I would ask you. That is—I have a thing I would like you to consider." He let out an agitated puff of air. "Advice, if you will."

Daisy, an organized woman with a practical mind, would likely dismiss him if he asked her directly what she thought of a future at his side. A plan formed in his mind, hastily and untidily, but entirely possible.

"Yes?" She blinked and the distance left her eyes, her attention returning to Harry. "You know I will always help you if I can."

"I have been considering other ways to help the people here, to solidify my future, and I have come to a conclusion that may sound somewhat drastic." He made a show of frowning and kicked a stone out of their path. "I think I ought to marry."

Daisy's step faltered, and he stopped a step after she did and peered down at her. She had a great deal of pink in her cheeks, but it faded quickly.

"Marry? But—"

"I need a partner in what lies ahead. Someone to talk things over with who has a real interest in what becomes of my ventures. And it would be beneficial to have a wife for all the social aspects of taking up my residence here." Harry presented the points slowly, as though uncertain of them rather than the fact that he made them up on the spot. "As I said, I need advice. Perhaps you could help."

She opened her mouth and closed it again, then frowned and started to speak—only to halt before doing more than emitting a squeak.

"You think it's a terrible idea," he said, trying not to grin. Her lack of answer might mean—at least he hoped it mean—she did not like the idea of anyone filling such a role in his life. It would necessarily replace her, after all. "I understand. I suppose I'm not the best candidate for a husband. Take away my fortune, and what am I?" He looked down as he scuffed his shoe along the grass, hiding his amusement. "Please, put the request from your mind. It is absurd." He took a step away but stopped when her hand grasped his forearm.

"I did not say that. You ought not to put words in a lady's mouth." She pursed her lips and he became very interested, for a short moment, in *her* mouth. "You merely took me by surprise. You have never even hinted at such a thought before. Do you— do you have a young lady in mind?" her voice rose on the last words and she cleared her throat hastily after speaking.

Harry stared at her, hope prompting him to speak some of the truth. "There is one lady I have found myself thinking of a great deal, especially of late."

She removed her hand from his arm and stepped back. "Really? Might I ask her name? Do I know her?"

"I would prefer not to tell. You see, I think she finds me a rather worthless sort. My holdings impress her very little. My wit, less so." He stepped away from the hedge, into a small meadow where a cow grazed. The cow likely belonged to the vicar, as the house was within calling distance.

Daisy followed close behind him. "That cannot be true. You are a good man, with a kind and generous heart." She walked around him, stopped before him, and glared. "Any woman who captures your interest is fortunate. I will tell anyone who asks the very same."

She stood so close. It would be an easy thing to bend down and brush his lips against hers, to find out what she tasted like. Today she smelled of sunshine and meadows, of brisk winds and cool forests. The last time he had seen her, she had smelled like fresh bread and roses. She was everything good and beautiful, joy wrapped in the image of a woman. He did not deserve her heart.

But he longed to give her his own.

"You are kind to say such things," he said, watching as her blonde eyelashes fluttered when she blinked. "What would you say to a woman to convince her I would suffice as a husband?"

It was an underhanded way to trap her into considering him. He was asking for compliments and praise where he deserved none. But if she could see the good in him, the ways he tried to be a better man, perhaps she would see the possibilities for the two of them to be together.

Daisy's color rose again and she turned away enough that her bonnet hid her face. She spoke quickly, "I am sure I do not know."

"Then I am without hope." He certainly had none if she could not think of one redeeming quality in him. "As my friend, and a very observant woman, I thought you might see what I cannot."

She took several steps away from him, the grass brushing against her hems, then turned to stare at him. What must she be thinking? Her eyebrows drawn together, her arms tightly folded across her waist. She appeared pained, and he nearly ended his ruse that instant. But she spoke first.

"I think you know quite well why a woman would agree to your suit, Horace Devon. I cannot decide if it is vanity or modesty that prevents you from saying so yourself. You are intelligent and kind. You are thoughtful of others and you are humble enough to correct your behavior when you are in the wrong. The people in your life are important to you. And you—you always make me want to laugh at my own foolishness and yours." She stopped, biting her bottom lip.

Harry watched as her eyes widened and her mouth fell open into an *O.* It was like watching a wave approach the shore, waiting for it to break, and he saw the moment Daisy came to her revelation. She spun around in almost the same instant, presenting him with her back.

§

What is wrong with me? I should be able to help Harry without falling to pieces like this. Daisy took several deep breaths, keeping her back to him, even while her heart attempted to break free of her chest with its pounding. Her throat closed up over the truth she dared not speak. *I do not want him to go off and find a wife. I want him to spend more time with* me.

But why?

She shivered when another breeze tugged at her bonnet, her spencer keeping none of the chill away.

A physical weight settled upon her, startling her from her thoughts. Harry's greatcoat closed before her, the sleeves flapping in the breeze while his hands held the thick fabric to her shoulders. She turned, reflexively reaching out to grasp the front of the greatcoat. Harry's hands fell to his sides and he offered a sheepish sort of smile.

"I would not wish you to catch cold," he said, his morning coat the only protection against the chilly afternoon. The heat he'd left in his wool overcoat warmed her. The fabric smelled like him, too. Like leather and sandalwood, and ginger and cinnamon.

Daisy took hold of his arm before he moved out of reach. "Thank you."

He stilled and his smile disappeared. He bowed. "Anything for you, Daisy."

Did he mean it? Anything?

She studied his lips, pressed in an earnest line. Then his blue eyes. Eyes that were bright and soft at the same time. Daisy still held his sleeve, she realized, but this thought did not make her let it go. Instead, she stepped closer to him.

"You are always kind," she said slowly.

He lowered his head slightly, perhaps in agreement. "You said that already. Is there nothing else to recommend me, Miss Ames?"

They stood so close, and she was as wrapped up in his gaze as she was in his greatcoat. *All of this to return a handkerchief.*

The square linen in her reticule had been nothing more than an excuse—a reason to be near him again without telling him how much she wanted to see him. Daisy no longer denied her attraction to Harry, but could it ever be more? What of her dreams, her plans, for the school?

Harry knew how important it was to her. Would he ask her to give it up? She wouldn't know unless she asked.

She wet her lips before speaking and saw his eyes dart down to watch the action. The world around them, already turning gray, darkened and blurred. Daisy stepped closer to him, determined to ask what he thought about her school, if he might consider *her* as a prospective bride.

"Harry—" She stopped, surprised at the low, soft quality of her voice. She hadn't meant to sound like that at all.

He leaned in, locking her to him with his stare. "Yes, Daisy?"

Bother. She forgot what it was she wanted to say, because all she could think about, all her attention, settled on one thought. *I wish he would kiss me.*

And then he did.

His lips brushed across hers before she became fully aware of him moving. Or had she moved? It hardly mattered which of them had closed the gap. She stood on her toes—his lips were gentle, pressed to her own, and his hands were at her waist. He pulled away first, enough to rest his forehead against hers. She lowered herself back to her heels.

"Do I owe you an apology, Miss Ames?" Harry asked, voice deepened by emotion, his eyes still closed.

Her hands rested on his forearms, holding onto him. "If you apologize for that kiss, I might never forgive you."

He chuckled and stepped back, releasing her waist to take up her hands in his. He studied her, the familiar playful gleam returning to his eyes. "Have you grown fond of me, I wonder?" He tilted his head to one side and Daisy mirrored the movement.

"I think I must have. I am afraid, Mr. Devon, I cannot possibly advise you on how to go about seeking a lady's hand. Not when I am wishing, all the while, that it is *me* you are searching for." It was a daring statement, and a bold red likely rose in her cheeks if the sudden heat she felt there was anything to judge by.

Harry startled her by laughing, his voice echoing in the empty space around them, bouncing off the vicarage itself perhaps. "You are much braver than I am. I have been trying to determine how to tell you that very thing for days."

Daisy gripped his hands tighter. "Truly?" He brought one gloved hand up to his lips and brushed his lips across her knuckles.

"Truly. If you are willing, I will ask your father for permission to court you properly. Make my intentions known."

Her heart shivered with joy.

And then she remembered the school and stepped back, gently taking her hands from his. "What about my desire to educate the children? I do not wish to give it up."

For a moment he appeared puzzled and she steeled herself for an argument.

"I would never ask you to," he stated. As simply as that, he removed her greatest doubt. Almost her only doubt. Except, there was that little voice tugging at her still. Until a short time ago, Harry Devon had lived for his own pleasure and did not give much of a thought to anything else. Was it possible he might tire of this new life? Managing an estate, and his other holdings, would not be easy. What if he decided it was not for him?

Harry grinned at her, and her worries dissipated like morning fog in the sunlight.

All will be well. She pulled his greatcoat more tightly around her and continued walking to the vicarage, he falling into step beside her.

"Perhaps you ought to speak to my father. Maybe not this evening." She glanced at him, trying not to smile too broadly. "I would like to have a little time to prepare him for the idea."

"When I come back from London," Harry said, reaching for her hand. He guided it through his arm and brought it to his lips for another kiss. "And not a moment later, Daisy."

She shivered in delight. Her sisters had warned her what it would be like, when she found a gentleman who caught her eye. She had scoffed at their romanticisms.

She owed them both an apology.

Chapter Seventeen

A smile continued to tease Daisy's lips, even after Harry had been away for three days. Every time she thought of his hand on her cheek, the touch of his lips upon hers, a pleasant warmth spread from her tingling lips to her toes. Whether she was dusting her father's books or ordering her notes and schedules for her classes beginning in January, she hummed to herself every happy tune she knew.

Drifting down the steps to the ground floor, ignoring the damp weather outside the vicarage, a harsh knock at the door finally startled Daisy out of her blissful fog.

No one rushed to answer it. Having few servants meant their occupation called them away from the front of the house all too often.

Daisy went to the door and opened it, a pleasant greeting rising to her lips.

Mr. Haskett stood on the doorstep, wearing a scowl as black as his coat. When he realized who had answered the door, his expression lightened somewhat. It went from darkly angry to mildly dismayed.

"Miss Ames." He bowed. "Good afternoon." He shifted, removing his hat. "Is your father at home?"

It was the first time she had seen him since denying his suit, as she had remained home from services with her father the day before. He'd developed a cold. Daisy couldn't allow for awkwardness between herself and the curate, however. A small community such as theirs would grow uncomfortable if she did not attempt some sort of friendliness.

"Good afternoon, sir. Yes, my father is in his study. Is he expecting you?"

"No." Mr. Haskett held his hat before him like a shield, protecting himself from her. "But I come on a most urgent matter."

Attempting to portray an ease she did not feel, Daisy stepped aside and waved him in. "Father is always happy to speak with you, Mr. Haskett."

He walked past her and she closed the door behind him, but before she could offer to take his hat, he was striding down the hall to her father's study.

Daisy shivered in the cold air she had let in along with the curate. She ought to find the shawl her sister sent, though it was not as warm as some of her others. The beauty of the Indian shawl always made her feel as though she wore a bit of summer. Rather than go in search of it right away, she trailed after Mr. Haskett to make certain her father received the curate kindly and to see if they needed refreshment of any kind.

When she stepped over the threshold, she caught the end of Mr. Haskett's rather fervent speech.

"—all of them torn down, right before winter. I confirmed it myself."

"It cannot be right. Surely the man would understand, would know what that would do to his position in the neighborhood," her father argued, though she saw the doubt of his own words fully upon his face. "Though it is something his father would have done."

Daisy remained standing where she was, uncertain as to what she walked in upon. Neither man noticed her.

"The man from London was taking measurements all day, refusing to talk to the tenants to tell them what he was about. But when I spoke to him, as he left, he told me the truth. He's been hired to demolish the cottages with a crew of workmen. He's even been asked to hire the men who live inside the cottages to lend a hand. What is this going to do to the families, Mr. Ames? We cannot let it stand."

Daisy leaned against the doorway, her mind putting together what was said. "Which tenants, Mr. Haskett?" she asked softly.

He barely spared her a glance. "Devon's."

Then he dropped his hand, and Daisy's heart dropped with it, before he started pacing before her father's desk.

"That cannot be," she said softly. "Mr. Devon would not put families out of their homes."

"None of us really know what he would do," Mr. Ames said, running his hands through his graying hair. "His father would have done it, after all."

"Sons take after fathers." Mr. Haskett made the pronouncement as if he were reading scripture.

Daisy shook her head. "I do not believe it of him. There must be some mistake."

"There is none. Mrs. Dempsey caught me as I walked along the road and asked if I could find out. She said she had a terrible feeling about the man roaming around, measuring things. I found him at the inn, and he told me everything. Devon hired this man, who claims to be a mason or builder of some sort, to demolish the tenant houses. The man came out to measure the property and provide an estimate of labor costs. It's barbaric." Mr. Haskett ceased his pacing and sat down in a chair.

Daisy did not believe it. She would not. It was impossible.

She hurried from the room and found her cloak, muff, and a bonnet lined with flannel. She donned the winter clothing with speed and hastened from the house, going to Whitewood. Harry would be gone, in London, but Mr. Ellsworth would be present. He would know what was going on.

The whole walk there passed by in a haze of denial and puzzlement. Why would Harry want to tear down the tenant cottages? There was no reason for it. There had to be a misunderstanding.

She arrived at the front gate of Whitewood and paused, realizing her course of action was not entirely prudent. Young women simply did not call upon bachelor households. It could damage her reputation.

163

But she had to know. Had she not given her kiss freely to Harry? Contemplating, as she was, giving him her whole heart gave her ample reason to worry.

Daisy walked through the open gate and went to the house, deciding to enter by the servant's door. That would lessen any whiff of scandal.

She obtained the kitchen door, her heart hammering from her rapid progression across the lawns of Whitewood. The door flew open after but a single knock, a footman standing before her.

"Miss Ames," he said. It was Mr. Howard, a young man she had practically grown up with. "What can I do for you?"

"I am here on a matter of business. Is Mr. Ellsworth here?"

The footman looked over his shoulder, and she saw the butler of the household standing down the hall.

"I am afraid he's not here, Miss Ames. He went to his father. Mr. Ellsworth, senior, is in a poorly way. A messenger came this morning calling the steward home, most urgently."

Daisy's shoulders fell. "That is terrible. I hadn't heard—" She took a step back. "I will have to speak with him another time then. Thank you, Mr. Howard. I will keep the Ellsworth family in my prayers." She took another step, then turned and tried to walk away with some steadiness of step if not steadiness of mind.

She could not run all the way across the countryside to question Mr. Ellsworth. Besides his poor father being sick, it was a great distance, and the autumn sun would set soon.

The Gilbert family. Daisy lifted her head again. *Mrs. Gilbert may know—she is his sister, after all.* She walked rapidly once more, determined to find answers for Mr. Haskett's pronouncement about the tenant cottages.

Harry would never tear them down. He must not. He would not. He had a compassion heart, after all.

Though he did seem rather keen on learning the ways of the estate, hoping to make it better than when his father had been in charge. Her steps slowed.

Daisy came to the road, her thoughts convoluted. What if it was true? What would she say if Mrs. Gilbert told her Harry's plans were to clear the cottages for some other project? Perhaps to bring in more sheep. She had heard of landowners who would do such things. Rid themselves of farmers in order to fill their fields with livestock.

Hadn't she heard somewhere that he bought a great many sheep at the market fair?

Doubt sunk more deeply into her heart, difficult to dislodge.

Daisy's steps turned homeward. Her certainty in a misunderstanding dwindled, and she had no wish to stand in Mrs. Gilbert's parlor while her heart broke.

Chapter Eighteen

The news of Mr. Devon's plans to tear down his tenant's cottages spread through the village, as only a plague could, and soon everyone had something to say on the matter of the gentleman's character. Most of the comments were whispered, but for the first time in her life, Daisy listened carefully to the gossip and rumors.

Mrs. Dempsey, one of the tenant wives, stopped to chat with Daisy on her way to market. She spoke of how Harry had arrived at her cottage one day to declare there would be no further rents paid. At first, though startled, she had been delighted by the news. Now she wondered if it was but a ploy to give him reason to evict all of them.

The seamstress, Mrs. Chandler, spoke when Daisy went to purchase new gloves. "My sweet granddaughter thought him kind for letting her pick blackberries from his bushes. But I wonder if he was not attempting to cover his character flaws with an act of generosity. It cost him nothing to let her pick berries, after all. When has anyone seen any real goodness from him?"

The household staff were somewhat loyal, as Daisy heard one of the newly hired footmen refuse to speak ill of him after church when some of his friends were asking why he worked for such a miser.

Public opinion turned soundly against Harry. Mothers who had tentatively introduced their daughters to him expressed gratitude that he had not "preyed upon" their dear girls. No one could produce true evidence of his wrong-doing, except the tenants of his cottages. But casting entire families out of their homes on the cusp of winter was, all agreed, evidence enough against his character.

The most frustrating thing of all was that Mr. Ellsworth could answer all of Daisy's questions, but after spending time with his ailing father the man had disappeared to visit some unknown relation a county over. Nothing could be explained to her satisfaction.

Feeling somewhat responsible for Harry's sudden interest in his holdings, Daisy stopped worrying for her school and instead helped the tenants on their hunt for new homes. Some of the families had been in those cottages for more than a generation, and leaving the homes they leased pained them.

No one spoke to the Gilberts on the matter, not wishing to offer insult to a family respected by the community. Daisy ached to ask Mrs. Gilbert if she knew anything of Harry's plans, but the Gilberts seemed happily oblivious to the storm of gossip and rumor surrounding them. Either they did not know what Harry had decided to do, or they knew and did not care. She thought it more likely the former.

Daisy walked slowly home from visiting with one of the cottagers, after helping the woman of the house pack crockery into an old crate. The family of six had decided to move in with a cousin for the time being, which would put strain on both families.

Daisy's mind was consumed so entirely by the matter that she did not notice a man had stepped into the lane ahead of her. Not until he spoke her name with familiarity.

"Daisy." His tone was soft and full of an emotion which caused her to wonder. How could he say her name in such a way and have such a cold heart?

Harry Devon grinned at her and approached, one hand outstretched.

She stopped walking and kept her hands tucked deep within her muff. "Mr. Devon," she said, measuring her words. "You are returned from London at last."

He lowered his head, almost like a boy expecting punishment, but his crooked smile said he meant to get out of it. "I am sorry I was away longer than I expected. I stopped to visit my sister, Rebecca, to tell her about the improvements at Whitewood. And about you."

Her heart betrayed her head, tingling as it did when she thought on his hopes for their future. To stop her emotions from getting the better of her, Daisy asked the question that had consumed the whole village.

"Are you tearing down the tenant cottages on your property?"

He released a long-suffering sigh and came closer to her, the outstretched hand lowering a fraction. "You have heard of the improvements? Yes. I hope we can have it all done with before Christmas. If the weather holds."

Daisy drew herself up taller. "And what will happen to the tenants, Mr. Devon?"

At last his hand dropped completely, his fingers curling into a fist. He rapped the fist against his thigh, studying her with obvious confusion. "I am hoping they will all be happy in their new homes."

She pulled in a pained breath at his callousness and nearly shouted at him. "New homes? Some of them do not even know where to go." Her entire body trembled as anger flooded her.

Harry raised both hands, making a calming gesture. "Daisy, it sounds as though there has been a misunderstanding."

"Then please, do explain." Daisy did nothing to disguise the bitterness in her words, and she ignored the way her heart jerked most painfully. "Explain how, exactly, casting families out of their homes when at winter's edge could possible qualify as an *improvement.*"

"Casting out—?" Harry's rather confused expression altered when his eyes darkened. "Has anyone spoken to Ellsworth? He is aware of the plan. And I'm sure if you asked—" He cut himself off, his wide eyes slowly narrowing while his brow drew down. "You believe that I'm tearing down the cottages, without regard for the people who live within, and nothing more. Am I understanding the situation correctly?"

Her frustration mounted. *Do I know him at all?* She had convinced herself, at first, of a misunderstanding. But nothing he said contradicted that yet. Nothing at all.

"The whole village believes you would do such a thing," she said, hearing and hating the defensive note in her voice. "You left, a man came to examine the buildings for demolition, and Mr. Ellsworth vanished—"

"He left on an assignment from me. It must have taken him longer than he expected." Harry spoke dismissively, as though it was unimportant that his steward was away, leaving rumor to run rampant. He had withdrawn into his own thoughts, a clouded look in his eyes. He'd turned pale, too.

A knot around her heart tightened. "What of the tenants' situation?" she asked. A winter wind snapped at her cloak. "How could you do this to them? They will leave, and I had hopes for their daughters—" She broke off as angry tears choked her. She'd dreamt of each of those little girls learning to read and write, doing sums, and bettering themselves through learning. Without homes, they would leave the area, and she would lose half the scholars she hoped to have in her school. They would lose the opportunities she anticipated presenting to them.

Harry drew back a step, his eyes focusing on her once more. His blue eyes, so bright but minutes ago, now dark and hard. "When these rumors started, you said nothing against them? Nothing in favor of my character?"

"How could I?" Daisy asked. "No one knew of our connection." *Something I am glad of now,* she added silently.

"Yes. I remember your abhorrence of rumor and gossip. Your desire to avoid linking your name with mine." He did not sneer or chide. The frigidity in his tone was more painful than both those things, but she pushed away the hurt and used her anger instead.

It was true. She might have spoken of Harry's character, given a reference outside of his family. Cast doubt on the rumors. But Daisy had not. She had listened, rather, to every ill word anyone said of him. Partly in horror that it might be true and she had nearly bound herself to him, and partly in defense of her heart.

Harry started pacing, taking a few steps away, then back.

"A woman's reputation is all she has, Harry. I'm not about to risk myself in that way, not when I know nothing of your plans, and that horrid man you had measuring the cottages said—"

He interrupted her, coming close once more. "You do not trust me at all, do you? I have never been anything but honest with you, I have tried to be a better man. It was easier for you to believe the worst of me than to hope the reasons behind my actions were motivated by a desire to do what was right."

Everything constricted, all her thoughts and doubts accusing her of exactly what he said. *I am not at fault. I cannot be. Everyone has been shocked by his behavior. How could tearing down the cottages be right?* And her father, the vicar, had said what everyone had been thinking. His words rose to her lips with ease.

"Your father would not have hesitated to do a thing which gave him a profit," she said. Her pride wounded, she meant the words to shield her from further harm. To protect her from his accusations.

When Harry drew back, his face pale and his mouth parting, she knew her shield had instead been a spear. And the words hit a fatal mark.

"I am nothing like my father." His voice was a whisper, his eyes empty. "Though it seems everyone in Annesbury is ready to condemn me for having the misfortune of being born his son." He took a step back. "Thank you for showing me exactly why I never wanted to return to Whitewood. Good day, Miss Ames."

"Harry," she called, her arm suspended in the air as though she could snatch him back, along with her unkind words. But why, if he was the monster throwing families into the cold, did she feel as though *she* had done something wrong?

He did not turn around, and in a moment was gone from her sight.

Though she longed to chase after him, to force him to change his mind about the tenants, Daisy remained where she stood.

Perhaps they did not suit one another after all.

Chapter Nineteen

Remaining at Whitewood, after knowing how the people of the village regarded him, was out of the question.

Harry used the desk in the library and wrote an explanation of what was to be done about the cottages and tenants. If Ellsworth had returned, Harry would have dispatched the man at once to clear up the matter. He had no wish to go himself to the tenant cottages, to see accusation in their eyes, the distrust and anger. Never mind it was all misdirected.

He called the butler and gave the servant the letter. "Have a footman deliver this to the tenants and read it to them." He said nothing else. He'd done all the explaining he intended to do in his letter.

Even if the people living upon his land lacked trust in him, he could not let them live in fear of losing their homes.

Once the butler left, Harry flung himself onto the couch in the library and slung an arm over his eyes.

Fleeing the village, the entire county, would be the easiest thing. Harry might go to London and take up bachelor quarters. No one there would think it odd. In a little time, spending money in the right places, popularity would follow and he might establish a name for himself. In London, he could buy his way into being well liked.

Except he did not care the sort of friends who could be bought.

Harry removed his arm from his eyes, stretched out and stared at the ceiling, attempting to find something to distract himself.

The chandelier was far too gaudy for a room supposedly dedicated to reading. Perhaps he would tear it out and replace it with more practical lighting. The heavy curtains were ridiculous, too. The room needed more light, not less. Rebecca, the youngest of his sisters, was a devoted reader. She had redone the library at her husband's primary estate so that, with all its lamps lit, it was as bright as day.

Maybe Rebecca would consent to redo the library for him. Possibly he could induce Christine to see to the stables and his sister Julia to put his stillroom in order. They could all come to visit and help him make the house into more of a home.

Except I do not want to stay where I am not wanted. He folded his arms across his chest and glared at the ceiling. He'd taken to imagining Daisy in the house, after all. Wondered, in fact, what she would do with the overly large place should she become its mistress.

I need not wonder about that anymore.

Harry pushed himself up and shoved his fingers through his hair before giving it a good yank.

Thinking of Daisy only deepened the ache in his heart. Had she ever believed him to be a good man? Why had she become his friend, kissed him, agreed she might one day be *more*, if she did not trust him?

He stood and left the room, walking the long, dark halls of his house. Around every corner, he almost expected to see a sister walking down the corridor. Or else to hear the tread of his father's step.

He stopped before the music room, considering the closed door. He pushed his way through and went to the piano. Julia had spent a lot of time in that room, practicing and playing everything she could. And it was here where one of Harry's few memories of his own mother lingered.

He had been very young when she'd died. He hardly remembered her. His sisters filled whatever place in his heart his mother had occupied, except for one small hole that ached when he wondered what he had lost.

Did Daisy play the pianoforte? What would she think of this instrument? When he sat down at the bench and pressed upon a few keys, he knew what he thought of it. *Needs to be tuned.*

Except he would not see it done. Not when he was considering leaving the house altogether. If no one occupied the home, there was no one to hear the keys played.

He stared down at ivory and black keys, not truly seeing them. Instead, he perfectly pictured the look on Daisy's face when he'd kissed her. Or she'd kissed him. Though uncertain as to who had initiated the moment, the memory had made him smile. He'd carried the taste of her kiss with him to London, grinning like a fool at the oddest moments.

He'd spent time learning of things that might interest her, too. As he went about his business, signing paperwork, he tried to learn more about the educational system of the Anglican church.

He'd gathered pamphlets, books, and spoken to experts on the subject. He'd arranged for funds to go to schools he found in the worst parts of London, where kind-hearted men and women struggled to teach children enough to lift them from the gutters.

Coming back home, full of all he'd seen, Harry's desire to speak to Daisy about everything had mounted with each passing mile.

He'd even prepared what to say to her father. It was high time he received permission to court Daisy properly, after all. Arriving home, he'd struck out on a walk to the vicarage to do that very thing.

Harry ran his fingers across the piano keys, not enough to play a single sour note.

Coming upon Daisy at once, on the lane in front of his home, had been like receiving a gift. His Daisy. Except she no longer considered herself attached to him. No longer wanted him. Her accusations, her distrust, pierced him deeply. How could there be love without trust?

Harry left the music room, trying to outrun his thoughts. But everywhere he went inside the house, he thought of Daisy. When had he started filling the corners of his heart and mind, the shadows of his house, with her image?

Dinner distracted him for a time, but only so long as he kept his eyes on his plate. Every time he glanced up to the empty chair at the other end of the table, he pictured it with Daisy sitting there, smiling back at him.

At last he laid in bed, hoping that sleep would bring him a respite from thinking of her. Though it was unlikely, given that he'd dreamt of her while he'd been away.

He couldn't live like this. He wouldn't stay at Whitewood. The house was obviously cursed for him, bringing him nothing but unpleasant memories and the thoughts of what would never be.

If only Daisy had trusted him.

Chapter Twenty

The gray of the morning sky's gloom seeped into Daisy's bedroom. She had hardly slept the night before and was awake before Sunday's dawn. The residents of their village would soon make their way to church. The previous Sunday, the first after everyone learned of Harry's plans for the tenants, Mr. Haskett had delivered an impressive sermon about the rich young ruler who would not give up his earthly possessions to take up the cross.

Daisy rolled away from the window, staring instead at her dressing table. Harry's handkerchief, still in her possession, sat folded on top of it. Why she still had the bit of cloth she could not say. Perhaps she kept it as a reminder of how mistaken one could be in another person's character.

Eventually, she had to rise from bed. Her father would not hear of her skipping church, not unless she was ill. Would Harry be there to glare at all the congregants for their harsh judgment of him? Or would he stay away, his true character revealed?

Personally, she hoped he would not come. She had no wish to see him.

Her heart cracked, and her eyes ached. She would most certainly *not* cry about the situation. She'd kept dry eyes all night. Morning would see her just as resolved to put Harry—Mr. Devon—from her mind completely. He was nothing to her. Not anymore.

She washed her face and prepared for the Sabbath. The house was quiet, as it often was on Sundays. Her father was in a contemplative mood and did not notice her own silence.

They had the dogcart brought around for the short walk to the church. The vicarage was on the Earl of Annesbury's property, the church nearer the village, and her father's health made the walk difficult for him.

When they arrived, one of the deacons helped her father step down, and then assisted her. She entered the church on her father's arm, too caught up in her thoughts to give heed to her neighbors. Except to notice one thing.

Harry hadn't come.

She and her father settled on the front pew, as they always did. Daisy adjusted her cloak and tucked both hands in her muff. Though the church was warmed by a stove, it was still too cold for her comfort. All rose and sang a hymn she knew by heart, then sat and waited for Mr. Haskett to read from a text.

"'Judge not, lest ye be judged.'" The words, spoken in Mr. Haskett's deep voice, reverberated through the church and forced Daisy to look up, in some surprise.

Mr. Haskett wore a solemn look, his shoulders were hunched, and he appeared rather pale. Sorrowful, almost.

"The people of this parish, myself included, have made a sore mistake. We leapt to conclusions about one of our own. We judged harshly, and with little evidence before us. Dear people, I speak of what I have learned only this morning. The tenant cottages on the Devon land are to be demolished."

Daisy ducked her head, her stomach tightening uncomfortably.

"But only after new cottages are built and the tenants moved into the safer, more appropriate housing."

There was an audible gasp from several in the room, including Daisy herself. She covered her mouth with her hand after the sound escaped and her attention focused more fully on Mr. Haskett than it ever had on his sermons in the past.

"The tenants received word of this last evening, and have given me the evidence of a letter written by Mr. Devon. As I was one of the first to spread word of what I thought was a cruel deed, I wished to admit my fault to all of you. I attempted to seek out

Mr. Devon this very morning, but he has gone again from home." Mr. Haskett lowered his head a moment.

Despite the upset from that piece of news, Daisy could not help but respect Mr. Haskett's humility in admitting his wrong. Before an entire church full of his parishioners. The bravery it took spoke well of his character and condemned her further for her previous silence.

Her father leaned closer to her and murmured quietly in her ear, "The curate would be a good match for you, Augusta."

That was what her father took from Mr. Haskett's announcement? Even now, with Harry's innocence and good intentions made clear, her father's first words were spoken in favor of the curate's suit?

Daisy stood. People shifted and turned to look at her. She could feel the eyes of every person in the room turned onto her back. Mr. Haskett stopped speaking—she had not even realized he'd continued to discourse on the subject of withholding judgment—and stared at her too. Though she knew her actions would cause speculation, and gossip, Daisy stepped out of the pew and walked down the aisle to the back of the church. She met no one's eyes. She simply left. Sitting still and quiet in the church, the curate's words added to the voice in her head to reprimand her, made the guilt roil until she felt certain it would burst from her.

She walked faster and faster toward home, the skirts of her gown flying up behind her. Her eyes stung, but Daisy did not realize she was crying until the icy wind hit the wet tracks upon her cheeks. While her dreams of opening a school were finally coming true, another dream had died before she had even given it a chance. Before she had given Harry a real chance.

She'd been so caught up in being better than he, showing him all the ways in which he lacked, how he had ignored his responsibilities. She'd lost herself in her own piousness, in her position as the vicar's daughter, that she had only thought to protect herself when the village turned against him.

Daisy had once told Harry, with some pride and some amusement, that as a vicar's daughter she had long since memorized many passages of scripture. That unfortunate truth haunted her now with words far wiser than hers echoing in her mind.

Pride goeth before destruction, and a haughty spirit before a fall.

How wilt thou say to thy brother, let me pull out the mote out of thine eye; and, behold, a beam is in thine own eye? Ye hypocrite.

She knew them all. Had been forced to write them out as a consequence to poor behavior when she was a girl. Her father and mother never wished her to forget those lessons, and it seemed making her write them out had done the job. But she remembered them too late.

Daisy made it home, went up to her room, and then shut the world out.

She had held her heart back from him since the beginning, even treating his friendship with skepticism.

Harry's expression, the pain evident in his eyes and voice, arose from her memory and further condemned her. A sob tore from her throat. *I've lost him. And I never deserved him.*

Chapter Twenty-one

O ne of the best ways to console oneself after a terrible disappointment, Harry had learned, was to play with his nephews and nieces. Luckily for Harry, his sister Rebecca had provided him with four such people to ease his troubles. Rebecca and her husband Christian had an eight-year-old daughter, twin sons of five years, and a three-year-old girl. Harry was spread out on the floor in the parlor of their home, constructing a block city with the twins.

Christian, Earl of Ivyford, was seated on the couch with Rebecca leaning against him, his arm curled around her waist and a hand spread over her expanding middle. The earl was reading a book, but Harry had caught his sister staring at him with a peculiar expression on her face.

The nursemaid appeared at the door, calling for the children to come wash before their dinner. There was a chorus of groans from the twins and the eldest daughter.

"Go on now," Rebecca told them, amusement in her eyes. "I will be up to read you stories before bed." After the children were herded out, Harry sat up and surveyed the impressive towers constructed from the blocks. "I think you may have some architects on your hands, Christian."

Christian closed his book and dropped it in his lap. "Last week when you visited, you claimed the twins would take up espionage."

"Given that they kept switching places, confusing me and everyone else about the place, I did think it would be a wise career for them. For king and country." Harry forced a grin, though he'd found ample humor in the twins' antics on his last visit.

Rebecca started to sit up, groaning a little as she did, and her husband adjusted to support her as she stood. "I do not know why it is so difficult for all of you to see the differences in those two boys." She put a hand to her back. "Though I do thank you for keeping them entertained the last three days. It has given me a respite."

"But," Christian added, "as grateful as we are for that, I must admit to some curiosity as to why you returned so swiftly."

"Christian." Rebecca turned around to swat her husband's shoulder. "We agreed we wouldn't ask."

"I did not ask anything, *carina*. I merely expressed curiosity."

Their easy exchanges had been difficult to watch the last several days, reminding Harry of all he wished for in his own life. Yet it was good for him, he knew, to see a match where there was so much faith and happiness. It gave him hope he still might find such a thing for himself. And they *had* been patient with Harry, allowing him into their home without asking questions, though he had barely been away for two days since his previous visit.

Rebecca had taken one look at her brother's eyes the night he arrived and welcomed him back, saying only, "We will talk about it when you wish."

Nothing even tempted him to talk about Daisy, about the whole horrid village thinking him a callous beast. He could go indefinitely without ever speaking of it again. But the concerned frown of his sister ought to be dealt with. She would worry about him, and in her condition, she ought not feel even the slightest of worries.

"Sit down, Rebecca," he said, pushing himself off the floor. "And I will abate your husband's curiosity." He shot Christian a grin, but it faded quickly. It was easier to keep up pretenses with the children nearby.

"Harry, you really do not have to—"

"Rebecca, let him get it off his chest," Christian interrupted her, his deep voice gentle. He took her hand and tugged her back onto the couch. "He will feel better, and you will stop fretting." It was easy to read the concern in Christian's expression, as he obviously thought the same as Harry regarding Rebecca's health.

"You will remember I spoke of Miss Ames when I was last here," Harry said, looking away from the couple now holding hands upon the sofa.

When Harry did not immediately continue, Rebecca spoke with a cautious tone. "Yes. I have always liked the younger Ames girl."

"You expressed your great regard for her desire to create a school for underprivileged girls." Christian, as direct as ever, did not leave off there. "Though I suspected you admired her for more personal reasons."

Of course Christian would suspect that. Harry had not said anything directly about his affection for the vicar's daughter, but he had not bothered to hide his regard for Daisy either. His whole soul ached when he thought of their parting, of the hurt and betrayal in her eyes. How could she think so little of him?

"Harry."

He pulled himself through the haze of regret to stare at his sister, realizing he ought to have started talking, explaining things, instead of losing himself to memory. He cleared his throat, which had closed up on him. His eyes burned. It was the first time he had allowed himself to think on Daisy without immediately changing the course of his thoughts.

"I am sorry." He cleared his throat again and tried to get hold of himself, rubbing at his eyes with one hand. "I wanted what you two have. I thought maybe I had found—maybe Daisy was the other half of my life. It felt so perfect, to just be near her."

He did not want to face his sister and see her pity. He turned his back to them and walked away several steps, until he could put his arm across the fireplace mantel and lean against it. "Everything fell apart. It was as if I stood on solid rock, only to find myself on a dune with sand slipping from beneath my feet. And just like that, it was over."

It was Christian's voice that rumbled, "You need to explain a little better than that, Harry."

So he did. He explained. He told them everything, from his first seeing her beneath a tree, calling for a stubborn cat, all the way to their confrontation about the cottages. He left nothing out, save the kiss. Why did it hurt so much to speak of what could never be?

Almost since the moment he saw Daisy, he had been working to prove himself to her, building a dream where he was good enough for a woman such as her. Though he tried his hardest, he did not measure up. He never would. All that he had done up to that moment now seemed pointless.

When he finished his tale of woe, silence hung in the air, and his whole body drooped in exhaustion. How did something emotional effect his physical being that powerfully?

Rebecca spoke first. "When do you expect to go back to Whitewood?"

Harry stared at her, somewhat incredulously. Had she not been listening?

"I have not given any consideration to when I will return," he said, somewhat slowly.

"But you are going back." Rebecca's statement was firm, and he saw her hand tighten over her husband's. "You must see the thing through."

Doubtful, Harry turned his attention to Christian. The earl was studying Rebecca, his eyebrows drawn together. "You are thinking of our first misunderstanding," the man said to his wife.

For a moment Harry felt as though he ought to leave, given the intimacy with which his sister stared into her husband's eyes. "Nothing had ever given me more pain than when I thought you did not want me."

Harry had been there when they fell in love, had watched it happen day by day, and he suddenly remembered what they were talking about. Rebecca had doubted that Christian wished to marry her, had thought he would dishonor their agreement and leave her reputation ruined, or that he would wed her and never give her the love of which she dreamt.

And he, her little brother, had been the one to say she must tell Christian the truth of all she felt. He'd been young, not even at university yet, inexperienced and hopeful for her.

"It isn't the same," Harry blurted into the quiet, bringing their attention back to him. "Not at all."

"Not exactly," Christian corrected. "But it is a betrayal of trust."

"Perhaps you are right, Harry." Rebecca spoke quickly, before Harry could do more than glare at Christian. "Perhaps she does not trust you and never did. But please, won't you consider the situation she is in? Men may prattle on about honor all the day long, but it is the woman who must guard against betrayal the most. If Miss Ames entered into an agreement with you, only to find you a villain, she would have ruined her life almost beyond repair. A broken engagement would end her chances at another advantageous match. It would put an end to her dream to teach. What parent would have her instruct their daughters? Marriage to a man without honor would be equally miserable."

Rebecca leveraged herself off the couch again, Christian standing with her this time to steady her as she tottered on her heels.

Harry sensed the conversation coming to a close, and he did not like the way it would end. "I never gave her cause to believe me anything less than a gentleman."

"Our father was a gentleman," Rebecca said quietly, "and a snake. Only those who knew him well, who saw the decisions he made leading to unhappiness, knew he could not be trusted. To the rest of the world, he appeared like the best of men. Miss Ames has known you a short time. You could easily present a good face to her and another to the rest of the world." She took her husband's arm.

"You wish me to leave?" Harry asked, ignoring the truth in her words. He loved Daisy, had fallen in love with her rapidly, completely—

Yet how well did she know him?

"Of course not," Rebecca said. "I wish you to think about how you will return and finish what you have begun. If you will both excuse me, I need to prepare for dinner." She did not curtsy and went from the room with less than her usual grace.

Christian watched her leave, and Harry watched Christian.

"She is right, of course." Christian smirked, speaking more to himself than to Harry. "She almost always is."

Harry said nothing, but collapsed into a nearby chair and dropped his head into his hands. "I need to think."

"Take all the time you need, Harry. Matters of the heart should not be rushed." Christian walked out, leaving Harry to the silence of his thoughts.

Chapter Twenty-two

Daisy would meet the girls of the village in an upstairs room above the seamstress shop. All was arranged. The rent already paid to Mrs. Chandler, the lessons organized, and Daisy had but to wait until January to begin teaching. Even the skeptical families had agreed that sending their daughters to her three mornings of the week could not hurt. It was a start, and a good one at that.

Daisy sat at her desk in the upstairs sitting room, considering the neat notes in the book before her, all her dreams coming together nicely. The local gentlewomen had offered funds and things necessary for teaching children, including books and supplies from their own children's school days. The support had largely been won by the countess's influence, which had come through Christine and Harry's connection.

What is Harry doing now, I wonder? Where did he go? And, more importantly, would he come back?

The door to her upstairs parlor opened and in came Katie, her eyes almost comically large. "Mrs. Gilbert here to see you—"

Christine Gilbert sailed in before the maid had finished speaking. "Miss Ames, I cannot keep silent any longer and you *will* see me."

The maid looked from Daisy to Mrs. Gilbert and back, her mouth hanging open.

Daisy came to her feet. "Thank you, Katie. That will be all." After the girl curtsied and shut the door, Daisy fully faced her neighbor. "What might I do for you, Mrs. Gilbert?" At least she kept her voice steady.

"You can tell me what you did to Harry." Mrs. Gilbert reached into her reticule and pulled forth a folded sheet of paper. "This is a letter from my sister. She has had the full story from Harry and I mean to know what you are going to do about it."

Not exactly prepared for a confrontation, Daisy tried to hedge the question. "Do about it, Mrs. Gilbert?"

The woman sat down without waiting to be asked, the letter clutched in her hand. Her dark brown eyes blazed with fury. "My brother, Miss Ames. You have injured him."

Daisy stepped away from her desk, standing behind a chair to keep it between herself and the rather upset woman. "The whole village injured him, Mrs. Gilbert." She lowered her eyes to the carpet. If Mrs. Gilbert and her sister had the whole story from Harry, did that mean he had spoken of their friendship? Of their shared kiss?

"Right under my very nose, I know." Mrs. Gilbert's tone was not at all friendly, but distraught. "I still cannot understand it. Why did no one seek me out? Why did *you* not come to me and ask about my brother's doings? It is as though painting someone a villain was far too entertaining, too delicious a scandal, to even try and find the truth of the matter. Was that what it was for you, Miss Ames? A drama too wonderful to disprove?"

Is that what Harry thought? That Daisy had wanted to believe the worst about him? She said nothing. The hypocrisy of her actions stung her anew. She prided herself on never giving heed to gossip, except, apparently, when it involved someone she was afraid to love.

"Miss Ames, please."

Daisy swallowed and met Mrs. Gilbert's eyes again, a blush rising to her cheeks. "What do you wish for me to say, madam? I know now that I was wrong, like everyone else. Are you going to each house in the neighborhood to demand explanation?" She snapped her mouth closed, hearing the defensiveness in her voice. They both knew why Mrs. Gilbert sat before her. Perhaps the woman was right, and Daisy was somehow trapped within a theatrical drama of her own making.

Mrs. Gilbert's chin came up and her eyebrows drew together. "I doubt the whole ire of the town would be enough to chase my brother from Whitewood. It truly only took the duplicity of one person to send him running."

Daisy turned away, giving her back to her visitor in perhaps the first instant of true rudeness she had ever enacted.

Mrs. Gilbert continued, most forcefully. "Quite possibly the same person who inspired him to stay and try to build a life here."

"Then it could not be me," Daisy said, staring at the wall, not seeing the paintings she had arranged and rearranged when the room became hers after her sisters married. "I have done nothing to earn his regard to such an extent."

The room fell silent, with such a stillness that Daisy could hear the branches creaking in the wind, outside in the garden.

When Mrs. Gilbert spoke again, after several moments of the aching quiet, it was with a different tone entirely. She sounded as if she was pleading. "Love doesn't *earn* things, Miss Ames. It makes gifts of regard, trust, and honor."

The truth in those words sunk deeply into Daisy's injured heart, burning as alcohol poured upon a wound, cleansing in its pain. "As you are making such bold statements, perhaps I should do the same. Are you saying your brother loves me?" Daisy closed her eyes against the answer.

"I am saying you ought to find out." A swish of fabric told Daisy Mrs. Gilbert had stood, was planning to leave. But then a hand landed on her shoulder and Daisy turned to look into the other woman's brown eyes. "My brother will return, Miss Ames. He does not leave things unfinished, and he has committed to improving upon the estate and the legacy left to him."

Daisy's heart trembled. "I am afraid I do not know how to make things right again, Mrs. Gilbert." She straightened her posture, tipped her chin up. "But I will try."

Mrs. Gilbert gave her arm a pat. "That is all I ask, Miss Ames."

It would not be enough. Not if Harry had loved her. She had hurt him too deeply to hope he still felt that way about her. Though Daisy had learned, over the course of time since he had left, that she had fallen in love with him. Her heart ached every time she thought of him, longing for him to come back, wishing she could change the past and prove herself worthy of him.

But that chapter had closed, and now she must write another. If only she knew how the story ended.

Chapter Twenty-three

Taking in a slow, deep breath, Harry readied himself to step out of his carriage. It was time to enter Whitewood again, to walk back up the steps, greet the staff, and pretend nothing out of the ordinary had happened. This time, he was prepared to face a village that did not trust him. People who would look at him with suspicion as they remembered his father.

It helped that he also knew that he had reinforcements coming. His sisters would soon be at the house where they had all grown up. Perhaps, together, they might make it a home again.

It did not take long to give instructions to the eager-to-please butler, and then take himself to the steward's office. Ellsworth answered Harry's knock immediately, calling for him to enter.

"Mr. Devon," he said, standing from his desk with a wide grin. "Welcome home."

"Ellsworth." Harry stood in the doorway, surprised by the man's enthusiastic expression. "I assume all is well with the estate." He came further into the room.

"Excessively. I was about to forward this packet of letters to your sister's home. The time you spent in London seems to have interested a great many people. I have notes from several political officials asking you about your interest in the education of London's poor." Ellsworth held up a thick packet tied with string. "And I have a collection of letters from newspapers asking if you intend to run for public office." He gestured to another stack of paper. "And finally, of course, personal notes from several local tradesmen. I have not opened those, but I can only imagine the contents are both sincere and contrite." He gathered up several folded letters and brought them around the desk to Harry.

"Contrition is not something I looked for." Harry took the papers and stared at them a moment, uncertain as to whether he should read them. Ellsworth could be mistaken, after all. "Thank you."

Ellsworth's cheerful expression faded. "Mr. Devon, I feel I ought to add my apology to the others you will likely receive. If I had informed the tenants of your intentions before leaving, a great deal of pain might have been avoided."

"I have never once resented you for any of this," Harry said firmly. He looked back down at the letters in his hands, almost wishing one might be from Daisy. But a young, unmarried woman would never write to an unrelated male. "If anything, I ought to be grateful. I understand now how my neighbors perceive me. I can act with greater caution in future."

"I hope we have all learned a lesson, and your neighbors will only regard you as the gentleman you are." His steward's eyebrows raised and his smile inched back into place. "But does this mean you are going to stay? Whitewood will still be your home?"

"Of course." Harry barely managed a grin. "A man ought to finish a thing he starts, after all."

"I must say, Mr. Devon," Ellsworth said, his tone more earnest. "It is an honor to be your steward. I could not wish to work for a better gentleman"

Finally, for the first time in days, Harry smiled without trying. "Thank you. I will accept the compliment. And the work. I had better start going through these letters." Ellsworth gathered the rest for him and soon Harry was at the desk in his own study, determining which letters he must answer personally and which he might consult Ellsworth about. He also started considering hiring a secretary.

After he sorted the last letter from London, Harry began going through the letters from the local tradesmen. Each were thanking him for his patronage, and some were even kind enough to offer him special services. But a few stated what he read between the lines in the rest. His neighbors were apologizing for not trusting him. By the time he folded the last and put it away, from the seamstress who offered to assist should he ever wish to order new maids' uniforms, Harry was exhausted. What was he to say when he met these people again?

He sat back in his chair, lifting his eyes to look out the window across from his desk.

Snow drifted from the gray skies, falling past his window in swirls. Standing, Harry went to the window and stood gazing out over the front of his property. The house sat upon a slight hill, allowing him to look down the lane, toward the road. He could just make out the blackberry hedges bordering his land.

A figure moved up the lane, coming to the house.

Harry's heart jumped into his throat and he leaned against the glass, as though it would help him see more clearly. A dark blue cape fluttered around the woman's figure as she walked at a quick pace.

It cannot be her.

It had to be a servant, perhaps returning from a village errand. He watched a moment more, then escaped the study. He started for the stairs, practically leaping across the landing in order to run down the flight to the ground floor.

Harry did not stop for his greatcoat, but went straight to the door, ready to fling it open—

He skidded to a stop, his heart galloping wildly, and hesitated to touch the handle.

"Are—are you going out, sir?" a voice asked, startling him. A footman stood in the entryway, staring at him with wide eyes.

Harry looked back at the door. "No." He took a step back. He should not be in a hurry to see her. If it even was her.

Of course it is Daisy. He released a shaky breath. "And I am not at home to visitors," he said firmly. Starting for the stairs, and ignoring the baffled footman, Harry stretched his mind back to the business of answering his letters. He went up the steps slowly, his ears straining to hear any sounds beyond the portal to his home.

After he gained the landing, Harry looked down. The footman had disappeared, going about his business again.

Who would answer the door when she knocked?

It hardly mattered. He'd already decided that Daisy would not see him. Not today. He wasn't ready for that. Of course, he wasn't sure he ever would be ready.

His hand was on the latch to his study when he heard the three light raps upon the door, echoing through the halls of Whitewood. Frozen, he listened for the steps in the hall. There they were, rapid, business-like. The front door did not creak when it opened—it was too well oiled. But he heard the lift of the latch. He released his study's handle and walked back to the landing, staying just out of sight.

"Good afternoon, Miss Ames."

Harry closed his eyes, imagining the way Daisy would look, framed by his front door, snow flurries and the gray sky her background.

"Hello, Jamison. How are you today?" Her voice, clear and comforting, flew through the house to him.

"I am well, thank you. What may I do for you, miss?"

"Is Mr. Devon home?" Did she sound hopeful? Of course she did. She had some wish to see him. But calling upon him in such a way invited scandal.

His eyes snapped open. *What is she doing here?*

"I am afraid he is not at home, miss. Would you like me to relate any message to him?"

"Oh. No. That is—could you let him know I called?" That sounded like real disappointment in her voice.

"Of course, Miss Ames. Good day."

She took her leave, and the door's latch clicked shut again. Harry's stomach tightened and his heart sank low against it.

I am the very worst sort of coward. He leaned against the wall, glaring up at the chandelier hanging over the entry hall. How could he turn her away? What more could she say to hurt him, after all? Hiding from Daisy Ames was impractical, foolish.

Harry groaned aloud, then raced down the stairs once more. The footman was there again, staring. The man might as well be useful.

"Fetch my overcoat," Harry barked.

The footman jumped to obey, going to a closet near the door and pulling forth a heavy gray wool coat. Harry did not wait for help putting it on, but snatched it from the man's hands before ripping the door open and charging through it. He pulled his arms through the sleeves, did not bother doing up the buttons, and ran down the lane.

"Miss Ames!" he shouted at her retreating figure.

She stopped, then turned deliberately around. Seeing her for the first time in more than a fortnight, Harry stopped his mad dash to catch up to her. Simply staring, he drank in the sight of her. Lovely as ever, her gray eyes were heavy and sad, her fair features framed by honey-colored curls.

"Mr. Devon," she said, her voice almost a whisper.

His feet started moving again, but slowly. "Miss Ames." Had he already said her name? Yes, he had, to call to her. To make her stop walking away.

"H-how are you?" she asked.

Harry stopped, several feet away from her still. "I am well. And you?"

Daisy took a step closer. "I have been miserable, actually."

That made him blink, and he tilted his head to one side. "I am sorry to hear that."

"I would think you would wish the very worst upon me." Her breath misted as she spoke, reminding him of the cold.

"Never, Miss Ames," he said, forcing a smile. "I would never wish any ill upon you." A large snowflake landing on one of his ears made him look up. He'd forgotten his hat.

"You are very kind." She stepped closer, now nearly within arms' length of him. "I have come to return your handkerchief." She pulled one hand from her muff, holding a square of linen.

Harry stared at the fabric, slightly baffled. "You still have it."

"You have never collected it. And I have tried any number of times to give it back." She did not hold it out, but looked down at it, as though studying the embroidery upon the edges. "It has adorned my dressing table for a long time now. I have seen it every day. It will be strange to have it gone."

Perhaps he ought to tell her to keep it. But no. A lady did not keep a gentleman's handkerchief. It was too personal an object, too intimate a thing to do. Yet Harry could not bring himself to reach for it.

"Is that all?" he asked, studying her bent head. "Is there anything I can do for you, Miss Ames?"

Daisy lifted her eyes to his, her soft pink lips pressed tightly together. For a moment she only stared at him, the snow falling around and between them.

"Would you give me your forgiveness?" she asked at last, her voice a whisper in the cold and her breath coming out in a puff of mist. "Though I know I do not deserve it. I failed you, Harry, as a friend. I have regretted my weakness and the pain I caused you every day since." She swallowed, maintaining eye contact. "I am deeply sorry for it."

A tiny piece of Harry's broken heart clicked back into place. "Then I forgive you freely, Miss Ames." He forced a smile, the moment laced in regret. "I have been informed that I was too quick to be offended. Misunderstandings are a common thing in life, even between friends."

"You are too kind." Daisy dropped her eyes to the handkerchief again, and he saw she ran her thumb over his embroidered initials as she held it. "Perhaps I am taking liberties, Mr. Devon. But I would ask one more thing, since you granted forgiveness."

"What would that be?"

§

Everything depended upon her next question, and Daisy had never been so frightened in her life. Despite the hopefulness she felt at his sudden appearance, he had every right to hold her in contempt. She had come this far. She must be brave.

"Might we be friends once more?" she asked, her voice quiet despite the boldness of the request.

Softness stole over Harry's expression, and a new emotion appeared in his eyes with it.

Delicate snowflakes landed upon her cloak, and his cheeks, melting nearly as soon as they landed. It swirled around them, hitting the ground between them. Daisy felt one large flake when it hit her cheek, melting at once, like a cold tear against her blush.

Without a word, Harry raised his ungloved hand to brush it away, his thumb gently caressing her cheek. The whole world went still, and Daisy stared up at him, a prayer in her heart. His hand stayed, cupping her cheek.

"Friends?" he asked, stepping closer, bending his head toward her. "Is that what you want, Daisy?"

She swallowed and her eyes flickered to his lips, then up again. He stood so close, she felt the warmth of his breath against her lips. "Yes. But I want more than that, too. I want *you*, Harry." She had never been so bold in her life, and there was only one thing more she could do.

Her lips found his, and the pieces of Daisy's heart came back together as he returned the kiss. He wrapped an arm around her, pulling her closer. Daisy savored the feel of being safely cradled in his arms. Her hands rested upon his chest, still clasping his handkerchief tightly.

When their lips parted, Harry rested his forehead against hers. "I am never taking that handkerchief back, you must realize that by now."

Daisy's cheeks warmed. "I never really intended to give it to you."

Harry narrowed his eyes at her. "I did not know that a vicar's daughter would turn to thievery. What would the neighborhood gossips say about you now, Miss Ames?"

She lifted her chin, unsmiling, and stated most firmly. "I do not care at all, Harry Devon, and you had better stop teasing me or I will call you Horace from now on."

He laughed and scooped her up in an embrace, twirling her in the snow while she squealed. When he sat her upon her feet again, Harry dropped a kiss to her forehead. "Come, let me take you home in a gig. And while I'm there, I had better speak to your father. I have every intention of marrying you, Augusta Ames, and I will need his permission to do so."

She tucked his handkerchief into her muff, then threaded her gloved fingers through his. "Harry—what about my school?" Although she thought—she hoped—she knew his answer.

"I am afraid you will have to change its name." He spoke with all seriousness. "Mrs. Devon's School for Girls sounds much better than Miss Ames's School for Girls, does it not?"

She squeezed his hand tightly, joy filling her heart. "It does sound rather perfect." And she trusted it would be exactly that.

Chapter Twenty-four

D ressed in a cream-colored gown, Daisy stared out the window, waiting for the carriage to arrive. Her father sat behind her, a book open before him. "It does not matter if we are late to the earl's ball, Augusta."

She bit back a smile, remembering the last time he had said similar words to her. "I know that, Father." Tonight, instead of the Gooches, Harry would come for them. And tonight, at the Earl of Annesbury's Christmas Eve ball, she would dance with Harry, and be introduced to all three of his brothers-in-law. Harry had told her, just after he asked for permission to court her, that his whole family would come to spend Christmas and New Year's at Whitewood. It was the first time they would all be together under that roof since Christine's marriage.

The whole idea of seeing Harry's sisters made her stomach twist in a strange manner, but Harry reassured her all would be well. And how could it not? She would be with him. He'd even invited her and her father to Christmas dinner.

The carriage arrived, its lamps glowing against the snow-covered ground, and Daisy nearly ran for the door. "He is here, Father!"

She threw open the door before a servant could appear, and hurried down the steps. Harry jumped down from the carriage, holding his hand out to her. His eyes took her in, from the ribbons in her hair to her slippers. He raised one of her gloved hands to his lips.

"Daisy, you are most beautiful tonight." Something about his voice made her breath catch in her throat.

"Thank you, Harry."

Her father appeared, leaning on his cane to avoid slipping. Harry released her in order to help the vicar, who grumbled about people giving balls in the dead of winter. Harry made certain her father was seated comfortably, then handed Daisy into the carriage, before climbing in to sit across from her. His grin flashed in the darkness.

"Are you ready, Miss Ames?" he asked.

"I should hope so, Mr. Devon."

"Have you a handkerchief?" he asked.

Daisy laughed, feeling her blush appear. "Always, sir."

Her father sighed, deeply. "I do not understand young people anymore."

She covered her lips to keep from giggling. It seemed whenever she was around Harry, she could not help but laugh. He had a gift for bringing forth joy in even the little things. He had helped her, just the day before, arrange for a table and chairs to be brought into the upstairs rooms at Mrs. Chandler's. He had helped hang up a map of Great Britain, and a blackboard. He'd stacked books for her in shelves. And all the while, working near her, he'd made her laugh.

Their courtship had been the talk of the village, perhaps the county, for three weeks. Everyone knew about it, and as often as Daisy could be seen on Harry's arm, she was. They shared a hymnal in church while he sat beside her. He escorted her father and Daisy home after services. He drove her through town in his open carriage, despite the snow, always at a moderate pace, and they stopped to speak to everyone they passed.

People had even begun to make sly remarks to Daisy about her prospects of becoming his bride. But apart from mentioning the name change for her school, Harry had not said another word of marriage.

Sitting across from him in the dark, Daisy tried to curb her impatience. Their courtship was, after all, quite wonderful. And she was assured, in every possible way, that he loved her. When it was the right time, he would ask her if they might have the banns read. She knew exactly what her answer would be, too.

The carriage stopped before Annesbury Park, which was lit with thousands of glittering lamps and candles in windows. Daisy waited for Harry to hand her down from the carriage, then slipped her hand onto his arm as anticipation built within her.

They were swept into the grand house with other guests before and behind them, the orchestra already playing. She looked up into Harry's eyes.

"This is going to be a wonderful evening," she said.

Harry's grin appeared somewhat crookedly. "I hope so."

§

With Daisy on his arm, Harry entered the ballroom, immediately searching out his sisters. They were all here, at his request, with their husbands. It did not take long to spot their group in the crowd. His sisters, all mothers and seasoned wives, were beautiful. And two of the three husbands were quite tall.

He led Daisy to his family's corner of the room, hardly stopping to greet anyone else. His heart pounded in his chest, with anxiety and pride both, as he introduced her. "Miss Ames, might I introduce my family to you? Some of them you know, of course. This is the Earl of Ivyford, Lord Christian Hundley, and his countess."

Christian bowed and Rebecca offered a grinning curtsy, despite her large middle.

"And Doctor Nathaniel Hastings, husband to my sister, Mrs. Julia Hastings."

Nathaniel offered his bow. "It is a pleasure to meet you at last, Miss Ames."

"And you know Mr. and Mrs. Thomas Gilbert, of course," Harry added.

"Quite well." Daisy curtsied prettily to the entire group, not betraying any of the nervousness Harry knew she must feel. "I am delighted to meet everyone."

The music was playing, and Harry was about to ask Daisy for her first dance of the evening when Christian stepped forward.

"Miss Ames, would you do me the honor of standing up with me?" he asked, his expression all seriousness.

Daisy blinked, as though startled, but agreed. "Of course, my lord." Before Harry could utter a word of protest, Nathaniel stepped forward.

"Might I have the next, Miss Ames?" he asked, his eyes darting from hers to Harry's, a glitter of mischief present.

Oh, no. Harry opened his mouth, but Thomas spoke next.

"And then I must have the honor of the next dance," he said, not even bothering to hide his grin.

Harry stood at his full height, pulling Daisy a little closer. "Now see here, what sort of brothers—"

"Are we all claiming Miss Ames's dances?" a new voice asked. Harry turned to see Lucas Calvert, the earl and a cousin to the family by marriage, standing over his shoulder and grinning. "How far have we made it?"

"If you wish it, you may be my fourth dance this evening, my lord," Daisy said, her dimple appearing. "I confess, I have never been so popular at a ball before."

"An absolute shame." Lucas tsked. "And yes. I will happily take the fourth dance, Miss Ames."

Daisy gave Harry's arm a gentle squeeze. "I will see you in an hour or so, Mr. Devon." She released him and took Christian's arm, while Harry watched incredulously.

Nathaniel and Thomas stepped forward, standing on either side of Harry. He looked from one to the other, deeply suspicious.

"Are you all trying to ruin my evening?" he asked. "You know very well what I have planned."

"They have to have their fun," Christine said from behind him.

"And it isn't our fault," Nathaniel added, "that you neglected to secure the first set with her."

Lucas grinned. "You best be quick about it, Harry. You still haven't asked her to dance. My brother Marcus is across the room. I think I'll see if he is interested in being the fifth—"

"You wouldn't," Harry said, almost panicked. At this rate, she would dance with everyone but him. "Lucas, I'm proposing this evening."

Julia gasped and pushed between her husband and Harry. "Really, Harry? Oh, that is wonderful!" Then she gave her husband a narrow-eyed look. "And you knew this when you asked Miss Ames to dance? I thought you were only teasing Harry."

"Of course I am teasing him," Nathaniel said, putting an arm around his wife's shoulders. "And we have a plan, my dear."

"Really?" Harry threw up his hands. "And what is it, exactly? Keep her too busy for me to get a dance, much less a word, with her?"

"Not at all. We are making certain you have the waltz," Thomas said, slapping Harry on the shoulder. "And the right moment."

Harry looked from one brother-in-law to the other, then at Lucas who nodded. He was surrounded by irritating, well-intentioned relatives. Perhaps having everyone come for Christmas had not been the best idea.

His eyes sought out Daisy's form on the dance floor, and he watched as Christian expertly led her through the steps.

"Oh, stop staring and ask me to dance, Harry." Julia put her arm through his, and Harry sighed. It seemed he had little choice but to put aside his plan and let his family take over, at least for the time being.

"Harry," Julia said when their dance had finished. "I want to tell you how proud I am of you."

That brought his attention away from Daisy changing from Christian to Nathaniel's arm. "You are?"

"All of us are," she said, her smile as serene as ever. "It is obvious you have found a place of real purpose, and you are building a strong foundation for your future. And your future family." She stood on her toes, placing a kiss on his cheek, then she stepped away and Christine took her place.

It seemed he was to dance with his sisters while their husbands danced with the woman he loved. Harry chuckled and escorted Christine to the floor.

§

Although being asked to dance by the rather intimidating Earl of Ivyford surprised Daisy, she found him to be a pleasant partner. He put her completely at ease, asking her questions about the girls she would begin teaching in a fortnight.

"I greatly respect what you are doing, Miss Ames. Harry has told me of your plans. I think he told everyone in London of what you are attempting to do. You ought to know," he added while they stood and waited for their turn to move down the line again, "there are many who have taken notice of *his* interest in education, too."

"Really?" she asked, raising her eyebrows at him. "What do you mean?"

His lordship's lips moved upward. "I should not be surprised if he is asked to join the ranks of the politicians in a few short years. Our nation is increasingly aware of the need for better education for the poor."

Daisy tilted her head to the side, studying the earl with interest. "Are you attempting to impress me with Mr. Devon's prospects?"

Lord Ivyford shook his head. "Harry needs no help from me, Miss Ames."

Then it was Doctor Hasting's turn to escort her through the figures of the dance. After a small exchange of pleasantries, the doctor lowered his voice and leaned nearer her. "I must admit, I have been concerned for Harry's welfare for some time. He did not have very much direction. Since meeting you, he has embraced his responsibilities in a way that ensures his success. Thank you for that."

Daisy blushed at the praise. "Mr. Devon is a good man. He found his way on his own, I am certain."

The doctor's smile was knowing. "It is fascinating how quickly a gentleman can find his way when inspired by a woman."

Then Mr. Gilbert claimed her hand. His usual friendly demeanor set her at ease, and he did not attempt to speak to her of Harry until he escorted her to Lord Annesbury. Just before giving her hand to the earl, he said, "Harry is a fortunate man to hold your esteem, Miss Ames."

She was blushing when she turned to the Earl of Annesbury, who looked as though being granted her hand was a great pleasure.

"Miss Ames, you are most popular this evening. People are beginning to comment." His lips twitched with humor. As she had known Lord Annesbury for the whole of her life, Daisy was not nearly so intimidated by him as she had been by the Earl of Ivyford.

"Two peers asking me to dance, a distinguished gentleman from the neighborhood, and a celebrated doctor from Bath also taking my hand would likely make people suspicious." She bit her bottom lip to keep from grinning. "Of course, as I have been in the company of Mr. Devon a great deal of late, and each of you have ties to him, I would wager most are watching Mr. Devon with equal interest."

His lordship laughed and exchanged hands with another woman on the floor before appearing in front of Daisy again. "You do not mind that we are making a spectacle of you?"

Daisy shook her head. "Not at all, my lord." She turned to find Harry along the line. Though she had not glanced his way before, attempting to give her full attention to her partners, she had known exactly where he was in the room at each moment.

Harry caught her eye and she watched his expression change from contentment to something else. His eyes darkened, his pleasant smile changed to an expectant, peaceful sort of look. Though they were half a room away, she could feel his affection in that one glance. Her heart replied in kind to the look of love.

"I thought I might torture Harry further by asking Marcus to dance with you," the earl said, bringing her attention back to him.

He grinned at her, his blue eyes sparkling. "But I think it best you step outside for a little fresh air after all your dancing."

Then he took her arm and guided her to the wide doors leading to the terrace. A moment later, Harry appeared, the Countess of Annesbury on his arm.

"My lord and cousin, your wife wishes to speak with you." Then Harry's eyes met hers and she could not look away.

"Excellent," he lordship said. "Miss Ames has need of some fresh air. An exchange of partners seems to be in order."

Harry's hand took hers, warm through their gloves, and then they stepped outside. Daisy did not care who was watching or what they might say. They stayed within sight of the open door, as was proper, the cold winter air cooling the heat in her cheeks. They kept their backs to the ballroom.

"I feel I must apologize for my family," Harry said, bringing them to the railing overlooking the snow-covered gardens. The warmth from the ballroom lingered, keeping Daisy from truly feeling the cold.

Daisy leaned her shoulder against Harry's. enjoying the feel of his coat against her arm. "There is no need. I quite adore them, and all they wished to do was assure me of all your good qualities."

He chuckled and looked down at her, light from the ballroom casting half his handsome face in shadow. "Then you are in good humor with me tonight?"

"The very best," she agreed readily, grinning up at him, grateful beyond measure to love such a man. "You have always had a good heart, Harry. Thank you for being patient with me, even when I forgot that wonderful fact."

Harry dipped his head toward her, his blue eyes earnest. "Daisy, I would wait forever for you, if it meant securing your heart to mine."

Her breath caught. "You have my heart. The whole of it. I—I love you, Harry." It was the first time she had spoken such words aloud, and her heart raced expectantly, hoping to hear—

"I love you, Daisy. I wish to be with you always, becoming a better man. Perhaps one day, I will deserve you. But until then, I hope to convince you to show faith in my attempt. Would you marry me, Daisy?" he asked.

"Yes," she whispered, her heart bursting within, as though a thousand fireworks had gone off inside her chest at once. "It is my honor to become your wife."

A voice loudly whispered from behind. "Is he going to kiss her?"

Daisy's cheeks warmed as she and Harry glanced over their shoulder to see all three of his sisters standing in the doorway, their husbands behind them, blocking anyone who might be trying to see from the ballroom but staring most unashamedly themselves.

Harry narrowed his eyes and opened his mouth, obviously prepared to offer a scathing retort, but Daisy laughed. His attention came back to her. Standing on her toes, Daisy lifted her lips toward his. "He had better kiss her," she murmured.

His mischievous grin appeared just before he swept her up in his arms and gave her an ardent, and most impressive, kiss.

Author's Notes

In the early nineteenth century, there was no education system in England controlled by the government. The Church of England had established schools throughout the country, but not enough to educate all the children. There were no laws in place governing the education of children either. In many parishes, it was the priests who taught school to boys and girls, and in London a man named Thomas Cranfield funded several "Ragged Schools" for the poor. Daisy Ames's desire to provide at least part time education for the little girls of her village was inspired by several accounts I found of women, usually noble or upper-class ladies, who offered "Sunday Schools" in their own homes. It wasn't until the late nineteenth century that there were laws enacted protecting a child's right to an education.

In regards to the end of this series, I hope you have enjoyed it immensely. I have loved these characters as I have come to know them through their love stories. I hope you revisit them again and again.

I also hope you enjoy my next series, titled simply Inglewood. Releasing in Summer 2019. There is a sneak peek in just a few pages.

Acknowledgements

There are always so many people to thank! I hardly know where to begin. I'll start with my husband, Skye, who has encouraged my every effort in the writing community and with all my books. He's helped me figure out fight scenes, boat tipping scenes, and kissing scenes. None of my books would be possible without his incredible support.

I must also thank my children, who are patient with Mommy's work. Darlings, I love you.

While I was writing this book, I received several texts and encouraging messages from my uncles and aunts. I've dedicated this book partially to them. "We are so proud of you" was texted to me by several of them, at a time when I needed encouragement. Thank you for loving me. I'll try to name as many characters as possible after all of you!

Thank you to my critique group, who always help me start strong, Joanna Barker, Arlem Hawks, Heidi Kimball, and Megan Walker, thank you for cheering me on. I have learned so much from each of you and I am honored to be part of our little group.

I'm thankful for Shaela Kay, my friend, alpha-reader, and cover-designer. You've brought my characters to life in more ways than one. I will forever be grateful we found each other.

To Jenny Proctor, who arrived late in the series and has been an incredible help as my editor. Thank you for helping me get the story and the words right, Jenny.

And to Sally's Sweet Romance Fans, my Facebook group for readers. You wonderful people keep me going with your kind words and encouragement. Here is Harry's story at last. I hope you love it!

Finally, I am grateful for the author groups The Writing Gals, American Night Writers Association, and Storymakers.

See you all next series.

Please enjoy this sample of Sally Britton's next novel,

Rescuing Lord Inglewood

CHAPTER ONE

March of 1814

E sther Fox kept her arm through her friend's as they walked past the stately homes of Grosvenor Square, the tall white townhouses looming over them like the cliffs of dover. A few paces behind, their maids followed. "We have all of summer before us to do as we please, and then you may try again," Esther said, more determined than cheerful. "You mustn't let one gentleman's lack of interest disappoint you so."

Miss Judith Linton, three years younger than Esther and certainly less experienced in the ways of the *ton*, continued to appear rather pale and tragic. Esther remembered feeling similarly at the end of her own first Season, and then at the end of the second. But coming to the end of her third, once more without an offer of marriage, she found it was not as bleak a situation as she had before supposed.

"He flirted so, and always danced with me twice," the young woman said, her eyes lowered to the walk. "I thought he would at least have the decency to make an offer."

"He is rather young himself. Perhaps he is not ready to give up bachelorhood." Esther thought that the most likely thing, given the gentleman in question was but twenty-one years of age. Gentlemen could afford to wait until they were forty, if they wished it, before even considering marriage. Ladies, on the other hand, were given half a dozen years to make a match before spinsterhood set upon them. As Esther's third season came to a close, and as she was now twenty years old, her time had begun to run out.

Putting that thought from her mind, Esther cast her eyes about to find something to distract Miss Linton. "Oh, look at the gardens, my dear. Are they not lovely?"

The garden park across the street was well tended, with rolling green lawns and beautiful flowers lining the walk. "Would you like to take a walk there?" she asked, preparing to step in that direction.

"No. The blooms make my nose itch." Miss Linton's unfortunate nose twitched at the very idea, it seemed.

What else might be a pleasant distraction? Esther ought to be adept at finding things to occupy the mind. She had done little else for herself for the past two years, living with her stepbrother and his wife while her natural brother was away at war. If she was not trying to take her mind off of her stepbrother's wife and all her demands, she was trying to forget that Isaac faced French soldiers and their bayonets.

Esther put those thoughts away again, as hastily as possible, and gave her full attention to her friend.

"Would you like to go to Gunter's this afternoon? My stepbrother will loan us his phaeton and driver, I am certain."

Miss Linton's lower lip receded slightly and her eyebrows drew together. "I do like the orange ice. It is most refreshing."

"I like the mint tea, too." Esther brightened, pleased she remembered Miss Linton's weakness for the cold treats. She looked ahead, at number 21 Grosvenor Square, and stopped walking immediately. "Oh, Miss Linton, look. It appears Lady Sparton is redecorating in the Greek style."

"Dear me." Miss Linton looked ahead, her eyes growing rounder.

There were laborers before number 21, uncrating a very large statue. Ropes dangled from a window three floors above street level as other men put a pulley system into place. The marble statue was larger than life, and when the last side of the crate dropped it was plain to see the Greek god Hermes in full motion, with winged sandals and flowing robes.

"My mother says people filing their homes with pagan statues is not at all appropriate," Miss Linton murmured, sounding scandalized.

"I think it interesting." Esther watched the men scurry about, more ropes going about the statue while two ropes with hooks were lowered from above. "Emulating an ancient society, while purporting to be modern, is something of a paradox. We dress our hair like Grecian statues, quote their philosophers, and still hold ourselves to the strictures of our society."

Miss Linton said nothing, and when Esther glanced at her friend, she saw the young woman staring at her, eyebrows drawn down and frowning in confusion.

"Never mind, Miss Linton." Esther gave her friend a pat on the arm. "Come, let us go closer so we might watch Hermes rise into the air."

"Hermes?" the girl asked, looking back to the statue. "Is that someone important?"

Esther refrained from giving an explanation, but hurried her friend along the walkway. They stopped perhaps fifteen feet from the statue, just as the men prepared to hoist it from the ground. Rocking forward on her toes, Esther could barely keep hold of her excitement. Others along the walk had stopped as well, further back, or across the street, to watch. She looked at the different expressions people wore, seeing some appear as disapproving as Miss Linton's mother would be, and others who appeared amused.

But a spectacle was a spectacle, and people would be speaking of Lady Sparton's redecoration for days, if not weeks.

Her eyes went back to the statue, now rising slowly from the ground, then to the men backing up as they pulled on their ropes. The path beneath the statue remained clear in all directions. People murmured and spoke, she turned when a child laughed to see a little boy in the arms of his nurse, pointing upward. Though Esther knew few of the people surrounding her, being in the midst of a crowd enjoying the same sight as she gave her a blessed moment of belonging.

She looked upward, studying the pulleys fixed to rods over the house, and let her eyes trail down the ropes. Was that rope fraying? Surely not. Esther shaded her eyes and peered more intently, not caring how unladylike the gesture might appear, and then she gasped. The rope *was* fraying. Several cords were sticking out, untwisting from the braid.

But there were two ropes, so even if one failed, nothing terrible ought to happen.

Except the balance would be upset. The man on the good rope might lose his grip.

She turned her attention to the men pulling the statue up, wondering if they were staring at the fraying rope as she had, seeing the possible dangers. The sun was in their eyes, which they had closed against the light.

Esther looked from the men to the rope, to the statue, to the distance Hermes must yet rise.

It is only a statue, she told herself. *If it falls, it falls.* She bit her bottom lip, knowing to cry out would not help the situation. Perhaps the statue would make it to the top before the rope gave way. No harm done.

Her gaze fell to the walkway and her heart stuttered. A man walked toward 21 Grosvenor Square, staring at the ground, and moving at a fast enough clip to give her reason to believe he would not stop. In fact, he appeared oblivious to the sight enthralling everyone else.

Without thought, Esther slipped away from Miss Linton, a cry of warning on her lips. Her eyes went up to the rope again and an invisible hand closed around her throat. In a moment of perfect clarity, she knew the rope would fully give way, and at the moment the unknowing gentleman walked beneath the statue. The small crowds watching were too preoccupied to see what she could see, a true horror unfolding before her.

Acting quickly, Esther ran forward as fast as she could, grateful for all the footraces she'd run against her brother long ago. She stretched both hands out before her. She heard the snap of the rope above her head. Esther did not slow, but ran directly into the body of the man with all the force at her disposal, knocking them both down to the ground. She landed atop him, a horrific crack sounding at the same instant her world went black.

***

One moment, Silas seriously contemplated whether there were any men of sense in the House of Lords, and the next her found himself flying backward to the ground. His arms came up reflexively, wrapping around the slim figure of the woman literally flinging herself at him, as though doing so might protect at least one of them from the fall. As he hit the ground with the woman atop him, the air pushed out of his lungs, his eye caught a white blur hurtling from above.

A horrific crack assaulted his ears and echoed against the houses on the square, and somewhere a person screamed. Or several people screamed. Then there was movement all around him, coming from everywhere, except—

He looked down at the head of deep brown curls upon his chest, realizing the woman in his arms had not moved since their inelegant landing. Silas started to sit up, cradling the woman against him. Was she hurt? What had happened?

As though hearing his muddled thoughts, a man knelt next to Silas and started speaking rapidly. "Oy, she's bleedin', sir. Looks like the rock clipped her on the head. Are you injured, sir?" Then the person turned away and shouted over the crowd. "Someone run for a doctor!"

People appeared in Silas's line of vision, pressing forward in clusters, women with pale faces and men with deep frowns.

"She saved your life, she did," someone said.

"Oh, Miss Fox," a high-pitched voice wailed, another young woman coming forward. "Is she dead?"

Silas looked down again, tilting the woman back in his arms enough to see her face. Long dark lashes lay against her pale cheeks, her lips were parted and her features were relaxed. Yet he could feel her breathing, could see the rise and fall of her chest.

Why did her face seem so familiar?

Moving carefully, Silas got his legs beneath him and stood, holding the young woman in his arms. He looked around, seeing white stones scattered about the pavement, white powder everywhere with it. A white foot, a face with staring eyes, helped him put enough of the pieces together to realize what had happened. He looked upward, where men were looking over an iron rail and gesturing wildly.

The woman in his arms stirred and groaned. Silas's eyes swept the crowd closing in upon them, then went to the house before which they stood. Lady Sparton stood on the steps, wrapped in a dressing gown, her hands pressed to her cheeks.

Silas acted. Standing about and waiting for someone to explain things to him would not do. He barreled toward the lady, up her steps, and past her into the elegant house. He ignored her startled gasp, looking about for a door. He went to the first he saw and kicked it open, entering what appeared to be a receiving room of sorts. There was a couch, and that was all he needed.

Silas took the young woman there and laid her down, as gently as possible, and as he eased his arm from beneath her head, he saw at last the blood the man on the street had spoken of. The gray sleeves of his jacket were coated in red where he had cradled the back of her head.

"Lord Inglewood, what happened?" a breathy voice asked from the doorway.

He looked up to see Lady Sparton, still pale, staring at him in horror. "Make certain the doctor knows where to come," he said, unwilling to admit he was still attempting to figure out all that had occurred. She nodded and started to withdraw. "And send a maid in—and her friend from the street."

"Of course, Lord Inglewood." She disappeared to do his bidding, no further questions asked.

Silas found a cushion for the young woman's head and attempted to reposition her on her side, keeping the injured place free of pressure. He inspected the wound himself, which was somewhat difficult given the abundance of brown curls in his way. Why did women wear their hair in such ridiculous twists upon their heads?

The sound of sobbing reached his ears, growing louder. He looked up as a young woman, the same who had been wailing outside, came forward. Two other girls, dressed in the plainer clothing of servants, appeared directly behind her, clutching each other's hands. Silas stood, but did not move from the unconscious woman's side.

"Miss, is this woman your friend? Do you know her?"

The weeping girl nodded, raising her hands to cover her mouth, completely overcome with her distress. Silas turned to the maids, fixing them with a stern glare.

"Who is this woman?" he demanded, pointing to her inert figure.

One of the maids stepped forward and bobbed a curtsy, as though maintaining proper forms was important in a moment such as this, and spoke in a near-whisper. "If you please, sir, she's my mistress. Miss Fox. Sister of Sir Isaac Fox. She must've seen the statue falling and she tried to help you...."

The rest of the maid's words were unimportant. Silas stopped listening and turned to look down at Esther Fox, the younger sister of one of his oldest friends. That explained the familiarity of her face, the feeling that he ought to know her. How many times had he seen little Essie trailing along behind Isaac, pleading to be included in their games? When was the last time he had seen her? Four years ago, perhaps. She hadn't been out yet.

And she had saved him from a falling statue.

"I found a doctor, right on the street," a man said, pulling Silas from his thoughts. It was the same man from before, holding a cap and twisting it, staring at Esther.

The doctor, a gentleman with gray hair and a narrow face, came inside with all haste. He knelt beside the couch, completely ignoring Silas except to ask, "How long since the accident?"

Silas did not know. Everything had happened too quickly, had been too confusing. He looked behind him at the largely unhelpful gathering.

"Not more'n ten minutes, sir," the laborer said.

Silas nodded his thanks to the man, then turned his attention to the doctor. He hated everyone standing about, gaping, intruding upon Esther's privacy. He opened his arms and waved, as though herding geese, to move everyone toward the door.

"Come, out into the hall. We must let the doctor work, and I have questions."

The sniffling young lady was the first to move away, then the maids, then the man from the walk. Lady Sparton joined them in the entryway, wringing her hands. Several of her servants stood about as well, though one did slip inside the room Silas had just exited, holding a bucket and a stack of towels. Good. Any indication of someone using their head in this situation could only be appreciated.

"I want to know exactly what happened," Silas said slowly, searching each of the faces before him. He let his gaze rest upon the man strangling his cap. "Why did that statue fall?"

The man shook his head, the lines of his face deep with worry. The man appeared to be young, his clothing well-worn. "We checked the ropes, sir—"

"Lord Inglewood," the woman of the house snapped.

Silas cast her a baleful glare. "Niceties are less important than this story, madam."

She turned red and crossed her arms over her dressing gown.

"We checked the ropes, my lord, and I thought one of them didn't look right. Mr. Lampton, he's the one in charge, said it would hold and we ought to use it. We didn't bring more rope and he didn't want no more delays."

"The statue ought to have been delivered last week," Lady Sparton added. Silas gave her another warning glance and she bit her lip.

"The sun was in our eyes, my lord. We didn't see the rope had frayed past saving or we would've lowered it carefully." He shuddered. "That girl—I'm sorry for it. I truly am."

"And where is the man who told you to use the faulty rope?" Silas asked with a growl.

The other man shook his head. "He left, my lord, before the accident even happened."

"Give information for contacting that man to—" Silas glanced around and settled on a footman. "To this man. I want his name, address, and place of business if he has one. He can expect to hear from me in regards to his negligent business practices. After you have given the information, you may deal with Lady Sparton. I am certain she has words she would like to say about the unfortunate loss of her statue." Each word concerning the lady's misplaced worry dripped with disdain. He had no use for the Spartons. They had always been more concerned with outward appearances than any matter of substance.

He turned to the trembling young woman, now being consoled by one of the maids while the other stared at the room where her mistress lay.

"What did Miss Fox do, exactly?"

"We were watching with everyone else, my lord." The young lady sniffled. "But she made us stand so *close*."

"Miss Fox is always daring," the most agitated maid said. "She was talking about Hermes."

Silas reached up to pinch the bridge of his nose, closing his eyes tightly. "Names, please."

"Miss Linton," the young woman said with a nod. "And this is my maid, Sarah. And this is Mary."

"Mary," Silas said while the maid dipped a curtsy. "You seem the most composed at the moment. Did you see everything that happened?"

She nodded. "Miss Fox ran out and knocked you out of the way. The statue would've hit you otherwise. When the statue hit the ground, pieces flew everywhere. One hit my ankle, though I was far back. Miss Fox slumped over like she was hit, too."

The account now fit correctly in Silas's mind. It seemed he owed Isaac's sister his life. "Very well. The doctor is with her now. I will stay with the young lady and I think it is best she is not moved until the doctor gives other instructions. Miss Linton, I suggest you return to Miss Hawke's family, with the very helpful Mary, and tell them what has happened. I am certain someone will wish to come see to her well-being. Are you far from Miss Hawke's residence?"

"It's a street over, my lord," Mary said, lowering her head.

"Then walking will be faster than ordering a carriage." He pointed to another Sparton footman. "You, lad. Go with them." The women were all obviously rattled, and the footman could return with whatever relative came in search of Esther.

Orders given, Silas turned and went back into the room occupied by the wounded young savior. He took in a deep breath as he approached the couch. The doctor knelt beside the couch, and a servant stood against the wall waiting for orders.

"You have had a nasty bump on the head," the doctor was saying, his voice low. Silas's eyebrows lifted. Had she wakened? "But it isn't so bad as it seems. Head wounds bleed excessively, even with the smallest of wounds."

The tightness in Silas's chest eased.

"Where am I?" the young woman's voice, a pleasant alto, asked. From his angle, Silas could not see her face from behind the arm of the couch.

"Lord and Lady Stanton's home," the doctor answered. "How does your head feel?"

"As though it has been cleaved with an axe."

The doctor chuckled, then covered the sound with his fist. He glanced up at Silas and immediately sobered. "I am told it was a stone depiction of Hermes that assaulted you, miss. And that your actions likely saved the life of another."

She took in a shuddering breath. "The gentleman. Is he all right?" She made as if to move, her skirts rustling and her brown curls lifting above the arm of the couch for a moment before she groaned and laid back down, assisted by the doctor.

"He is perfectly fine, my dear. Please, lie still. I do not think you ought to move for at least an hour. Rest. You will likely have a headache, perhaps some nausea. It is best you do nothing to excite yourself for the rest of the day, at the very least." The doctor stood. "I believe you will be well again after some rest. I suggest you clean your hair very carefully, lest you reopen that wound. But you ought not need stitches. Merely time to heal."

"Thank you, doctor." Her voice was soft, resigned, Silas thought.

The doctor approached and fixed Silas with a most serious frown. "You heard my direction to the young lady. I trust you can ensure she rests peacefully and is returned home with the least possible excitement."

"Yes, doctor. Thank you." Silas started to bow but the doctor interrupted the movement with a quick shake of his head.

"I do not think you have considered all the ramifications of what has happened today, my lord. That young woman saved your life, that is certain, but I am concerned that she will pay for her kindness with more than a nasty bump on the head."

Silas narrowed his eyes. "I am not sure what you mean, doctor. I will see to it that Miss Fox is granted the rest and care she needs to recover from the ordeal."

The doctor did not look as though he believed Silas. He pulled gloves from a pocket and put them back on his bare hands. "I will call on the young lady tomorrow morning. Fox, you said?"

Esther's low voice came from the couch, evidence that she remained awake and alert. "I am staying at the home of my step-brother, Mr. Aubrey."

The doctor's forehead wrinkled. "Then it is there I will call upon you tomorrow, Miss Fox. Good day to you." He bowed to Silas. "And to you, my lord." The doctor left the room, so only a servant, Silas, and Esther remained.

Silas let out a slow breath as he moved to the couch. He looked down at Esther, whose eyes were closed, her head resting on a cushion. He traced her features with his gaze, trying to see the girl he remembered in the lines of her face. Her cheeks were not so round as they'd been in childhood, and they were pale rather than sunburned or freckled. Her hair had been a lighter brown with golden tips, but now the rich curls tumbling freely down her shoulders were dark. Little Essie had grown into something of a beauty.

And Isaac would have Silas's head for thinking any untoward thoughts about his sister. "Esther?" he said aloud, going down to one knee beside the couch.

Her brow furrowed and she opened one eye to look at him, then the other came open as both went wide. "Lord Inglewood."

Right. They were not children any longer. He saw ample evidence of that in the changes of her features. The fact that she recognized him immediately did not escape him. "Miss Fox. Good morning." Was it still morning? It felt more like it ought to be evening, or another day entirely.

"Why are you here?" she asked, her lips pursing in puzzlement over the question.

"You do not remember? I am the man you flung yourself at on the walkway." He tried to grin at her, to adopt the teasing tone from their childhood. It made the experience a little easier to bare, thinking back on those summer days. Esther had followed her brother and his friends wherever they went, whether it was in the trees, the attics of houses, or along the sandy beaches. Despite being five years their junior, she was determined to be part of all their doings.

Her color came back into her cheeks, but faded away again. "Truly? And you are unharmed?" Her eyes darted from the top of his head down to his knees, as though looking him over for injury.

Silas raised his hands and turned in a circle. "It is touching that here you are, injured, and your concern is for me. I am well, Miss Fox." He lowered his arms and bowed. "Thanks to your quick thinking."

"I am glad of that, my lord." She smiled weakly and closed her eyes. "Even if my head does pound rather terribly."

He pulled one of the chairs in the room closer to her and gestured for the footman to bring his towels and basin nearer. "Perhaps a cool cloth will help with that." After removing his gloves, he prepared one of the smaller cloths by dipping it in the clean water. The doctor had left a towel beneath Esther's head, which was spotted with blood—not nearly so much as what was on Silas's sleeve. How much of her blood had been spilled on his account?

Isaac would have something to say about it, were he present.

Silas folded the cloth over and then carefully laid it upon her forehead. She released a gentle sigh, her pale lips parting. "Thank you, my lord."

"Does it pain you to speak?" he asked, lowering his voice to an almost-whisper. "Or for me to speak to you?" Sitting in silence for however long it took someone to come for her might be best, but curiosity over his rescuer's circumstances nipped at him. He had not heard word of Isaac in some time, or of their family.

"No. I would prefer to talk. It might take my mind off my stomach, if not my head."

Yes, the doctor said she might feel sick. He looked about for the bucket he had seen before and then pointed to it, catching the eye of the footman. The servant put the basin of water on a table, then fetched the bucket from near the hearth and brought it to Silas's side before returning to his post against the wall.

That precaution taken, Silas studied the woman before him. She wore a fine gown, appeared to be in good health aside from the wound recently acquired for his sake.

"Do you hear from Isaac often?" he asked. Speaking of her brother might be best, since he hadn't seen Esther in years. Nor had he ever really taken much time in getting to know her.

"His letters come as regularly as the post allows." she kept her eyes closed, though her expression tightened. "From what I can tell, his duties in the army keep him extremely busy. Thus far, he remains safe."

Isaac, as a baronet, had no obligation to serve in the British military. Yet he had purchased his own commission and went across the channel three years previous, to fight Bonaparte. Silas had not understood his friend's need to take up arms, but he respected Isaac for it. "I am glad to hear it. I admit, I think of him every time the idiots in Parliament speak of the war effort."

"I hope that means you do what you can to aid Isaac from home." One of her eyes opened again, fixing him with a rather stern gaze. "He will not return until it is all over and done."

"Which ought to be soon, since we expect France to surrender at any time." Everyone knew Napoleon's defeat at the hands of Russia had crippled the French army. The self-proclaimed emperor's own generals had begun to turn against him. Talk of war likely was not the best way to occupy her mind. Silas cleared his throat and changed the subject. "How have you amused yourself in your brother's absence?"

"As anyone in London does. I go to balls and card parties." Her lips twitched slightly. "And I do my very best not to mortify my step-brother's wife. She is determined to see me wed and is forever in despair of failing me."

Although the activity of seeking husbands for young ladies was not a secret, rarely had anyone spoken to Silas so openly of the pursuit. That Esther would amused him. "I suppose it is kind of her to take such an interest in you."

"Mm." The sound of amused agreement made him relax. "Diana, Mrs. Aubrey that is, promised my brother she would look after me while he was away. She is quite tenacious in keeping that promise."

"And how is your stepbrother?" Silas recalled little of the man. He had already been at university when Esther's mother, the widow of a baronet, married the senior Mr. Aubrey. From all accounts, the match had been a good one for both families. Isaac had been raised by a good man, though it took the Fox children away from Woodsbridge and entirely out of Suffolk, where they had grown up together.

"He is a harried soul, or so his wife says." Her lips parted in a grin before she winced and raised a hand to the cloth.

"Ah, I have neglected your headache. Forgive me." Silas reached for the cloth, his bare fingers brushed the cool, damp skin of her forehead. He swallowed, somewhat guiltily, as he damped the cloth and wrung it out again. He carefully laid it back upon her brow, arranging it to stay out of her eyes.

Her hand came up again, gloved, and took one of his in a gentle grasp. Silas made eye contact with her, surprised to see a reassuring look to her eyes. "This is not your fault, Silas," she said quietly, his Christian name slipping most naturally from her, causing an odd sort of prickle in his chest. But of course, how often had she shouted at him to slow down, come back, stop playing tricks on her? She had always called him Silas, until they had gone away to live with their step family. "I will be fully recovered in next to no time, and I would do it again."

Caught in her deep brown eyes, Silas did not look away, nor loose his hand from hers. He leaned forward, lowering his voice. "If Isaac was here, he would berate me soundly for needing to be saved by his little Essie." Her eyebrows raised at the childhood name. "If I had been paying attention, none of this would have happened."

The moment stretched long, until he became aware of the way their breaths had synced, quiet and deep. The sunlight filtering in through the tall windows warmed the room, though he thought something else likely caused the heat to rise in his cheeks and the answering blush on her own.

A loud slam startled him out of the silent exchange. A tightness in his chest, one he hadn't been aware of, gave one last squeeze before vanishing. Silas stood, ready to investigate the noise, when the rather shrill voice of a woman filled the entry hall beyond the closed door.

"Where is she? Where is my Esther? Is she well? Oh, she is ruined, even if she is well," the voice loudly proclaimed.

Frowning, Silas looked down at Esther, who suddenly appeared paler and more pained than she had in the entire time he had been sitting with her.

"Diana," she whispered, then squeezed her eyes shut. "Good luck, Lord Inglewood."

Silas did not have time to be disappointed in her use of his title before the door to the parlor opened, another footman scuttling out of the way of a rampaging woman.

Mrs. Aubrey proved to be a formidable looking woman, nearly as tall as Silas, dressed in deep purples, she looked like an oncoming thunderstorm. She brought into the room both a sense of urgency and an overwhelming scent of gardenias.

"Esther," she nearly shouted, causing even Silas to wince. "Oh, my poor girl, my poor sweet child." She hardly spared a glance at Silas, though he stumbled backward out of her way, before throwing herself on the ground next to the couch. She took up one of Esther's hands and began patting it rather forcefully.

"Are you fainted, my dear? Are you able to speak? I have heard the whole of it from that feather-brained friend of yours, and your sweet maid. You poor darling. What were you thinking? My little heroine." She abruptly stopped her patting and withdrew a handkerchief directly from her bosom, using it to stop a suddenly onslaught of tears.

Esther had opened her eyes, though she winced, and attempted to speak several times only to be cut off again by the exuberant Mrs. Aubrey. Silas might have been amused, had he not seen Esther's discomfort.

"Mrs. Aubrey," he said, presuming to forgo an introduction. "Your sister-in-law is injured. The doctor has asked that we keep her from overexcitement."

The woman's tears stopped as abruptly as they started and she rose to her feet with almost an unnatural swiftness. "*You*," she said, pointing a gloved finger at Silas's chest with as much force as one might put into a rapier thrust. "What are *you* going to do about this?"

Silas, hands raised defensively, narrowed his eyes at her. "What do you mean, madam?"

She drew herself up to her rather impressive height, a large silk blossom in her hat waving dangerously. "You have *ruined* her."

Esther drew in a sharp breath, and Silas glanced down quickly to see her face turn pale enough for him to finally make out a few freckles on her cheeks. "He has what?"

About the Author

Sally Britton lives in the desert with her husband, four children, and two rescue dogs. She started writing her first story on her mother's electric typewriter, when she was fourteen years old. She knew romance was the way for her to go fairly early on. Reading her way through Jane Austen, Louisa May Alcott, and Lucy Maud Montgomery, Sally also determined she wanted to write about the elegant, complex world of centuries past.

Sally graduated from Brigham Young University in 2007 with a bachelor's in English, her emphasis on British literature. She met and married her husband not long after and they've been building their happily ever after since that day.

Vincent Van Gogh is attributed with the quote, "What is done in love is done well." Sally has taken that as her motto, for herself and her characters, writing stories where love is a choice each person must make, and then go forward with hope to obtain their happily ever after.

All of Sally's published works are available on Amazon.com.

Made in the USA
Monee, IL
12 October 2022

15747188R00128